THIN AIR

THIN AIR

Kate Thompson

SCEPTRE
LIR

Grateful acknowledgement is made to The Society of Authors as the Literary Representative of the Estate of James Stephens for permission to reprint the extract on page 196, which is from James Stephens' *Fairy Stories*.

First published in 1999 by Hodder and Stoughton
A division of Hodder Headline PLC
A Sceptre book

10 9 8 7 6 5 4 3 2 1

A CIP catalogue record for this book is available from the British Library

ISBN 0 340 73957 6

Typeset by Palimpsest Book Production Limited,
Polmont, Stirlingshire
Printed and bound in Great Britain by
Mackays of Chatham PLC, Chatham, Kent

Hodder and Stoughton
A division of Hodder Headline PLC
338 Euston Road
London NW1 3BH

For Brigid Ruane and Brendan Dowling

Acknowledgements

My thanks to the Tyrone Guthrie Centre in Annaghmakerrig, to the Ennistymon Library, and to Jane Tottenham, all of whom have kindly helped me by providing that essential commodity; work space.

Part 1

The End

Night

The old pick-up roared and clattered through the night. From the passenger seat, Trish watched the hedgerows emerging briefly from the darkness and vanishing into it again behind her. There had been a bit of a gathering after the sales; a few drinks, and it had got late. The narrow roads they were travelling on had long been empty.

Her boss, Gerard Keane, drove with an arm draped out of the window. He never seemed to feel the cold. He would be out and around the farm in shirtsleeves, even in the dead of winter. Trish envied him. She never seemed to be warm. She pulled her jacket closer around her now and snuggled down into the corner of the seat against the door, looking forward to home and a hot water bottle. But a moment later she was sitting up again as Gerard pulled the rig into the side of the road.

'There's a mare and foal here that a fellow wants to sell,' he said as he pulled up the hand-brake and turned off the engine.

'Haven't you enough of them?' said Trish.

'Too many,' said Gerard. 'Are you coming to have a look?'

'In the dark?'

Gerard didn't answer, but dug the sheep lamp out from behind the seat and held it up. Trish shook her head and huddled against the door again. She watched the beam of the lamp as it swung away across the field, then turned on the cab light and picked up the crumpled sale catalogue. In the trailer behind her the new fillies moved restlessly, causing the pick-up to rock on its springs. One of them was called Harpist Bizarre, by Strange Dancer out of a mare called O'Carolan's Lass. Trish liked her. She had already nick-named her Harpo. The other one wasn't registered. She was a lot plainer and not as easy to like or to name. Trish decided to leave it to Martina. She was sure to like the filly; she liked anything or anyone that was a bit awkward, misfitting, like herself.

While she mused, the torch-beam came back across the field, fencing shadows. Trish put down the catalogue, but Gerard didn't get back into the cab. Instead he came over to the passenger-side window.

'Come and have a look,' he said.

It wasn't quite an order, but it wouldn't have been easy to refuse.

'All right.' Trish opened the door and dropped down on to the gravel of the hard shoulder. As she followed Gerard over the gate a gust of wind blew her down from it and into the quagmire that the horses had created on the other side. The mud dragged at her feet, and for a dreadful moment she felt that the darkness behind her was dragging at her soul in the same way. She struggled through and ran on after the retreating light.

There were a couple of mares in the field, and one of them had a new foal, but Gerard had not brought Trish into the field to look at them. As they got to the three-sided corrugated-iron shelter where the horses stood, he took her arm and led her around to its furthest side. She was off guard, disarmed by the night, and when he pushed her against the wall she couldn't believe what was happening. Clumsily, he tore at her clothes and pressed hard, tense lips against her face.

Trish was so shocked that she could barely react. She was accustomed to his lascivious stares and suggestive jokes. She had given as good as she got and felt comfortable with it; a harmless kind of slagging between a middle-aged boss and a young employee. She had never expected anything further.

He thrust his hips against her and tried to push his tongue into her mouth but by now she had found her strength. She succeeded in getting her hands between their bodies, and pushed him away.

'Come on, Trish,' he said, trying to close in again. 'I'm mad about you. You know that!'

She ducked out under his arm and made for the gate in the darkness. He came after her, the torch beam wavering behind her and making her shadow loom and shrink and lurch. Inside the gate he caught at her arm. She snatched it away.

'Get off me!'

'Oh, for fuck's sake!' The fury in his voice frightened her, but she climbed carefully and headed towards the pick-up. The light was still on in the cab, and she got into the driver's seat, but he had taken the keys with him. The road was dark and empty. Trish turned on the radio, but without the key in the ignition it wouldn't work. In the trailer, the fillies were quiet now, as though they too were awaiting their fate.

Trish listened to the night for what seemed like a long, long time. It occurred to her to get out and walk, even though they were miles from anywhere. But the night was too dark, and the gusting wind too fickle, and no matter how hard she tried, she couldn't rid herself of the feeling that there was something out there, and that it wished her no good.

When Gerard eventually returned he seemed diminished. He started the engine and pulled away again, and drove too fast along the empty roads in a grim silence. Finally he said: 'You led me on.'

'I did not.'

'You did. You were always coming on to me, you little bitch.'

Trish looked out at the passing darkness, afraid of the malevolence in his voice. But he said nothing else, and before long they had passed through the deserted streets of Rathcormac and were turning into the boirin that led down to the farm and the houses. Relief washed through Trish's bloodstream. For the first time she began to think beyond the present moment, about what the consequences of what had happened might be. She began to think about leaving.

They unloaded the anxious fillies in the yard and shut them into a waiting box together. Gerard leaned against its door as though he was looking in at them, but he wasn't.

'Brigid and I . . .' he said. 'We don't . . .'

Trish shrugged and moved away. 'It doesn't matter,' she said. Gerard helped her to lift the front ramp and secure it.

'See you tomorrow,' he said. He seemed contrite. Trish was beginning to feel sorry for him.

'You said I could stay off tomorrow,' she said.

'So I did. What's that you were going to do?'

'I might be changing my car. In Limerick.'

'That's right. Good luck, so.'

'Goodnight.'

Trish went into the old cottage. It had been the farmhouse, until Gerard had married and built a grand new house on the other side of the farmyard. Gerard's father, Thomas, had stayed on in it for a year or two, until they had built him a bungalow at the edge of the lake. Usually it was comfortable enough, but now it was damp and cold, and it was too late to go about lighting a fire. Trish was tired and unhappy. For all its failings, the place had been her home for more than a year. It would not be that easy to just up and leave it. And there were other factors as well; friendships and loyalties, matters of pride. She decided to go to Limerick and look at the car, as she had planned. By the time she came back the next evening she was sure to know what to do.

But by that time, a new set of circumstances would make her problems insignificant. By that time, Martina would have disappeared.

7

Day

On the evening that followed, Aine dropped her schoolbag inside the back door and ran through the house. No one was there. The range was warm, not hot. She found the right tool and lifted the plate above the fire-box. A few red embers lay half buried among the drifts of soft ash. Aine threw a few sods of turf in on top of them, puffing and waving at the ash clouds that rose, then replaced the plate and went to the bottom of the stairs.

'Martina!'

There was no answer. Aine went back into the kitchen and looked into the fridge, the bread bin, the fitted presses above her head. There was plenty of food, but the sight of it made her realise that it wasn't really food that she wanted. It was a welcome. She picked up her bag again and went out. Behind her the ashes slowly dropped and settled in a thin, barely visible layer, over everything.

Further on down the boirin, Aine wandered through another hallway and went through another empty house before eventually being greeted on the back doorstep by Popeye, the lurcher, who led her out to the vegetable garden at the side of the house.

Thomas was clearing winter weeds from the wet, sour-looking soil.

''Lo, Granddad,'

Thomas turned, the wrong way at first and then the right way.

'How're you, Aine. Are you well?'

'I am,' said Aine. 'And yourself?'

Thomas shrugged and turned back to the garden. 'Sure, I have one leg in the grave, God help me,' he said, but he was grinning; winding her up as usual.

'As long as you don't put the other one in,' said Aine, as she had heard her mother say once.

'I will, begod,' said Thomas. 'I will some day.'

He continued with his work, turning the earth slowly with the fork, slowly shaking loose soil from the roots of the weeds he pulled, then throwing them slowly aside. Aine sat beside Popeye on the wall and noticed that it was the first really warm day of the spring. The lake in front of the house was calm and still; dark in the middle, paler towards the edges where reeds grew. Thomas picked a stone from the soil and examined it carefully from every angle before he tossed it aside.

'Martina's not at home,' said Aine. She meant to tell Thomas that there was no provider and that she was hungry.

'She's out on Specks,' said Thomas. 'I saw her go off.'

'Oh.' He had not understood. Aine jumped down and went nearer. He was inspecting another stone, pushing the damp mud from it with his thumb.

'Why are you looking at it like that?' said Aine.

'Eh?'

'What are you looking for?'

Thomas grinned as though he were embarrassed. 'I'm not rightly sure,' he said. 'I suppose I'm looking for one with a signature.'

'Whose signature?'

'I don't know,' said Thomas, and then his grin became mischievous. 'God's?'

Aine helped him to look for a while and as soon as she forgot about being hungry he said that it was time they had some tea.

Joseph was on the school bus, coming out from town. The girls sat at the front end and the boys sat at the back and made a lot of noise. The front end smelt of cheap deodorant and the back end smelt of musk and methane. Joseph was saying: 'He'll never let me. I'm supposed to be studying.'

'We all are,' said Stephen, who lived in Rathcormac beyond the lake. 'It's Friday, isn't it?'

'Yeah,' said Joseph. 'But he still wouldn't let me.'

'Don't tell him, then.'

'What. Just go?'

'Yeah. Come now. Stop on the bus.'

'Jaysus,' said Joseph. 'He'd kill me.'

'He hasn't yet, has he?'

'Jaysus,' said Joseph again, but he was grinning and there was a spark in his eyes as he said: 'Will I?'

Aine and Thomas drank big mugs of sweet, milky tea and

ate slices of Thomas's home-made bread covered in red jam. Afterwards, Thomas said: 'Will we go to the island?'

Stephen's mother had chicken sticks and chips waiting on the table for him when he came in. When she saw Joseph behind him her face fell and she went to the freezer to get some more.

'I'm all right, Mrs O'Neill,' said Joseph. 'Honestly.'

'You share what's there,' she said, 'while I put some more down in the microwave.'

'Feckin' chicken feckin' dippers!' said Stephen under his breath. 'She still thinks I'm a three-year-old.' He picked one up and dipped it into the bowl of ketchup carefully set beside the plate. 'Yech!'

'They're all right,' said Joseph, tucking in. Stephen nibbled the end of one; rounded it into a finger or a phallus.

'Chick dipper,' he said.

Joseph giggled. 'Chick sticker.'

Stephen picked up a long chip. 'Big fucker.' He dipped it in ketchup and sucked it off.

'Big sucker!' said Joseph.

They straightened their faces rapidly as Mrs O'Neill came in with more limp and steaming chips.

'Do you want Pop Tarts?' she said.

Stephen doubled up with mirth. Joseph went bright red.

'No thanks, Mrs O'Neill,' he said.

She shook her head disgustedly and went out.

'We do, Ma, we do!' Stephen called after her. 'We want Pop Tarts! Big, juicy ones!'

'Shut up, Stephen,' said Joseph. But they were both laughing, giggling helplessly, dropping towards Mrs O'Neill's fitted carpet.

Aine bailed with a cut-down Coke bottle while Thomas rowed.

'There's no need,' he said. 'We could row out and back ten times and she still wouldn't sink.'

But Aine bailed anyway, because it made her feel safer. She didn't stop until she felt the prow scraping shingle as they pulled up against the shore of the island. Then she stood up, wobbling.

'Can we drive, next time?'

There was a causeway at one end of the lake, built in the eighteenth century by the landlord of the time. It was still used by Anthony Daly, the current owner, for getting cattle on and off the island.

'Hardly, I'd say,' said Thomas. 'You can't drive, and I can but I won't.'

He stepped out of the boat into the shallows. Stones slipped and slithered beneath his feet. The water didn't quite reach the top of his wellingtons. He steadied himself, then hefted Aine up on to his hip.

'God. What a weight.'

'Bicycles, then,' said Aine.

'Oh, that's right. There was some talk of bicycles, wasn't there?' He sloshed through the water and dropped his granddaughter on to dry land. He was winded to the point of distress but he was not about to admit it. Aine sat on a rock and waited while Thomas tied the painter to an out-hanging branch. By the time he had finished he had enough breath to speak again.

'Bicycles and birthdays,' he said. 'A bicycle with horns, wasn't it?'

'Bull horns,' said Aine.

'A bicycle with horns,' said Thomas. 'What next?'

He sat down on another rock. Aine got up and kicked along the beach. Now and then she picked up a stone and looked at it carefully and turned it over and looked at the other side, and then plunked it into the lake.

Thomas took out his pipe and began to poke at its crusty black innards.

'How can a stone have a signature, anyway?' said Aine. Thomas put his pipe back into his pocket and stood up.

'Find me a flat one,' he said, 'till we see can I skim it.'

Stephen bought fags at the Korner Stop and they smoked in the main street. Stephen was open about it. Joseph held the cigarette backwards and tried to look casual. The smoke scorched his palm and turned it yellow. They dropped the butts and stood on them before they got to Mick's house.

'We can't put it on yet!' he hissed, closing the kitchen door on his mother and younger brother. 'Are you mad or what?'

'When, then?' said Stephen.

'Tonight. They'll go down for a drink. They always do on a Friday.'

'But that's hours!' said Joseph. 'I can't stay that long.'

'Then you won't see it, will you?'

'Shit!'

Mick hustled the others out of the house again and back into town. The sun sent slanting rays among the buildings. Mrs Reilly passed along the street, heavily laden with Korner Stop carriers. The boys moved aside as she wheezed and scuffed and rustled past.

'Give me a fag, Stephen,' said Mick. 'Are you staying, or what?'

Aine and Thomas skimmed flat stones until they got a Book of Records score. Thomas said it was sixteen, but Aine said she had counted all the little bubbly ones at the end and there were twenty-two. Thomas conceded and lit his pipe.

'I'm going up to the fort,' said Aine.

'Good for you,' said Thomas. 'Must be great to have young legs.'

'Will you wait here?'

Thomas pointed with the mouthpiece of his pipe to the old church on the shoulder of the hill. Only the gable was standing and the sun was golden behind it.

'I might be up there,' he said, 'and I mightn't. You'll find me anyway.'

Aine didn't doubt him, but turned and began to climb the steep hill towards the summit. Part of the way up she stopped to catch her breath. The broad sweep of the lake between her and the mainland was bright with evening gold. The shadow of the island fell across the other half and left it black as sump oil. There was a city down there somewhere, Thomas said. Aine wasn't sure whether she believed it or not. On the mainland something glinted; her mother's car, creeping down the boirin. All the windows in the house shone with gold as though the sun were inside it. Her mother stopped the car and got out of it. Aine called and waved, but she was much too far away. Her mother went inside.

Joseph and Mick and Stephen went into Whelan's Fast Foods and sat on stools at the side counter. Mick bought curry chips. Joseph scraped up the price of a Coke. Stephen laughed at the three straws and handed round the fags again.

'Are you staying then, or what?'

'I dunno, do I?'

'Well I don't know, do I?'

'I have to give it back tomorrow,' said Mick.

The doorbell pinged and the boys turned their heads in unison. The girl who came in glanced sideways at them, then fixed her gaze at the opposite wall.

'Karen McCarthy,' said Stephen, quite loud. Then, under his breath, 'The titless wonder.'

Joseph burst out laughing with the Coke straw in his mouth and sprayed the lot of them.

'You dirty bastard,' said Mick.

Karen McCarthy continued to look at the white-tiled wall.

'Hello!' Brigid sang through the empty house. 'Hello!'

The only reply was the soft whisper of a sod settling into its own ashes inside the range. Brigid held out her hand, judging by the heat how long the house had been empty. She opened the back door and called again, then returned. There was a pile of washing-up in the sink. Brigid had never asked Martina to look after the kitchen or to put on the dinner. On the contrary, she had often told her that she shouldn't; that she should be careful not to allow herself to become a skivvy to the rest of the family just because she was around. But Martina always did it anyway, and Brigid had become accustomed to finding the dinner on the go when she got home. Despite herself, she was irritated.

The phone rang. It was Joseph, phoning from a call-box in town, asking if he could stay the night with a friend. Brigid agreed, relieved to have one less mouth to feed, and had put the phone down before she remembered that Gerard had ruled against it. Joseph's Junior Cert exams were coming up in a few months' time. He wasn't supposed to go out until they were behind him.

Suddenly furious with everyone, Brigid stormed across the kitchen and opened the freezer. She dragged a gigantic pizza out of the depths and a huge, rumbly bag of frozen chips. Then she rolled up her sleeves and set about stoking up the range.

The island covered about a hundred and fifty acres altogether. Parts of it were wooded and other parts were craggy. It was roughly circular and no part of it was ever far from another, but it was very steep in places.

It had been inhabited since the Stone Age. Apart from

the church and the fort there was a holy well, the huddled remains of a group of monastic cells and the roofless walls of several cottages dating from the times of the Penal Laws. Here and there the ground still held the memory of gardens in ridges and furrows, always running downhill, towards the lake. Aine passed through some of them as she climbed. The shapes were as familiar to her as her own hands and feet. Thomas had been bringing her here for as long as she could remember.

She crossed the remains of a foundation wall and climbed on up towards the fort. The route that she took was the same as always, passing the blocked-up entrance to the souterrain. Thomas had a story about it and why it was closed, but Aine didn't like to think about it. The place sent a shiver down her spine. She gave the jumble of stones a wide berth and soon the first green wall of the fort came into view. She was panting from the climb, but was determined to get to the top without stopping. The last hundred yards was an ordeal but she pushed hard, and then she was there, standing inside the inner ring, looking out at the surrounding lake.

'I'm up, Grandda,' she shouted, expecting no answer and getting none. The fairy ring, her mother called it, but Thomas said it was Cormac's Dun; Cormac Mac Ruadh, who was drowned by an enchanted bull and who was living still in the dark city beneath the lake, waiting for the day when his bride would come and join him.

Aine found a spot that was free from cowpats and sat down on the damp grass. There were daisies and violets, and clusters of primroses on the steeper parts of the banks. Martina said she wasn't to pick the wild flowers because they were getting scarce, but Thomas said there would be wild flowers still when the people were all dead and gone.

Gerard was still singing the song that had been playing on his car radio when he went into the kitchen. Brigid looked up from reading the *Television Guide*. She got the smell of sweat and horses from him despite the carefully maintained distance between them.

'When's dinner?' he asked.

'I'm only in the door,' said Brigid.

She cooked lunches in a hotel in Ennis. She had been doing it for nearly a year, now. It was the first paid job she had ever had.

Gerard turned on the television and watched a troop of Australian teenagers chase each other across a sandy beach.

'Joseph is staying the night at Stephen's house,' said Brigid. To her surprise, Gerard just nodded.

'Do you want a coffee?' she went on.

Gerard shook his head. 'I'm after getting a load of feed. I'd better unload it. And The Nipper has gone lame on me again. I'll have to take him down and stand him in the lake.'

'How did he get lame again?' said Brigid. 'I thought you had him turned out.'

'Well, you thought wrong, didn't you?' said Gerard. He went out into the back porch and Brigid heard him taking off his shoes and putting on his wellingtons. She closed down the damper of the range to let the oven heat, then pulled the heavy kettle on to the hottest part of the top. On the television, the Australians seemed to be helping each other to take off their clothes.

Thomas made his slow way up to the church and sat on one of the scattered headstones. Across the water he could just make out the shape of a man crossing the stable yard. It might have been himself, thirty years ago.

Abruptly the light changed as the sun dropped behind the grey summits of the westerly mountains. A sudden chill came with the change, and Thomas saw the man in the yard hesitate and look up before he looked up himself and caught the ponderous flight of a pair of ravens passing over.

On the hill-top, Aine felt the chill too and saw the ravens and heard their wings cutting the golden air, over and over again. She had been day-dreaming, and now the grass was suddenly cold and damp and her arms were all goose bumps. She pulled down the sleeves of her jumper and was about to set off back down the hill when something caught her eye. She wished that it hadn't. She wished that she could pretend she had never seen it. She promised herself that she would come back tomorrow and look at it then. But it was too late. Something stronger than curiosity turned her face away from home again.

Thomas got up and pulled his jacket closed. He peered up towards the top of the hill, but he could only just see the edge of the outer fortification; no more. The child was surely all right. The flapping ravens were gone, the hill was sweet and green, there was still more than enough light to get safely home. He walked across the side of the hill, one leg longer than the other, to meet the child as she came down.

Aine took a few steps forward. Between the inner and the outer wall of the fort, a set of white bones was lying. She crept forward again. She had seen bones before, many times, but never bones like these.

Whatever owned these bones had died on its back. Its spine was long and straight, and at the end of it, long, straight legs stretched out, as of a creature that walked upright. But it wasn't a human skeleton. The neck was twisted around at an impossible angle, and at the end of it was a cow's skull, set in an agonised gape.

Aine stepped forwards, and then back. The bones had been picked clean, but here and there a few shreds of skin still clung, and the smell which rose from them was frightful. She made to turn away, but needed one last look. At the end of the legs, and of the inwardly bent arms, cloven hooves sat on the bones, like two pairs of ill-fitting shoes.

Thomas stood on the hill, waiting. The boat was below him, still snug against the shore. She had taken on a bit of water, enough to set the bailing bottle afloat again. He could see the man and the horse walking down to the opposite shore. They stopped briefly at the water's edge, then walked on in and stood in the speckled shadow of some tall ash trees.

The weather was clear and still. There were a few clouds, but not of the type likely to produce one of the squalls for which the lake was notorious. Even so, Thomas was keen to get home.

'Go up and see what's keeping her,' he said to Popeye. Popeye wagged his tail and sat down.

Stephen went home to see if he could blag some more money. Joseph sat with Mick in Whelan's and tried to think of something cool to say. But all he could think of was his father and what he would say the next day. He was beginning to wish that he hadn't come.

Aine came lurching and skidding over the brow of the hill, stopped like a hunted creature, looked around. She saw Thomas and raced towards him. Popeye met her halfway and circled them both as Aine launched herself at her grandfather and brought the two of them sliding down on to the grass.

'There's a dead thing up there,' she said. 'I don't know what it is.'

'Is it big or small?' said Thomas.

'Big. Very big. Very tall.'

'A sheep?'

'Bigger. It had cow's feet.'

'It was a cow, so, wasn't it? Is it long dead?'

'I don't know. It smelled very bad.'

'Long enough dead, then. Wouldn't you think Anthony would do something about it, instead of leaving it to rot up there?'

They got to their feet. Thomas brushed himself down. The dog stood at a distance and sniffed the air.

'Will you come and look?' said Aine.

'Not a chance in the world, young lady.'

'Please?'

'No, no Aine. I'll not go up to the fort again.'

'Never?'

'Well. Maybe one day. If I started out very, very early in the morning and came back very, very late at night . . .' He had assumed his familiar, playful expression and Aine felt her fears begin to melt. She punched his arm, quite hard, and continued to swipe at him as she followed him down the hill.

As they crossed the water a pair of swans swam out from the island and watched them, as though to make sure that they were really leaving.

'They'll be nesting, I suppose,' said Thomas.

'There's a new girl in our school,' said Aine. 'She's from England. She says that nobody is allowed to kill swans. She says it's because they belong to the Queen.'

'Is that what she says?' said Thomas.

'Is it right?' said Aine.

'No,' said Thomas. 'Irish swans don't belong to the Queen. Irish swans belong to themselves.'

'Are we allowed to kill them, so?'

'We are not,' said Thomas. 'Because you'd never know who they once were or who they might become.'

'Like the children of Lir?' said Aine.

'Like the children of Lir,' said Thomas.

*   *   *

Gerard and The Nipper were still there, still standing in the shallows as the boat drew towards the shore. A few early midges danced around their heads, but they hadn't started to bite, yet.

Aine was still bailing, and the horse snorted as the boat glided towards him. He stepped away until the rope in Gerard's hand brought him to a halt. Thomas punted with an oar and stopped the boat. The dog fell off the prow and then, pretending that he had jumped off, began to snap at minnows, real and imagined.

'Still lame, then?' said Thomas.

'He has my heart broken,' said Gerard. 'I was certain that he was right.'

'You put him back into work?'

'He was sound as a bell, Dad. You wouldn't have known that he was ever wrong.'

The horse had begun to come back towards Gerard, mainly to see what the dog was after. Thomas slipped out of the boat and waded across to him. He felt the leg, the only white one. The water made it look pink.

'You've no patience, that's your trouble,' said Thomas to the surface of the lake. Gerard looked towards the sky and made 'here-we-go-again' faces at Aine. She laughed and threw water at him from the Coke bottle.

'Jesus, Aine!'

'Sorry.' She was shocked. She hadn't meant it.

'You ought to have turned him out,' said Thomas, dropping the white leg and slowly straightening his back. 'I told you that a month ago.'

Gerard glared at Aine, who looked down at Popeye. The Nipper blew hot breath into Thomas's pockets.

'You'll have to do it now, anyway,' Thomas went on. 'If you don't you'll never get him right.'

'There you all are!'

Aine turned to see her mother standing on the shore. 'You might have said you were bringing her off with you!'

'Ah, sure, we only went over to the island,' said Thomas.

'And it's nearly dark. How was I supposed to know where she was?' No one answered, so Brigid went on: 'Bring her over, will you, Ger?'

Gerard gave the horse to Thomas and lifted Aine out of the boat. She dropped the Coke bottle and put both her arms around her father's neck, loving him more than was possible. He was so strong, so warm, so safe.

'I saw a big giant,' she said.

'A big giant? Did you?' His boots sloshed through the water. 'And did you see the whale?'

'What whale?'

'Don't be telling her stories, Ger,' said Brigid. 'Your father's bad enough.'

Gerard winked and dropped Aine on to dry land. Her mother put an arm around her shoulders and hugged.

'Have you seen Martina?' she asked.

Gerard shook his head and waded back out to Thomas and the horse. The boat was beginning to drift. Thomas went after it and the dog jumped in.

'Goodnight, Grandda.'

'Night, Aine.'

He had one foot in the boat and the other in the water. She would bring him up to the fort. He would never die.

'Do you know where Martina is?' said her mother as they walked together across the dewy fields towards the house. Without thinking, Aine shook her head.

Night

While Aine helped her mother to clear away the pale and pasty remains of the meal, Gerard lit the fire in the sitting room. He watched the *News* while Aine started a favourite jigsaw and Brigid tidied around them, then they all settled in to watch *The Late Late Show*. Gay Byrne was interviewing a woman who had written a book about how women ought to behave towards men if they want to keep them. Nobody said anything, but it seemed to Aine that her parents were involved in one of those awkward silences, like when they were angry with each other. She hoped she wouldn't be sent to bed. The show was boring but the woman talked about sex a lot so it was bound to be up for discussion in the playground on Monday.

Thomas finished washing up and turned on the TV. On the mat beside the fire, Popeye pricked up his ears and listened to the night going on outside without him. He looked up at Thomas with the sorrowful gaze of a prisoner. Thomas sat down heavily in the battered armchair. The dog sighed and went back to sleep.

*   *   *

When the ad break came up, Gerard stretched and said: 'I'd say Martina's met up with some of the lads.'

'I suppose so,' said Brigid.

'They'll be down in Duignan's I'd say.'

Brigid sighed deeply. 'And you'll want to go and find out, I suppose?'

'I don't mind,' said Gerard, showing a momentary interest in a lager ad. 'Do you want to go?'

'Well we can't both go, can we?' She nodded towards Aine who felt suddenly conspicuous.

'I don't mind,' said Gerard again. 'You go if you want to.'

'As if I would,' said Brigid, under her breath.

'What?' said Ger. 'What did you say?' Aine tensed, hearing the anger enter her father's voice.

'Nothing,' said Brigid. 'You go.' She stared fixedly at the television. Gerard did, too. Gay Byrne came back on and everybody in the audience clapped. He introduced a new band, who launched into a loud song. Brigid and Gerard seemed to be watching, but Aine could tell that they were really both waiting.

'Do you like the song?' she asked.

'I don't know,' said her mother. 'Do you?'

Gerard stood up. 'Right, so,' he said.

Brigid said nothing. She didn't look at him.

'See you later, then,' he said, and closed the door behind him. Brigid stared at the TV. The loud song ended and Gaybo said: 'Well done, well done.' Aine became aware of a terrible sadness in the room. She remembered the thing on the island with the long bones and the cloven hooves, and she abandoned the jigsaw and crossed the room to snuggle in beside her mother on the sofa. If she was lucky, she wouldn't be sent to bed at all.

Mick's parents eventually gathered themselves together and went out.

'Jesus, fucking Christ,' said Mick. 'I thought they'd never go.'

They went into the sitting room where Gay Byrne was saying, 'Well done, well done.' Mick's younger brother was watching him.

'Bed,' said Mick.

'No way,' said David.

'Bed, I said.'

'Dad said I could watch the *Late Late*.'

'Well we're not watching the *Late Late* are we? So sod off. Now.'

'What are you watching then?' asked David.

'A video.'

'What video?'

A car crawled along the street outside. Joseph listened, every nerve on edge, waiting for his father to burst through the door in righteous rage. The car passed on. Joseph breathed.

Mick grabbed David by the elbow and dragged him up from the sofa. David wriggled like an eel, freed himself, and dropped back on to the cushions. Mick set his jaw.

'Anyway,' said David. 'I know what video it is.'

'What is it then, smart-ass?'

'It's the one everyone's been watching. About those two girls.' The others' silence told him that he was right. 'And I'm watching it.'

'No way, José.'

'Or I tell Dad.'

'Oh, let him, for God's sake,' said Stephen. 'They'll be back before we get the flaming thing turned on!'

'But he's only eleven!'

'So fucking what?'

Mick seethed. 'If you tell Dad, you're dead. You hear?' He went up to his bedroom and returned with two cans of lager and the video in a cracked case. Stephen cheered. Joseph listened as another car passed by.

The street outside Duignan's was lined with cars. Gerard stopped in the middle of the road and studied them. There was no sign of Trish's car, and he drove on until he found a place to pull in. A fresh breeze was blowing crisp packets and sweet wrappers along the street as he walked back towards the pub. Trish's car was definitely nowhere to be seen, and he was about to put his head around the door and look in when he remembered that she had gone to Limerick with the intention of changing it. He examined the line of cars again. Some of them he knew but there were plenty that he didn't. Any of them could have been Trish's new one. He hesitated. If she was there she might think that he had come looking for her and not for Martina at all. Already he could feel his face beginning to colour with anger and embarrassment. He didn't need it. Martina was sure to be there. She always was on a Friday.

A lad and a girl came out, glued together at the armpits. Gerard nodded and stepped back to let them pass. Beery warmth accompanied them. Gerard turned and walked the other way down the street towards his own regular, O'Loughlin's.

Aine snuggled down deeper into the hollows of her mother's body. Gaybo's voice began to echo and boom. Thomas was trying to dig his foot out of the entrance to the souterrain with the fork. Stones moved, then rumbled and heaved with the pressure of something inside. It seemed to be a sheep-turd, but it wasn't. It was the bull, which emerged like a newborn creature, shoved out of the earth by some inner force. It was mean and dangerous, and was accompanied by the dreadful smell of dead things. Aine jumped and sat up, grabbing at her mother's cardigan, staring wide-eyed at the middle of the room. Brigid put both arms around her.

'What's wrong? Bad dream?'

On the television, Gaybo was talking to a man who kept laughing.

'I saw a big giant today,' said Aine.

'Did you? A big giant?'

Aine knew that she was being humoured. She nodded anyway. 'On the island.'

'On the island. A big giant. I hope you chased him off.'

Aine shook her head. 'He was dead.'

'Oh. He was dead. Well, then, we have nothing to worry about, have we?'

Aine shook her head. She turned over so her mother couldn't see her and put her thumb into her mouth. It wasn't the idea of the bull that scared her so much as the thought of it emerging from the earth like a worm or like the calf that she had once seen being born, coming out of a hole in its mother. The embers of the fire drew her in and showed her hag faces. She closed her eyes and tried to think about a new bicycle.

The beginning of the tape was bent and scratched. Dim shadows moved behind crackling white fizz.

'Jaysus, this is brilliant!' said Joseph. He was sitting on the sofa, squashed in between Stephen and David. Mick sat on the armchair, swearing. David fidgeted nervously with the tail of his shirt. Stephen cracked the tab on a can. A feeble froth bubbled out.

'Ooh,' said Mick, heavily camp. 'Suck it off, Jo, quick, suck it off.'

Joseph laughed and leaned across. As his lips got close to the can, Stephen lowered it and wedged it between his legs. Joseph followed it for a few seconds, then caught on. Mick howled with glee. Joseph gave Stephen a shove.

'You bollocks!'

'Shhh!' said David. On the TV, a woman's voice could be heard, saying: 'Now what are we going to do?'

The mist cleared. There were two women standing beside a car with a flat tyre. One of them was blonde and the other one was dark. They were both wearing shorts, high heels, and lots of make-up. They both had large breasts barely concealed inside skimpy T-shirts.

'The blonde's mine,' said Mick.

'No way,' said Stephen. 'Here, I'll fix the flat. I've got a pump.' He worked an imaginary bicycle pump above the beer can in his crotch. Joseph giggled.

'Shhh!' said David.

Two guys had pulled up in a flashy car. They got out and started talking to the girls. Their voices didn't match what their lips were doing, but it didn't seem to matter. They were both dark and stubbled and dressed in black leather and sunglasses. It was quite clear that they were bad news but not, apparently, to the two women, who were delighted to get into the car with them.

Thomas rebuked Gaybo and switched him off. The dog leapt up and preceded him to the back door. Outside, a fresh breeze was getting up, but it wasn't about to be a storm. Not yet. Above the scudding clouds a bright moon sent light to make the dark surface of the lake gleam. Thomas listened to the night. Popeye listened too, then chased off about some important business. In the hazel behind the house, something rustled and flapped and was still again. The wind brought the sound of a car, but it might have been a mile away. Thomas called for the dog, who appeared from nowhere and sat down at his feet. Something nagged at the back of Thomas's mind, something that he ought to have attended to but had forgotten. He couldn't get at it, and it slipped away among all the other things that mattered once but no longer did. The dog sniffed the air, reading it but unable to translate. The man was aware of the comparative poverty of his senses. They were growing shallower, too, so that at times he seemed barely to be connected to this world but to another, more subtle one. Sometimes it frightened him, but at other times, like now, that waiting world seemed much more exciting. It was ancient and quiet but none the less vibrant for all that. It was, he realised now, the place that the stories came from. More real than the heaven that the priest described because it was here, now, and it always had been. It was just that people tended to forget it, somehow.

He looked towards the big house. It was full of lights, but the people inside it were dark and mean, turned in on themselves, selfish like the whole of their generation. There would never be an end to all they could want and all they could get. They were hardly the same breed as the old people. And yet they were.

The dog set out again, but Thomas called him back. Reluctantly, he followed the old man into the house.

There was no more giggling. The action had moved to a huge, ancient mansion owned by the two dark men and their father. Somewhere in the house, the blonde woman was taking a bath while the old man watched in hiding. In the meantime, his sons were sorting out the dark woman in the cellar. She was spread-eagled on a four-poster bed, tied hand and foot. While one of the men looked on, the other slipped a sharp knife up the inside leg of her shorts.

33

Joseph was torn between conflicting pressures, one at his groin, the other somewhere inside, untouchable. He knew that it should be all wrong, what he was watching, but the woman was giving little fearful animal gasps and cries, tossing her head from side to side, her eyes half closed, her breasts arching upwards.

He squirmed on the sofa, somehow succeeding in keeping his hands off his cock. He could hear Stephen's heavy breathing beside him and he wanted to look, to see if he had a hard-on, but he couldn't tear his eyes from the screen. The woman was completely naked now; all her clothes cut off. In her struggles to free herself, she thrust up her pelvis. But the man with the knife stepped away and, as the woman squirmed and grunted, the other brother stepped forward, undoing his flies.

The barman flicked the lights on and off and called time. It was Gerard's round and he watched another twenty pound note reduced to small change. It was too late, now, to go back and check the other pubs for Martina. He didn't know what all the fuss was about. The girl was nineteen, after all. She was an adult. She'd be furious if she thought her dad was going around asking for her. And quite right, too. Wasn't she well able to take care of herself?

Brigid found herself thinking about Kevin and wishing that he was still at home. She could imagine him there beside her, watching the television in companionable silence, providing the solid male presence that she seemed to need in her life. Gerard no longer provided it. She couldn't remember when he had changed; become cold and rejecting. A long time ago. Years. And as for Joseph, he hardly seemed to be there at all. He was like a shadow, a person without substance. She didn't understand him. Her own blood, but none the less a stranger to her.

She had intended to stay up and watch the late film, but now she found that she hadn't the energy. As she got up, the sleeping child stirred and sighed and stretched into the empty space. Brigid moved the thumb out of her slack mouth and covered her with the patchwork quilt from the back of the sofa.

The two men had finished with the dark woman and disposed of her. Now they had shifted their attention to the blonde one. Joseph was so excited that he was afraid he would come in his pants. From the way Stephen was sitting, he suspected that he already had. On his other side, David was rigid and pale.

'You dirty little bastards!'

Joseph sprang up with a reflex action and turned to see Mick's father, Brian, standing in the doorway. He had the impression that he had been there for some time, looking over their heads at the screen.

'Who brought that into this house?'

Joseph's hands were dangling in front of his genitals but he knew he was hiding nothing. Mick's mother was staring straight at him, straight through him. He turned and bolted through the kitchen and into the bathroom. Mick's father roared down the corridor after him.

'Come back here!'

But Joseph slammed the door and slid the bolt across. Cold water. He turned on the tap and tried to splash himself. The water soaked his shirt, his jeans, everything, but it had no effect on the problem. Tears of fear and humiliation fell down his cheeks.

From the sitting room he could hear the rise and fall of angry voices; loud questions, mumbled answers. There was a rapid drumming sound which might have been his own pulse and might have been heavy footsteps in the hall. He could tell that the little brass bolt wouldn't hold for long if someone gave a half-decent shove. The water in the tap was becoming hot. He turned on the other one, ran it on to his hand and tried to rub it on to his cock. The moment he touched himself he came, doubling up with the intensity of it, shooting spunk past his own chin and on to the soap-smeared mirror.

'Joseph?' Someone called down the hallway.

His breath caught in his throat as the spasms continued, an eternity of terror and shame and ecstasy.

'Joseph! Come out of there!'

'Just a minute, Mrs Burke.'

His voice sounded old and tired. He was exhausted and disgusted. He looked at himself. There were white globs of spunk on the mirror, and there was no toilet paper.

Brigid dozed. She woke when she heard Trish's car pass along the boirin at the back of the house. She woke again when Gerard's car pulled in, and again when he got into the bed beside her. And she woke once more when she heard the back door open and close, and footsteps come quietly upstairs. It had to be Martina.

After that, she slept soundly.

Day

Trish opened her eyes at first light. Something had woken her, but she couldn't tell what. She cast around for the dream she had been having but there were only bad feelings, and she remembered that she had been trying to decide whether to go or whether to stay. Several times over the past twenty-four hours she had made up her mind that she was leaving, but each time the initial euphoria was replaced by anxiety. She had formed attachments here. She had nowhere else to go. As often as she decided to leave, she decided against it. And when she found herself in that defeated state of mind, she began to wonder whether she had been responsible for what had happened; whether she had, in fact, led Gerard on without realising it. Women, after all, were usually to blame for these things.

She turned towards the pale blue light at the window, just as the sound came again. This time it was quite clear, the chink of a loose shoe on the concrete yard at the back of the house. There were horses in the boxes there but there shouldn't be any in the yard.

For a while she stayed where she was. The horse would be

all right and there was nothing else to get up for at that hour.
But as soon as her mind was free of distraction it returned to
the same old circumambulation. Would she or wouldn't she?
Should she or shouldn't she? In sudden fury with it all she
threw back the bedclothes and got up.

The stabled horses were awake and looking out over their
half doors. The two fillies were still clinging together anxiously
like a beast with two heads, and The Nipper was as hungry as
ever. He whickered and knocked the heavy door with his knee
but, for once, Trish ignored him. The sound of the loose shoe
had come from Specks, Martina's roan cob, who was standing
outside the yard gate, looking in. He had a saddle on but no
bridle. His martingale was broken and trailing from his girth.
Trish's blood ran cold.

Aine was wrapped up in the patchwork quilt watching early
morning cartoons when Trish poked her head around the
sitting-room door.

'Hey, Aine. Is Martina around?'

Aine shrugged and turned back to the television, but she
listened to Trish's quick footsteps going up the stairs and
the creak of floorboards overhead. There was one last, quiet
moment and then the peace was shattered. Her parents' voices
lifted in bewilderment, then anxiety, and white terror swam
into the house.

Brigid burst into Joseph's room.

'Have you seen Martina?'

'What? No!'

'What are you doing here, anyway? I thought you were staying at Stephen's'

'... came home.'

'I thought you were Martina coming in. Why did you come home?'

It all seemed to be a continuation of last night's nightmare; the fury of the Burkes, the long walk out along the dark road. Joseph didn't want to have to face it. He said nothing and turned over to go back to sleep.

'Get up, will you? Help us to look for her!'

'Where?'

'I don't know where! Everywhere!'

Joseph jumped up, energised by a note of panic in his mother's voice that he had never heard there before.

In the sitting room, Aine heard her father and Trish go out of the back door and over the boirin towards the cottage. She pulled on her socks and was hunting under the sofa for her runners when her mother came in.

'Did you know that Martina was out riding yesterday?' she asked.

Aine froze. She had known. Thomas had said it.

'Did you?' Brigid's voice was high; frightened.

'No,' said Aine. 'Why?'

But Brigid was gone, out through the kitchen and beyond the back door to catch up with the others. Aine's face was flushed with fear. She found her shoes and pulled them on.

'Oh, Jesus,' said Gerard. 'Oh, Jesus.' He walked around Specks, who watched him uneasily. Now that Gerard had

40

seen it, Trish pulled the saddle off and threw it up on the gate.

'Poor old Specks,' she said. She had never liked him; said he was an ugly old cob, but she didn't blame him for it. Despite the bit of white that showed in his eye there was no badness in him.

Brigid had come up to the gate and was looking at him.

'The saddle was on him,' said Trish. 'But no bridle.'

'No bridle?' said Brigid. 'Dear God. What on earth has happened?'

'It's possible he was tied up somewhere,' said Trish. 'If he pulled loose he might have left the bridle behind.'

Gerard nodded. 'It's possible,' he said. 'Or if she fell and held on to the reins she could have pulled it off.'

Between the big house and the stable yard, Joseph stood, afraid to come too close. Aine was beside him, clutching at his shirt sleeve.

'In any case, we'd better start looking,' said Gerard.

Gerard sped off up the boirin in the pick-up, then abruptly slowed down. She could be anywhere. She could have been coming home; right under his nose. He would have to be careful.

He turned his head from side to side as he drove. The boirin was a mess. On the left, the boundary was a rusting straggle of barbed wire and broken sheep netting, through which brambles and nettles were growing and spreading in all directions. A few tumbled stones showed that there had once been a wall, but Gerard couldn't remember it being there.

He did, though, remember putting up the white electric tape to keep the horses and cattle in. It was supposed to have been a temporary measure.

The farm was running down. Gerard had got out of sheep and into sport horses at exactly the right moment, before the grants came in and everybody wanted them. He had sold dozens of home-bred youngsters, and they had expanded, bought more stock and built the bungalow for Thomas. Everything was booming, growing, improving. But the market had flooded and Gerard hadn't had the foresight to move quickly enough into anything else. The cattle were keeping everything ticking over, but there was nothing to spare; nothing for post and rail fencing. All the same, he had to admit that it would have cost nothing to clear up the mess; drag the rusty wire to the dump and burn the old posts. He could hear Thomas's disapproval nagging away at the back of his mind. It would never have been neglected like that if he was stil running the place.

He had come to a stop where the boirin met the main road and he sat looking left and right, wondering which way he was going. With a shock that sent acids cutting through his circulation, he remembered. He turned to the left, and as he did so he saw Brigid in the Kadett behind him, inching up to the junction, turning the opposite way. He was ashamed, certain that she knew he had forgotten, the way she knew everything about him; everything about everyone.

He crawled for a hundred yards along the road, scanning the hedgerows. It was difficult, even at that speed, and he wished he had brought someone with him. Where was she, for God's sake? There must be some obvious answer, some safe and happy outcome. His mind ran down various alleys of possibility. They were all blocked.

Brigid turned right on to the main road and then immediately left again, up a single-track road that led towards the mountains. She was surprised that Gerard had not gone that way. It seemed the most obvious place to look.

They had cattle up there, about thirty of them, all bullocks, ranging on a hundred acres of hillside. The land didn't look like much in farming terms, but Brigid knew they were lucky to have it. The area was limestone based, and the mountains were almost entirely bare rock. Some said that it was a natural process of erosion that had taken place over the millennia, and others said that it was the result of over-grazing by the livestock of nomadic peoples in more recent times. There might, in the end, be no way of knowing for sure, but the consequences were beyond doubt. The bald mountains acted as heat-banks, and along the sides of them alpine shrubs and flowers grew. On the best-sheltered flanks were areas where between the rocks, grasses and other fodder plants thrived throughout the year. These areas were generally left to the wild goats during the summer, but in the winter they could support small numbers of cattle without any supplementation at all. Except for water. Despite its high rainfall, the region was classified as desert, since it possessed hardly any natural reservoirs, and the run-off from the rocks passed directly into underground bores.

The place was famous. People came from all over the world

to visit it, but for the life of her Brigid couldn't imagine why. It was grey and dreary. Counting the cattle up there was just another chore on a list. One that she never undertook. One that Martina and Specks regularly did.

Brigid's voice ran a commentary, a continuous loop inside her head. 'It'll be all right. It has to be. It'll be all right, please God.'

She jammed on the brakes. There was a flash of colour in a gateway; bright blue and black, but even before Brigid stopped, she knew. It was plastic. Fertiliser bags and bale-wrap scrunched up together and stuffed down behind the gatepost. Brigid put a hand to her face and closed her eyes. Her heart was banging in her chest, frightening her. She gritted her teeth. The stupid girl was probably fast asleep in a comfortable bed somewhere. And when she found her, she would kill her.

Gerard got out of the pick-up and pushed open the gate into one of Dan Flaherty's fields. It was badly hung and he had to drag it across the muddy ground, ploughed and pitted by the feet of standing cattle.

He decided not to drive in and went back to turn off the engine. He would be able to see more on foot, and he began by closely examining the ground. One or two of the prints there might have been made by a horse but he couldn't be sure. As he dragged the gate shut again, it occurred to him that he was wasting his time. The cob could jump, he knew, but he probably wouldn't. If he had lost Martina in this field he would still be here, stuffing his ugly face.

All the same, Gerard found that he had to look; had to be

sure. He walked across to where a pair of parallel green banks marked the beginning of the ancient road known as the Old Line. It had always been a favourite riding place, even for him, as a boy. It was long and straight and soft and green. The horses seemed to find it as inviting as their riders, and always danced across the grass like racehorses going to the start. When he was young, if he opened Flaherty's gate and Kelly's gate Gerard could gallop for more than half a mile in a long, graceful curve exactly parallel to the lake-shore. But Flaherty's gate was gone now and the gap closed up. The old road ran underneath the hedgerow and vanished. On the other side, Matty Kelly had ploughed up the land and reseeded it. Gerard had been shocked. He was still shocked, all these years later. Nowadays it wouldn't be allowed.

There were only three or four hundred clear yards left of the Old Line, but even so it was still a fairly decent gallop. Martina often came here with the cob and Trish sometimes came with her, to give some young horse a pipe-opener. The banks weren't high, but Gerard walked along the top of one of them anyway, to get the best possible look at the surrounding land. Dan Flaherty's cattle lifted their heads from their grazing and watched him as he passed. There was nothing unusual to be seen, and the few horse prints that he did find were old and blunted by rain.

Joseph went down to the bungalow to tell Thomas. He hated going down there, hated the tacky new house, hated having a grandfather who lived out the back. He was afraid of finding Thomas dead; had been since Thomas told him that he had found his own grandfather dead when he was a teenager. He was also afraid of finding Thomas engaged in some kind of private and repulsive activity, like masturbating or pissing in the sink. He was particularly in dread of these things since last night.

'Grandda?'

The back door was open and the dog came bounding out. Joseph rubbed its ears. He had never heard it bark and it crossed his mind that perhaps it couldn't, for some reason. Maybe it was a freak. Maybe Thomas had had it de-barked. He wondered if there was such an operation and, if so, could his sister get it. He heard Stephen's voice. 'Imagine that! A woman that didn't talk back!' and was immediately ashamed for thinking it, especially in the circumstances.

Thomas came to the door, a cup of tea steaming in his hand.

'Ah,' he said, stuck for a moment, embarrassed because he could not, could never remember Joseph's name. He was the quietest of all of them; the darkest and the most distant. Somehow they had never hit it off.

'You're about early,' he said, in the end.

'Martina's gone missing,' said Joseph. 'The horse came home this morning without her.'

Thomas's face seemed to collapse. 'Oh, dear,' he said. 'That isn't good. That isn't good at all.'

He went back inside, pulled a chair out from under the kitchen table and sat down on it. That, Joseph thought, was a lot of help.

*　　*　　*

It wasn't long before Gerard was quite certain that Martina wasn't on the Old Line, nor had been. But he also knew that if he turned back before the end he would always be wondering. He dropped down on to the road again, remembering every step of it. There had been charioteers here once; real ones. An archaeological survey in the fifties had shown that the track had once run all the way around the lake, but for some reason the banks on the other side had been lost. They had found chariot hand grips and bits of wheel hubs. Celtic ones; Irish. Thomas used to say that charioteers still raced along the road on nights of the new moon. He said they went straight through the gates and hedges as if they weren't there, all around the lake from one side to the other and back again. He said that if you heard them you should lie down and close your eyes and pray to Saint Patrick. He said he had heard them himself one time, coming back across the fields from the mart in Ennis with Jackie Flynn. But Jackie Flynn got annoyed if he was asked about it, so Gerard could never get the truth.

Not that he didn't know what the truth was. He was sure that Thomas didn't believe the stories himself, but felt under some sort of ancestral compulsion to hand them down to anyone who would listen. A chill went through him and he looked out over the lake to where the island stood, bull-like, in its own early-morning shadow. Gods. Fairies. He had never been able to work out which was which, or whether they were the same things, or who it was that had been banished to live under the ground when the Milesians had come to rule the surface of the land.

He had come to the end of the field. He looked across into the next one, but there was no reason to go any further. Martina couldn't have anyway, unless she had jumped the cob over the hedge. He turned and started back the way he had come. Surely to God the girl had turned up at home by now. She was probably sitting at the range, drinking a hot cup of tea. Maybe she had hurt her leg. Or her head; got a knock, perhaps. On the road.

He broke into a run. Why was he out here, wandering around the fields when he hadn't even thought of phoning the hospital?

As soon as the others had gone, Trish thought of it. Her brother had died of tetanus when he was seventeen and she had been a realist ever since when it came to life and death. She had no problem imagining Martina in a hospital bed; comatose, brain-damaged. She parked Aine in front of the television in the cottage while she phoned; first Ennis, then Limerick, and finally the Galway Regional. Martina wasn't in any of them.

Brigid turned off the metalled road and drove up a long, gently curving boirin which ran between green, sloping meadows and on up into the grey crags where the winterage lay. She drove slowly, watching carefully, finding no clues. Grass grew in between the stony tyre-tracks and Martina was in the habit of cantering all the way up. It was the main reason that she was always so willing to ride up there to check on the cattle. Brigid tried to imagine the thrill of it, of speeding along the track on horseback, but she failed. It had never appealed to her. She admired the horses from a distance but had always been afraid to get too close.

The track narrowed as she got higher, but remained passable for the Kadett right up to the end. There was a space to turn, a gate, and on the other side of it, a concrete water trough fed by a trickling spring. Other than that there was nothing. Just rock. As Brigid got out of the car the sun appeared over the easternmost hills, casting sudden shadows, creating contrast. Brigid opened the gate and went through it and past the dribbling trough. A cattle-path led on upwards, winding among the spurs and faults of the grey crags. The going was awkward enough, and Brigid was fairly certain that Martina always left Specks tied to the gate when she walked in to look at the cattle. The limestone was flaky and criss-crossed with grikes, some a few inches deep, others twenty feet or more, their dark depths concealed by ferns and mosses that grew on their walls, far beneath Brigid's feet. Even where a thin covering of soil allowed for the growth of coarse grass there could be holes. Brigid had always considered the shoes she wore to be sensible, but now she wasn't so sure. The heels were not high but they were narrow and unstable. Already her ankles were beginning to tire.

She walked on, rounding a shoulder of rock which hid the trough, the car, all signs of civilisation from her view. The path now seemed less like a path and more like an invitation, a tendency perhaps, the most obvious way forward. She was now quite certain that a horse could not have come up here, but once started she couldn't turn back. Just around the next turn, or the next . . .

She found that she was walking with an urgency that hurt. There were pains in her thighs and in her calves, and her pulse was racing at her throat. There was now no hint of a track at all. Instead there was a desire to be up high; to reach a vantage point and to look out over the landscape from it; to be able to see everything. Brigid was surprised by herself, by the soundness of the instinct that had led her there, and she stopped to look back.

She had climbed into shadow again, on to a flat area of grike-covered pavement, one of a number of terrace-like levels that stepped their way up the mountainside. Vegetation was minimal around her, but ahead, between where she stood and the next craggy terrace wall, was an area of low hazel scrub, waist-high perhaps. It was grey as the rocks around it, except where a taller ash tree rose out of it, and then it was white. In a few weeks' time everything would be bursting with green, but it was hard, now, to imagine it.

A raven flew over, its wings so noisy in the air that it frightened her until it came into view. She watched it as it circled above the place where the car was and came back over her head again. She was certain that it was looking at her; checking her out. It gave her the creeps. The whole place did. It was dry and lifeless, ancient and cold. Godless.

She shivered, pulled her light jacket around her and went on.

Thomas and Joseph walked up to the yard just as Trish and Aine returned from the house.

'Where have they all gone tearing off to?' said Thomas.

'They're looking for her,' said Trish.

Thomas shook his head as he opened the gate and went into the yard. He inspected the cob carefully, bending double to look at his belly and to run a practised hand down his legs.

'There's not a mark on him,' said Trish.

'No,' said Thomas, straightening up slowly. ''Tis very queer.'

Specks nudged politely at Thomas's pockets. Thomas found a few crumbling horse nuts and gave them to him. 'And come here to me,' he went on. 'Was there any talk at all of going around to the neighbours? Of doing the thing right?'

Trish shook her head.

'I might as well wait and see,' said Thomas. 'Have we looked around our own fields yet?'

Gerard closed the stiff gate and got back into the pick-up. The road was too narrow to turn in, so he drove on to the end, to where Dan Flaherty's house was. As he turned the truck, he looked out beyond Dan's little landing-stage at the still waters of the lake and was suddenly struck by a horror that he could barely comprehend. There were nine miles of shore, not including the island. Within riding distance there were a dozen places where a road or a track met the water's edge. Every seven years, it was said, the lake claimed a victim. Gerard's mind began to wander back towards the last one, but he diverted it; stopped the engine and got out. Dan Flaherty's dogs were choking with fury and curiosity inside their closed shed, and his ancient donkey, still woolly from the winter, watched in amazement as Gerard passed by.

*   *   *

Brigid walked on towards the hazel scrub, stepping carefully, aware of how dangerously tired her ankles were becoming. She could see the process of erosion at work, where flakes of limestone had broken from the bedrock exposing fossilised mud-layers, some with shells in. She began to notice plants as well; the dark-loving ferns in the grikes, and anemones, and tiny, primitive rose bushes with millions of soft little thorns. All her life she had lived within sight of these mountains. She drove through them several times a week, on her way to Ennis. Now she realised that despite their growing fame as a tourist attraction, she knew nothing about them at all. The schools had brought all her kids on field trips and they had drawn pictures in their copy books. But she, herself, knew nothing.

There were three wooden boats upturned on the grass beside the landing stage. One of them belonged to Dan and the others to a nephew of his who brought fishing parties down from Dublin. The water was murky along the shoreline, but the bottom was just visible. In the summer the algae grew so thick that it covered the surface completely and nothing could be seen. Two dogs had died there the previous year from swallowing water in the shallows, and people were being advised not to swim there any more. All the local farmers had been asked to reduce the use of nitrates on any land that might drain towards the lake. Gerard knew exactly who would comply with that request and who would ignore it.

There were no hoofprints anywhere around. Gerard scuffed

backwards and forwards for a while and threw a large stone into the water, watching the mud rise and settle, feeling child-like, feeling helpless. Out in the lake, the island was slowly brightening like a living thing waking up. Martina often rode out there, sometimes even walked across the fields and brought a picnic. It was one of her favourite places. The last time that they had ridden together, before Gerard came off The Nipper and damaged his back, before he had employed Trish, that was where they had gone.

Gerard had tried to persuade Martina to sell Specks and to help himself and Trish with the youngsters they were always bringing on. There would never be a shortage of riding and he had promised never to put her on anything hot or brainless. She had refused, said that she loved Specks; she felt safe with him and would never sell him. It was a stupid attitude. The cob was pig-ugly. He had a weak shoulder and a hollow back, and his action was so bad that it was a miracle he didn't break his own legs. Even Trish agreed with that, though she reckoned that he was clever as a cat and always knew where his feet were. She thought she knew it all, Trish did, the little cow. But who was clever now?

Brigid had come to the edge of the hazel and was looking for some sign of a pathway through it when she realised that she had been quite mistaken about its nature. What she had taken for sparse, waist-high bushes were in fact the tops of much taller trees and bushes which had their feet in a declivity; a glen which dropped steeply down from where she stood.

There was something sinister about the place. The descent,

down ten feet of damp, mossy cliff was treacherous in itself. Worse, it seemed to lead into darkness. Anything might be down there.

But what? Brigid ran through possibilities in her mind but there was nothing dangerous at all that she could think of. There were no snakes, no poisonous creatures or vicious ones; no bogs, no briars, not the slightest chance of strangers. Yet still she stood, reluctant. The sun rose higher and dispelled the shade. Time was pressing. If she crossed the glade and climbed the next shelf, she would be high enough to get the view across the valley that she wanted. If she wasn't going to do it, she should turn and head back now, and waste no more time.

On the edge of her vision something moved. Brigid looked up and around. The grey hills seemed to shimmer and pulsate, as though they were alive and alert; aware of everything that was happening. Brigid tried but failed to erase the impression from her consciousness. Nothing seemed to make any sense, but at least things could hardly get any worse. The bottom had already fallen out of her world. Brigid took a deep breath, pushed through the perimeter of low bushes and began to descend.

Trish and Aine set out to search the surrounding fields. They started in the orchard behind Thomas's house where Specks lived, then continued on around the boundaries of the farm and along the lake-shore until they met Joseph and Thomas and Popeye coming back the other way.

'No luck?' said Thomas. Trish shook her head.

'God, I don't know,' he said. Aine took his hand and he squeezed hers.

'Don't be worrying,' he said, but she knew that he was.

Trish looked out across the lake. She had the stories from Martina and Thomas, or some of them at least. That the lake demanded a sacrifice every seven years. And, worse, that Cormac Mac Ruadh came out by night looking for a bride to drag down to the watery city in the depths. The ones that didn't measure up to his expectations he let go again, to float up to the surface. But when he found the right one, she would never be seen by mortal eyes again.

'She couldn't be in the lake, anyway,' said Joseph. 'Sure she couldn't?'

'Course she couldn't,' said Thomas. 'How could she?'

Dan had got up at last. He was standing at the door in vest and braces looking from Gerard to his truck, which was lying across the road where he had left it, in the middle of a three-point turn.

'How're you, Ger?' he said. 'What's going on?'

In the shed, the frustrated barking turned into sustained howls.

Brigid inched carefully down into the glen, holding on to the stems of hazel, straight and strong. Once she grew accustomed to the shade she was surprised by how bright it was, and how green after the grey rocks above. Every stone was coated in soft moss and between them the ground was covered in shamrock

55

and wild strawberry. Brigid stood still. Narrow, purposeful paths wound between the trees. Not far from her feet was the earthy opening to a lair of some kind, and a musky scent hung in the air above it. The place frightened her. Even though she had been born and brought up in town, she believed that her years on the farm had brought her to an understanding of the countryside. Now she knew that she was wrong. The atmosphere in that mountainy place was as alien to her as a foreign land. She was an intruder there; she did not know the language or the laws or the currency. Nor could she be certain about what she was doing there, even though it had all seemed so clear a few moments earlier. Martina was lost, but wherever she was, it certainly wasn't in here.

Specks was still loose in the yard when Trish and Aine got back. He was licking his saddle and Trish took it down from the gate and brought it into the tack room. The first thing she saw when she went in was a New Zealand rug, neatly folded, exactly as she had left it.

She swallowed down a rising anger. The rug belonged to one of the older brood mares who had been suffering from pneumonia. When the weather was mild they took it off her during the day, but she still needed it at night. Clearly Gerard hadn't bothered to put it on her the previous evening. It was typical of his negligent style.

Aine was waiting for her in the yard. As Trish closed the tack-room door she said: 'Do you think it was Specks's fault?'

'No way,' said Trish. 'Was it, Specks?'

The cob huffed at her pockets and she patted his neck. Aine reached up for a handful of his mane and bent her left leg at the knee. Trish bumped her up. Specks showed no sign of noticing and followed Trish to the feed shed.

'Whose fault is it, then?' Aine asked.

Trish closed the shed door to stop Specks walking in behind her. He turned his head and sniffed at Aine's foot.

'We don't know if it's anybody's fault,' said Trish, emerging with a double handful of nuts and dropping them on to a clean patch of concrete. 'We don't know what's happened, or if anything has happened, so we can't say if it's anybody's fault, can we?'

'Ooh, er,' said Aine, as Specks's head went down to pick up the nuts.

'You're all right,' said Trish, returning to the feed shed. 'Just sit up straight.'

The Nipper was banging furiously at his door, maddened by the sight of Specks eating. Trish came out with a full bucket and a scoop. Aine sat up, balanced herself and began to plait a few strands of mane at Specks's withers.

'What if somebody knew she was missing and never said anything?' she said.

'Why would they do that?'

Aine shrugged. 'But if they did?'

'Nobody would do something like that,' said Trish. 'Why would they?'

She went into The Nipper's box and pushed past him to the manger. She knew by the way he moved, even before she felt the white leg.

'Oh, for fuck's sake,' she said. But she said it under her breath, aware that Aine was just outside the door.

Gerard phoned the hospital from Dan's dark and grimy kitchen. The dogs snuffled at his legs and his groin from behind and shrank back slyly each time he turned round.

Dan moved around heavily in the adjacent bedroom, unconscious of his grunts and farts. The hospital took ages to answer, and then ages to find the woman who should have been at the admissions desk. Gerard turned his back to the wall and let fly a kick at the dogs, who slunk into an aggrieved huddle beside the cold, greasy range. Above them, a dozen joints of rank, home-cured bacon hung from a beam. It was years since Gerard had been in the house. It hadn't changed at all.

With an effort of will, Brigid remembered her purpose. Quietly, holding her breath, she stepped forward on to the floor of the glade. Wild garlic bruised beneath her feet and filled the air with its pungency. The delicate leaves of the shamrock bent and sprang back. A yellow-breasted bird with a coal-black cap chattered on a branch. Brigid was just beginning to breathe more freely when a loud report, sudden as a gunshot, froze her to the spot. She looked around but she could see nothing. She was out of her depth or tuned to the wrong frequency, and she was frightened.

The sound came again, and this time she identified it as a brisk snort. She knew the sound, and all at once she located its origin. Thirty yards further on, the ground began to slope

58

steeply up as it met the foot of the next craggy shelf. Among the mossy rocks, considerably higher than Brigid, a wild goat was standing, looking straight at her. Brigid stared back, disarmed. She wasn't surprised to find goats there. They often came down into the lower meadows and had to be chased off the good land and back up into the rocks. What did surprise her, however, was the poise and confidence in the creature's bearing. This was not a servile farmyard animal but something quite different. No one owned her. No one ever would. This place was her place. This time it was Brigid who was trespassing.

The goat was brown and white. She stood absolutely still. And then, as though her brain had suddenly cracked some visual code, Brigid could see them all. There were black ones and white ones, a grey kid and a piebald one and one that was almost the same colour as Specks. All of them stared at her, their yellow eyes narrow and remote. Smoothly, in complete agreement with one another, they moved off. They were lean and strong and agile. Brigid did not count them.

Instead she turned and started to make her way back out of the glade the way she had come. Some sort of insanity had brought her in here and she was wasting her time and her energy.

Trish put a head collar on Specks and he followed her out through the gate of the yard and down the edge of the turn-out paddock. Aine sat as if she was in an armchair. Four neat plaits hung down on to the cob's shoulder and she was working on a fifth. Trish led them through the gate into the jumps field, then gave the rope to Aine.

Specks's head went down and he began to graze. Trish left Aine to battle with him about it and walked on into the field. She looked closely at each jump as she passed it, keeping an eye out for the bridle. A fall at a jump would be an obvious place to lose one.

The admissions woman eventually came on to the line, just as Dan emerged, fully clothed from the bedroom. They both spoke at once. Gerard turned to face the wall again. Dan kicked the dogs outside and filled the kettle noisily. Gerard put down the phone.

'Not there, anyway,' he said.

'I'll tell you what you'll do, now,' said Dan. It was typical of him, always knowing best. Gerard turned away to hide his irritation.

'You'll go on home,' Dan went on, 'and get a bit of breakfast for yourself. By the time you have that done, I'll have a few of the lads gathered down at your house.'

Gerard bottled an impotent rage.

'The way we'll have the whole place covered,' said Dan. 'And then we'll be sure to find her, God bless her.'

Gerard nodded and went out to the car. Despite his annoyance with Dan he knew that he was right. He needed to relax, be methodical, take things a step at a time. But as he completed the turn and drove away he was aware of the island behind him exerting some kind of force. It sent shivers down his spine.

*   *   *

When Brigid emerged from the hazel a brown hare, gilded by the sun, loped off across the rocks and vanished into the hillside. Brigid made her way carefully back. At every step a different kind of flower seemed to be growing out of some little toe-hold in the limestone. Brigid said their names like a rosary and felt comforted. Only once did she look back. The goats were at the top of the next step on the mountain, standing against the skyline, watching.

At the far side of the jumps field a circular track had been beaten out of the grass by the passage of many hooves. This was where Trish and Gerard lunged the young horses and got them jumping. Trish didn't like the system. She felt that Gerard put the jumps up too high too fast and, although the horses usually developed a tremendous athleticism, most of them came out of the education over-anxious and inclined to refuse. Trish preferred to start the youngsters more slowly, over trotting poles and brush-piles, gradually progressing to low walls and barrels. But Gerard was impatient and said they couldn't afford to spend that amount of time. The horses got educated his way.

Just as everything else had to be done his way. The woman that Trish had trained with ran a tight ship; everything tidy and orderly. The horses learned at their own speed and their needs came above those of everybody else. Trish had loved it. But Gerard's operation couldn't have been more different. It was a rusting hulk; undermanned and leaking.

Trish stopped at the edge of the lunging ring and looked back across the field to where Aine had won the battle with

Specks and was riding him round in a tight, left-handed circle. Trish was fond of her; fond of all the children in the family. It was a shame that people had to have parents.

As soon as he was out of sight of Dan's house, Gerard stopped and turned round in his seat. The island was still brightening in the morning sun; becoming green and fresh. But the feelings it engendered in Gerard were uniformly unpleasant. Monks had lived there once, and when he was a boy he had teased his brother Peadar about their ghosts. He had given them names and different-coloured cowls, and he described them all so vividly that Peadar swore he could see them as well. With a shock, Gerard remembered how he had felt when Peadar said that; how a monstrous fear had loomed at the edge of his consciousness. What if they had actually become real? What if the clear delineations of the actual world had broken down and left the human race open to an invasion by its own imagination? It had scared him far more than it ever scared Peadar. He had suddenly seen Thomas's stories everywhere; in the ground, in the water, in the fallen stones of the monastery and the cottages and the fort. Unable to cope, he had relegated them to a sealed cell in the deepest recesses of his mind where they still lay, unregarded and untold, corrupt and terrifying. He suppressed them with television, with drink, with the solid, patriarchal comfort of the mass. But as he watched the island now they threatened to emerge, and fear crawled up his spine.

Specks was tired of walking round in a circle. He stopped

and put his head down to graze again, pulling Aine forward so that she either had to let go of the lead rope or fall off down his neck.

'Trish!' she yelled. 'I need another rope!'

'Let him eat,' she called back. 'You can ride him properly later.'

Trish sighed and returned to her search. One of the jumps on the lunging track was very high, getting on for four and a half feet. It was clear that while she had been away on her day off, Gerard had been pushing somebody very hard. She remembered the heat in The Nipper's leg and swore under her breath. It was the last straw. As soon as things settled down, she would be out of there and gone.

Brigid drove back to the main road, but she wasn't ready to go home, yet. Instead, she took another mountain lane and turned on to the unmetalled famine road which ran for several miles along the mountainside parallel to the lake. The fierceness of her concentration was making her tired and confused, and just as the light glanced off the pale rocks and hurt her eyes, so her own thoughts were beginning to cause darting pains in her solar plexus.

There were several good vantage points along the road, but Brigid didn't get out of the car again. When the boirin rejoined the tarred road she drove straight home. The back door of the house was open but there was no one about. Despite the sun which blazed down outside, the kitchen was cold, and its silence was unbearable. Brigid turned on the radio, looked at it for a moment, then went back outside.

*   *   *

Gerard couldn't tear his eyes away from the island. Despite his resistance, a ghoulish flood of memories was being unleashed and he was in their grip. There was supposed to be a money-hole somewhere underneath the old wall that ran along the bottom of the north-facing slope. Thomas said that Cormac Mac Ruadh, the chieftain who had built the fort, had buried his gold there and set a trusted warrior to stand watch over it. At Cormac's request, the warrior swore to guard it, dead or alive, and there and then, Cormac struck off his head. The story told that his spirit, in the form of a man with a bull's head, still waited there, and if anyone ever came close to discovering where the money-hole was, a terrible fate would befall them. Thomas said that two of the archaeologists involved in the dig had met with mysterious deaths, but Anthony said that they never went anywhere near the island at all.

As he finally turned to drive away, Gerard realised that he had always preferred Anthony's versions of the truth to Thomas's.

Thomas got back into the car, disturbing Joseph's dreams, causing him to sigh and sit up. They were outside Anthony Daly's house on their way round to gather all the neighbours.

'Dan has already phoned him,' he said. 'He says there's no need for us to go around. Everybody's letting some other one know.'

Joseph reached forward and made another attempt to find

his favourite station on the car radio. Thomas wished he could take to him.

'Can you think of anywhere else we should look?' he said.

Joseph found the wavelength at last and leaned back in the seat, looking out towards the lake, seeing nothing.

'Are you on this planet at all?' said Thomas.

'Yeah,' said Joseph. 'Course I am. Are you?'

Thomas started the engine and they drove home in silence.

Brigid saw Aine on Specks and went over to her just as Trish completed her circuit of the field.

'Do you really think it's safe to do that?' Brigid asked.

'Do what?'

'Leave the child on the horse.'

'Specks is all right.'

'You could be wrong, you know,' said Brigid. 'We don't know yet what has happened to Martina.'

Trish patted the cob noisily on the shoulder.

'Specks is safe as houses,' she said.

He stretched out to investigate Brigid. She pushed his nose away and reached up for Aine, who slid off into her arms. Trish's anger spoke inside her head as she unbuckled the horse's head collar and pushed him away to graze. 'He's an awful lot safer than some people not a million miles away from here. Ever think of getting him gelded, Mrs?'

Brigid cut across her thoughts. 'Is he supposed to be in here?'

'No,' said Trish. 'But there won't be any jumping done today.'

Specks wandered off to a muddy patch of ground and dropped himself carefully, knees first then haunches. He rolled clean over first time, then back, then back again.

'That makes him worth three hundred pounds more than we paid for him,' said Aine. Brigid took her hand and led her out through the gate. She wished she hadn't said that to Trish, who knew far more about the horses than she ever would. She had no reason to mistrust the girl, but she did, and had done from the day she took up the job.

Trish watched them go, the woman clumsy in her silly shoes, finding the muddy going difficult. She expected to feel the familiar resentment at unearned mistrust, but surprisingly she didn't. She pitied her.

Aine turned round and waved. Trish waved back.

'We phoned around the hospitals, Mrs Keane. She isn't in any of them.'

Brigid turned.

'Me and Aine,' said Trish, in case she had been wondering.

Gerard's pick-up drew up at the front of the house, closely followed by Thomas's Golf. Brigid hurried in, leaving Aine to drift in more casually behind her.

'Any news?'

Gerard shook his head.

'Oh, Gerard,' she said. She thought he might reach out to her, hold her, offer her comfort, but he never had, and it was clear that the current crisis changed nothing. He went on through to the kitchen and pulled out the frying pan. She followed him.

'What are you doing?'

'Making breakfast.'

'How can you make breakfast?' For an instant she thought it was a joke, and looked towards the door, expecting Martina to dance in and say 'Boo!'

'How can you make breakfast?' she repeated.

Aine slipped away to the sitting room, away from the gathering tension.

'There's an explanation for all this somewhere,' said Gerard. 'In the meantime, we have to eat. Has anybody been on to her friends?'

Brigid shook her head.

'Why don't you do that, then? Instead of flapping around like a headless chicken and worrying about what other people are doing?'

Joseph came in and went straight to the cupboard. He pulled down two packets of cereals and put them on the counter-top. Thomas came in more slowly.

'Any news?'

Brigid got out milk and closed the fridge. Gerard opened it again and got out rashers and sausages. Both shook their heads. Joseph poured two different cereals into a bowl. Brigid left the milk in front of him and went out to the phone.

Aine liked the programme that was on, but she couldn't sit still. She bounced on the sofa even though it wasn't allowed, and when no one came in to stop her she bounced harder, then ran across the room and jumped on to it, then did it again. A terrible kind of energy possessed her and she ran and jumped and ran until she was too tired to do it any more, and then she went back into the kitchen, red in the face with her own heat.

None of Martina's friends had seen her. When Brigid came back into the kitchen, Gerard went out to phone the Guards. Joseph was standing over the fry and Aine was standing at his elbow, looking into the pan.

'Can I have that one?' she asked, pointing to a long sausage with a little crisp nodule at the end.

Joseph gave her a wink. 'You want the one with the knob on?' he said. 'We'll have to see now, won't we? Have you been a good girl?'

Aine shrugged. She knew it was a joke but it made her feel uncomfortable all the same.

'Haven't buried any sisters lately?' Joseph went on.

'Joseph!' Brigid strode over and took the fish-slice from him.

'What?'

'How can you talk like that? This is serious. Don't you realise that?'

'She'll turn up, for God's sake! What can have happened to her, after all?'

In the silence that followed, Brigid dished up the fry and Thomas buttered bread and stacked it in the middle of the table. His lips had a blueish tinge which would have worried

Brigid on another day. Joseph stood with his hands in his pockets looking sulkily out of the window. Aine watched as her mother gave the sausage with the knob on to Thomas, but she didn't dare say anything.

Gerard phoned the sergeant's house but he was out. His wife said that she would tell him when he came in, and that in the meantime he ought to find a good photograph and get on to HQ in Ennis. Gerard said that he would, and he sat for a long time on the chair in the hallway trying to work up the courage. It seemed too serious, somehow, or melodramatic. It would move Martina's absence into another category. He couldn't bring himself to do it.

By the time he went back into the kitchen, the others had finished breakfast. As though he had disturbed something, everyone began to move at once. Joseph cleared a chair for him and began to gather dishes. Aine dragged Thomas into the sitting room to watch television with her. Brigid pulled on rubber gloves and began to run water into the sink. From there she could see the mountains, pale and grey against a paler, greyer sky. She was aware of a sense of defeat, as though she had tried to scale them and turned back. But that wasn't what had happened. When she thought of it, of the hazel and the wild goats, it set her nerves on edge again. But she remembered why it was that she had wanted to get up high, and it was suddenly more important than ever.

She took off the gloves and dropped them in a pile beside the unfinished dishes.

'I'm not staying here,' she said. 'I just can't.'

Aine tried both the channels. There was a boring black and white film on one of them and pop music on the other. She had posters all over her walls and stickers all over her school copies, but she wasn't really interested in the music the bands played. She turned it off and tried to turn Thomas on instead.

'Daddy says Specks is a tinker's cob,' she said.

'Does he?'

'Yes. Is he?'

'No. He just says that because he doesn't like him. He says it because Specks is the kind of horse the Travellers like.'

'Why did you buy him?' said Aine.

'Because Martina was frightened of the young horses here.'

'I wouldn't be.'

'No. I dare say you wouldn't.'

'But why Specks?'

'Because he was quiet and good.'

'Yes, but why Specks?'

Thomas was on the verge of impatience when he realised what the child was asking.

'Ah,' he said. 'You're looking for a story.'

Aine nodded

'But, sure, you have heard that story a hundred times.'

'Tell it again.'

'I won't,' he said, but he was smiling and she knew that he would.

As soon as Brigid was gone, Gerard began to feel restless.

He finished his breakfast quickly and dropped his plate into the abandoned suds. Joseph was clearly in a dream. He was standing with the dishcloth in his hand, wiping the same bit of the table over and over again. Gerard swallowed a rising anger. He knew that he should try to renew his relationship with the boy. He also knew that he couldn't do it now.

The phone rang and he answered it. It was the sergeant, who took an eternity to offer plenty of concern and no help at all. Gerard did his best to remain polite, but it was almost more than he could do.

Brigid parked the car in the same place and climbed over the gate. The hazel was further away than she had remembered and the unexpected heat of the spring sun seemed to be magnified by the bare rock. At that moment it felt very much like a desert, despite the tiny pools of water that still lay in the shell-holes in the rocks, left there by recent rain.

She could hear a tractor moving in the valley below but, far from being a comforting sound it intensified the eerie atmosphere and increased the sense of isolation. She had intended to take the same route as she had earlier, but now she found that she was already further to the left than she meant to be. It was mildly irritating, but what was worse, and already causing problems, was that she had not had the sense to look for some wellingtons before she came. Her ankles were aching. For the first time she understood why walkers often used sticks. A stick now would help with balance, and with feeling out good ground. She wished that she had one.

'Oscar took hold of the gold bracelet to pick it up off the ground,' said Thomas, well into his stride by now and beginning to enjoy himself. 'He gave it a good old tug but it wouldn't come up.' He mimed someone leaning forward and trying to pull something out of the ground. Aine watched, entranced.

'Still it didn't come,' Thomas went on. 'So finally he planted his two feet, like this, and hauled away. And you know what?'

'What?' said Aine. Gerard had come into the room and was hunting around on the mantelpiece for something, but neither of them took any notice of him.

'Up it came,' said Thomas. 'Up it came, but guess what came with it?'

'The bull,' Aine cried. 'It was a big ring through the end of the bull's nose!'

'The bull was on the end of it,' Thomas confirmed. 'And Oscar was in a right fix, wasn't he?'

Gerard found the photo he was looking for among a pile of magazines. 'Is that a good one of her, would you say?' he said.

Aine and Thomas took turns to examine the photograph. It had been taken by Trish the year before, at the Galway Races. Martina was wearing a smart tweed trouser suit, the kind of thing she was never seen wearing at home. The wind was trying to blow her floppy hat away and she was laughing, hanging on to it with one hand and holding a long cigar in the other.

'She didn't usually look like that,' said Aine.

'What do you want it for?' said Thomas.

Gerard didn't want to tell them. He shrugged.

Aine didn't like the photograph. It didn't represent the warm, comforting Martina that she knew. That person at the races was someone else, someone not known to her at all.

'Trish has some other ones,' she said. 'Better ones.'

'We have better ones ourself,' said Gerard. But when he came to think about it, he wasn't sure that they did.

When he went back into the kitchen, Joseph was still wiping the corner of the table, over and over, as if he were stroking it. Gerard fought down the impulse to hit him. Instead he snatched the cloth out of his hand and hurled it at the draining board, where it sent a dozen knives and forks clattering to the floor. Joseph said nothing, but went into the sitting room.

'Round they went,' Thomas was saying, 'Round and around and around until there wasn't a tree left standing on the island, what with Oscar running and the great black bull running behind him. And once all the trees were gone there was nowhere else for Oscar to go but back to the shore. But when he got there, expecting to exchange the gold ring for a lift in the hag's boat, what do you think he found?'

'Nothing,' said Aine.

'Nothing,' said Thomas. 'That's exactly what he found. The hag was gone, and the boat and all. And Oscar must have thought his final hour was come.'

Joseph picked up a magazine and dropped quietly on to a chair.

'And it would have been,' Thomas went on, 'except that a speckled trout jumped up out of the water. And what happened to it?'

'It turned into a horse,' said Aine.

'It turned into a speckled horse,' said Thomas. 'A speckled horse the very same as Martina's Specks out there in the field. And it told him to ride on its back, so he did. And when the bull saw the horse with Oscar on top of it jump back into the water, it let go the gold ring for it was mightily afraid of the water and wouldn't step into it at all. So Oscar got safely away from the island with the hag's bracelet. And do you know who the horse turned out to be?'

'James Bond,' said Joseph, from behind his magazine.

'You shut up, you,' said Aine. 'It was Aengus, wasn't it Grandda?'

''Twas indeed. And when I saw Specks at the fair in Ballinasloe I said to myself, "Now. That horse there mightn't be Aengus at all, but it might be. And if it is, wouldn't I be the fool who didn't make some attempt to buy him!"'

Aine laughed delightedly. 'And is he Aengus?' she said.

'What do you think?' said Thomas.

The front door banged loudly and, a moment later, Gerard's car could be heard starting up and pulling off along the boirin. Thomas stood up.

'Is that why the hole on the island is blocked with stones?' said Aine.

'No,' said Thomas. 'That's another story altogether.'

'Tell it!' said Aine.

'Go on,' said Joseph.

But Thomas was back in the dreadful present, and the other story was a grim and frightening one, even for him.

Brigid passed a small cairn of flat stones. She peered briefly in among them but not too closely, afraid of what she might see. Far from finding the mountainside easier to manage this time, she was more frightened than ever. She had a feeling that she was being watched and kept looking out for the goats. But this time, they were nowhere to be seen.

She stepped on a huge flake of limestone which wobbled noisily. The hare she had seen earlier, or perhaps another one, appeared from nowhere and loped off towards the hazel. Its coat shone red-gold in the sun. When it got to the edge of the woods it sat up on its haunches in the shadows and was camouflaged; one vertical line among many. Brigid kept her eye on it for a while, but the grikes demanded her attention and when she next looked up it was gone.

But it had calmed her, because of its familiarity perhaps, or because it had distracted her from the morbid thoughts that were scratching away at her consciousness but which she was not yet prepared to confront. By the time she reached the edge of the hazel woods she had one thought only and that was to cross through them and climb up the crag beyond, from where she could look down into the valley below.

Rathcormac was barely more than a village, but it had eleven pubs. Gerard visited them all. One or two of them were open for the desperate cases and the odd morning coffee, but most of them were still closed. It wasn't a problem. Gerard knew all the publicans and none of them minded opening their doors to him, even though one of them had clearly got out of bed to do it. Some of the bars were still as they had been at closing time the previous night, the tables covered in overflowing ashtrays and sticky spills. Others were neatly swept and clean. All of them smelled of sour beer and fag-ends. By the third or fourth one, Gerard was beginning to find the smell nauseating.

Trish finished her breakfast and washed the few dishes, then turned the two fillies out into the paddock to stretch their legs. The boxes were in dire need of mucking out, since Gerard always did the bare minimum when she was away, but she decided to go and find out what was happening at the house first. Joseph was in the kitchen. He pointed with his chin at her frayed jeans and thick sweater.

'And on the cat-walk now, we have Patricia Kelly in the hottest Paris fashions . . .'

Trish ignored him and went on into the sitting room to talk to Thomas.

None of the publicans had seen Martina. Most of her friends had moved away from the area, but those she still hung around with had been in town. By the time Gerard had checked the most likely pubs, the situation was looking grim. But he went on to the less likely ones and asked there, and even brought the photograph into the ones where

Martina wouldn't have been seen dead. He was wasting his time.

His last stop was O'Loughlin's. He knew Martina hadn't been there because he had been there himself. But he needed a small bit of comfort. Just one.

When Father Fogarty arrived, Joseph put the kettle on and retreated to the sitting room to fetch Thomas.

'He's afraid of the priest,' whispered Trish.

'Why wouldn't he be?' said Thomas, a little too loud. 'Sure hasn't he got sin written all over him?'

If Father Fogarty heard, he gave no indication of it. He was genuinely distraught at Martina's disappearance. He came as soon as he heard, he said. His anxiety made Aine uncomfortable and she clung to Thomas as he settled himself beside the range in the kitchen.

'You all right, then?' said Joseph, hovering at the door.

'We are not,' said Thomas. 'Come back here and make the tea.'

'How is your mother taking it all?' said Father Fogarty.

'She's fine,' said Joseph.

There was a pause, then the priest turned to Thomas. 'She fell off the horse, then, did she?'

Thomas discovered a hardness within him and felt it growing. He was angry with Joseph for his total self-concern and he was angry with the priest for his youth and his arrogant assumption that he was required here. He didn't feel like playing the game.

'We won't know that until we find her,' he said, and the

omission of the word 'father' felt like a crime. 'We'll know nothing until then.'

Father Fogarty nodded, effectively silenced. Joseph poured water on to the tea.

'Have we any biscuits?' he said, rummaging in a cupboard. With an effort, Thomas lumped Aine up on to his lap. He didn't normally do that and she was a little uneasy about it, but too polite to get down.

'Tell me this,' he said to her. 'Did you ever see a rabbit eating a slug?'

Aine made a face and shook her head.

'And did you ever see a slug eating a rabbit?'

'No. Of course not!'

'But wouldn't it be handy if they did?'

'Why would it be?' said Aine.

'Because there'd always be plenty cabbage then, wouldn't there?'

Joseph giggled. 'There always is plenty cabbage, Grandda,' he said.

'I suppose there is, now you say it,' said Thomas. 'All the same you'd wonder, sometimes, wouldn't you?' He raised his eyebrows to the priest who smiled awkwardly and wondered if he had missed something.

Joseph got cups out and poured the tea. Father Fogarty could think of no way to relieve the uncomfortable silence, but was rescued by the arrival of Mickey O'Grady and Anthony Daly, eager to help with the search. Soon after them, Maureen Griffin came with a tray full of sandwiches, as if it was a funeral. After that, Meg and Jamesy Kelly arrived with their two teenage daughters, Niamh and Jeannie. Everyone wore boots and carried jackets. Joseph emptied the teapot and put the kettle on again.

Some wanted to go straight away, but Thomas suggested holding on until more people arrived and Gerard came back. So they waited, spreading themselves out around the kitchen and catching up on all that was known. Before long Patsy Davitt arrived, then John and Sandra Mullins, and the questions and explanations began again until, to everyone's surprise, a contingent of English hippies arrived from the New Age settlement on the mountainside. For once, the local people were glad to see them.

Brigid passed through the hazel without hesitating and climbed out the other side. It was like a test, an ordeal, and she had succeeded in it. She took a moment to congratulate herself, then remembered why she was there and turned to address the crag which climbed steeply away from her.

The goats had left clear indications of the best ways to go. Their paths, the goat streets and highways, were marked by wear, by dusty little passes between rocks, by the occasional broken tuft or earth-fall. Their droppings were everywhere, some fresh and shining like chocolate sweets, some older and paler and crumbly. If there was any smell from them it was too subtle for Brigid's senses.

She followed the steepest trail. It was a climb rather than a walk, but although her shoes were inadequate the footholds and handholds were plentiful and it wasn't dangerous. Twice she stopped for a breather, looking down into the darkness of

79

the thicket below. Once the raven passed across the rock-face and its shadow brushed her body; a touch that was somehow more intimate than a kiss. A tingle of energy moved up her spine. She climbed on.

It was tough; another ordeal, another achievement. At the top she made sure of her footing and turned around, seeing at last what the goats saw, what the ravens saw, what she had come up there to see. Beneath her the valley and the lake were spread out like a map.

Some of the hippies knew Martina but some of them didn't. More photographs were found and handed around. Martina on Specks. Martina on the beach at Fanore with Popeye, hiding behind a towel with a starfish on it. Martina looking cold and miserable at a horse sale. There was a strained silence as the photos went around, and then everyone talked at once.

When Gerard came back he had to leave his car halfway up the boirin. He recognised most of the other cars as he walked among them, and when he saw the priest's his stomach lurched. The first thought that entered his head was his attempt to seduce Trish, and he thanked God that he hadn't forced himself upon her. Only as he reached the back door did another thought occur; that the priest might have come to administer the last rites. A cold flood of panic washed through him and was followed by nauseous guilt. At the back door he paused and listened. It sounded as though there was a party going on in there.

Aine was being entertained by Niamh Kelly, who was down on all fours in the sitting room pretending to be a bull. A sudden hush fell over the kitchen and she crept out to the hall. Her father was standing in the doorway opposite, his face very pale. There was a mumble of voices.

'How're you, Ger. Any news?'

He shook his head, and it seemed that everyone in the room began to breathe again. They all moved backwards or sideways to make a kind of circle. The table was covered with knapsacks and flasks and half-finished cups of tea but it was cleared in seconds when Joseph dug out the Ordnance Survey map for the area. Then the huddle closed in around it and Aine could see no more. She turned back to Niamh but she had joined the throng and was clearly not playing any longer. Suddenly alone and frightened, Aine went back to the sitting room and turned on the television.

Thomas took a general's role, giving lots of orders and declining to do any of the footwork himself. No one objected. The young New Agers bent over backwards to be helpful, as though their purpose in life was to atone for the original sin of being born English and they had been presented with a rare opportunity. One of them, a bearded young man called Sam, raced off to town to get parts of the map photocopied. The others stayed and offered everything they had: themselves, their dogs, their horses, bits of rope, a method of sending smoke signals if anyone should find Martina.

Gerard stayed quiet and let his father make the decisions. When Trish came in, he ignored her. More people arrived. Everyone had suggestions. Everyone was heard. Sam came back with the maps and they were distributed. People formed themselves into small groups, and Thomas teamed Joseph up with Father Fogarty to search the lake-shore. Both of them were surprised to find themselves included among the searchers, but neither of them had the neck to beg off.

It took a surprisingly long time for everyone to get organised and out. Trish had her own idea and Thomas agreed to it. Gerard elected to go to the island, and when Thomas suggested he should take someone with him he chose Popeye. Sam offered him a copy of the relevant piece of the map and he managed to be civil as he declined it. On the doorstep he turned back and called to Thomas.

'Where's Brigid?'

Thomas shrugged. In the sitting room, Aine heard the question and the silence. She tried hard to think where her mother might be, but she was sure that this time she really didn't know. A nasty kind of worry tried to wriggle into her head, but she hummed loudly to keep it out, and turned up the volume on the television.

From her perch on the crag Brigid saw the straggling convoy of cars, vans and tractors crawl up the lane from the house and disperse. She was moved by the sight. Year by year the community became more disparate as the old people died off and strangers moved in. Everyone filled their time with their own business and seemed to have none of it left to spend with others. Yesterday Brigid would have said that the community was dead. She could not say that now.

She could see a lot from where she stood but not as much as she had expected. The valley was full of hedges and hummocks and trees, any of which could be concealing a prostrate figure. A couple of times as she scanned the landscape inch by inch her heart skipped at a flash of colour in a hedge or a gateway but by now she had come to recognise a certain shade of yellow and a certain shade of blue as belonging to fertiliser bags. She was sure that Martina had no clothes in either colour.

But she could not picture what Martina might have been wearing. She had not been up when Brigid had left for work the previous morning; most days she wasn't. Still scanning the valley, wishing that she had a pair of binoculars, Brigid tried to imagine her daughter's day.

She would have got up late; ten o'clock or so. A small breakfast; she was always on a diet. Where would Gerard have been? She must ask him what he knew. But then what? What did Martina do with her days? Would she phone someone? Was there a boyfriend somewhere, perhaps?

Brigid realised how little she knew of her daughter. They were polite to each other, but not warm, not intimate. Now that she came to think about it, she saw that Martina always held something of herself in reserve; hidden. Not like Kevin. She knew everything about him. When she thought of him her heart warmed. But Martina was just Martina. Always there; dependable as daylight.

But maybe there was more. Maybe there was a whole side to Martina that Brigid didn't know at all. Something that was always turned away from her, like the dark side of the moon.

One of the search party cars had turned on to the road which led up towards the mountain. It stopped at a gateway and two people got out. Then it carried on for another hundred yards or so and parked. Two more people emerged. They spread out across the fields and a dog skittered here and there between them. Brigid could have saved them a lot of walking. Even so, she was glad that they were there.

Was there a boyfriend? Martina was nineteen, nearly twenty. If there wasn't a boyfriend then there ought to have been. Maybe there was and she had been keeping him a secret. Maybe this whole thing was an elaborate ruse to cover an elopement.

Without thinking about it, Brigid had begun to descend, holding on to the rocks at either side to steady herself. She was remembering an incident that had happened a few years before and it was making her very uncomfortable.

Martina had been sixteen and had just finished her Junior Cert exams. She got a summer job in a hotel in Limerick and moved into a flat there with a few of the girls she worked with. It all seemed to be going fine until Gerard called in on them one morning without warning. The door was opened by a young man, and that was the end of Martina's job.

Gerard had refused to hear any explanations. He stayed in the street until Martina came out and then he put her in the car. Then he waited until they were at home with Brigid before he launched his attack. He called Martina a whore, a slut, dirty and disgusting, not fit to be seen by decent people. Brigid had stood aside, her support for her husband not active but assumed. Martina had not come to her for shelter but absorbed her humiliation alone. She didn't go back to work that summer. She hadn't worked since.

Brigid tried to remember what she had felt at the time. She knew that Gerard had gone over the top, but then he often did, particularly at Joseph. She saw his temper as a weakness in him and forgave him for it, assuming that the children did, too. She remembered her intention to speak to Martina afterwards, but she couldn't remember doing it. One hour had drifted into another; one day into the next. As time had drifted through and past her for all the rest of her married life. Where had it gone?

She found herself back in the glade. Somehow she had come down most of the cliff-face on automatic pilot. Her own thinking was shocking her. The truth was that she had said nothing. She had not challenged her husband or consoled her daughter because she was a part of the same culture; the same authority. She shared his fear and disgust of women's sexuality. She despised it in herself as much as in her maturing daughter. Gerard's voice had represented her voice. He had spoken for her.

The air in the glade was fresh and cool after the dull dry atmosphere of the rocks. There was a damp, mossy fragrance like mountain streams. Even the light was crisp and clear. Nothing moved. It was no longer threatening in there. It was peaceful.

Brigid sat down on a moss-covered stone and loosened the strict, dusky-pink blouse that was buttoned tight to her throat. A blackbird called from a nearby bush and was answered almost immediately. Brigid sighed deeply and leant against a cluster of narrow hazel limbs. She wondered how it could have been that all her life she had accepted values that were damaging to her; adopted them wholesale and without consideration. In doing so she had diminished herself and her daughters, and everything that was feminine in society except for self-sacrifice. She had a sudden, lucid vision of herself among a line of girls going into school to be taught there that they were sinful and grasping; the cause of all evil.

The glen made her think of fairies, so green was it, so otherworldly. She imagined herself sitting cross-legged, wearing a pointed hat and smoking a little pipe. She began to laugh, and realised that she was crying. She hoped that Martina had eloped, but she feared that she had not.

As Gerard drove off up the boirin, Popeye turned around in the passenger seat and looked back, as though he was having second thoughts.

'Sit down,' said Gerard. 'You'll survive.'

Popeye gave him a bunt on the cheek with a wet nose and continued to look back. Gerard wiped the wet spot. He didn't like dogs and had never kept one, even for the children. Once a skinny bitch had strayed in to the farm, her coat mangy, her dugs dangling. He threw stones at her and shouted, but the kids fed her when he wasn't looking. A couple of days later, he caught her in the night when the children were asleep, and tied her into a sack and threw her into the lake. Throughout the whole operation the bitch shook from head to toe but didn't once make a sound. Despite himself, Gerard hadn't slept that night. It still made him feel queasy. He could never do such a thing again.

Popeye gave a little whimper like a sigh and turned to face the front. Gerard hoped he wasn't going to be troublesome.

Trish replaced a few nails in the loose shoe. It was a duff job but good enough for the moment. It would last until the blacksmith came again.

Afterwards Specks slept while Trish tacked him up, using one of the jumping bridles in place of his own. He woke for just long enough to co-operate when she picked out his feet, then dozed off again. But as soon as Trish got up on him, he went off eagerly with a long, active stride, high head and pricked ears. She knew then why it was that Martina loved him. Everything was wrong; his conformation, his action, his dreadful blotchy colour. But his heart made up for his failings, and more. Trish gave his ears a friendly tug and let him go on a loose rein. She wanted to interfere with him as little as possible. She wanted to see which direction he would take.

At the top of the boirin he swung to the left without a moment's hesitation and strode along, tossing his head, enjoying the slack rein and the sunshine. Trish took out a cigarette and lit it.

Gerard accelerated along the main road, looking neither right nor left. His blood was running hot and he was driving too fast. He had to jam on the brakes to make the turn down towards the island, and the dog fell forward against the dash and on to the floor. A cold sweat broke out on Gerard's back. More slowly now, carefully, he drove between the high stone walls of what had once been an estate. The entrance into

87

the old house was on his right. He glanced down it as he passed. Anthony had been doing some clearing in there, finally cutting up fallen trunks and branches that had blocked the avenue for years. It was clear right down to the house, which stood four square, heavy, still dark inside despite having no roof. Gerard wondered what Anthony was up to. Property values were increasing in the area, but Anthony would sell his own internal organs before he would part with a square inch of land.

A hundred yards further on, the tarmac abruptly ended and the road forked into two gravelly tracks. Gerard took the right-hand one, which brought him down to the causeway. The gate was at the landward end of it and, for reasons of their own, Anthony's cattle had crowded around it. Gerard had intended to drive through, but the gate was tied shut with baler twine and the knots were so many and so complicated that it wasn't worth the effort. He went back to the pick-up to get the dog, then climbed over the gate.

The cattle ducked their heads and blew steamy billows and walked backwards. A swan that had been sitting on the bank of the causeway walked into the water and swam away. From the other side of the gate, Gerard examined the knots closely. Anthony's farm was large and wealthy, but most of it was held together with baler twine. There was no point in trying to work out who had tied these particular knots. It could have been anybody.

Gerard turned and went on. He was impressed, as he always was, by what a great piece of building the causeway was. The middle of it was still beautifully level after all the years and the sides sloped with a perfectly even camber down to the water. Anthony said that it had never been touched since it was built, but Thomas said that it was resurfaced as part of a famine relief project in the 1840s with stone drawn from the quarry and broken to small gravel by hand.

The quarry was there, all right, at the end of the left-hand fork in the road. Gerard and his brother, Peadar, had swum there and built tar-barrel rafts, even though they were told not to, and that it was more dangerous than the lake. They had made a death-slide as well, with a rope slung all the way across. Peadar had fallen off it and into the middle of the quarry one time. Gerard, watching, had been terrified until Peadar stood up and waved. The water only came up to his chest. There were deep parts, though, and that was why it was dangerous; you could never be sure where they were.

At the end of the causeway the land opened out into a broad, green field which rose gradually towards a copse of hazel, ash and oak. The monastic ruins were just visible from where Gerard stood. Proof of the arduous existence of the monks was embossed on the surrounding slopes. The ridges were grass-covered now, but they must have once looked like the raised beds that Thomas still dug every year to grow his few potatoes and his annual surplus of pigeon-pecked, wind-battered cabbage. He was a stupid old man, full of stupid old stories. They didn't even make sense; they contradicted each other and jumped backwards and forwards over the centuries, from the early gods to the Normans and back again.

'Martina?'

He stood quietly, waiting for a reply.

'Martina!'

Nothing. Popeye looked at him as though he was mad, then raced off across the causeway, his nose to the ground. Gerard wondered whether it had been such a good idea to bring him. He was lean and powerful, bred to run and perpetually longing to prove it. If he put up a hare or a rabbit he could be gone until night-time, hunting up and down the island. Gerard didn't need that kind of hassle.

At the end of the causeway the dog stopped and waited for Gerard then went off up the first field, quartering the ground. Maybe it wasn't such a bad idea after all. If Martina was on the island, he was sure to find her.

Thomas went down to his house to look for his pipe and Aine went with him. At the door of the house a swan was standing. It hissed as they approached. Aine ducked in behind her grandfather. To her it was a very big bird.

Father Fogarty and Joseph walked along the shore, together but separate. The priest had already tried to get the boy talking on several different subjects but had failed. He tried again.

'You were never interested in the hurling, sure you weren't?'

'No.'

'Nor the soccer.'

'Not really.'

'Up there on the racehorses the whole time, I suppose.'

'Sport horses.'

'Oh. I see. Hunters and jumpers, that sort of thing, is it?'

'That's right.'

'I thought your father kept racehorses.'

'No.'

'Oh. I see. You ride the hunters, then, do you? The show jumpers?'

'No,' said Joseph. 'I hate them.'

The silence descended again, as though it had triumphed. They had been walking along a narrow shingle beach but now it came to an end and was replaced by a belt of dense, black reeds. Between them the water was scummy and dark.

'Are we going through or what?' said Joseph.

'I don't see much point, really. Do you?'

Joseph shrugged.

'She would hardly have ridden through there, would she?'

Joseph shrugged again. 'I don't really know what we're looking for,' he said.

The priest was beginning to wonder whether the boy was the full shilling. He began to walk away from the water's edge, looking for the easiest way to circumnavigate the reeds. The wellingtons that he had borrowed were too big. He felt clownish in them.

'Do you really not know what we're looking for, Joseph?' he said.

'My sister,' said Joseph. 'But we're wasting our time.'

'How come?'

'She'll turn up.'

'How do you know?'

Joseph shrugged.

'Do you know where she is, Joseph?'

'No.'

'Has she gone missing before?'

'No.'

'How do you know, then?'

''Cos she's my sister. I just know.'

The priest wondered if he did. He led the way over a wobbly barbed-wire fence and got caught by the crotch of his trousers. Joseph turned his back but his shoulders betrayed his laughter. When it was his turn to cross he got hooked the same way and blushed crimson. Father Fogarty laughed openly. He thought it might break the ice but it didn't. He spoke before the silence could settle on them again.

'There's a lot of stories about the lake, I hear,' he said.

'They say it claims a victim every seven years,' said Joseph.

'And does it?' said the priest.

Joseph shrugged.

Reluctantly Brigid left the glen. As she climbed out over the green velvet rocks she found a stick lying across her path. It was not particularly straight as hazel rods go, but it fitted her hand and her height perfectly and might have been made for her. Brigid examined it closely. It was light as a feather and surprisingly strong. Someone had cut it at some time, but not recently. It was like a stick that a farmer might have used for herding cattle, except that no farmer or cattle ever came in there.

Brigid looked around her. Everything was still and silent but she could not rid herself of the impression that there was somebody there. She went on, using the stick to help her. It didn't seem at all strange in that world that it should have been provided for her. She had asked for it, after all.

Gerard started on the lower, south side of the island, within sight of the lake-shore. He passed through the old graveyard with its handful of crude headstones then checked the walls of the church, inside and out. The dog was never still, searching here and there, leading the way on up the hill to where a stand of strong trees stood sentry around a waist-high cairn. Gerard had met an archaeologist in the pub one night and asked her about the cairn. She had been vague; said she couldn't tell without seeing it, but some of those things were quite recent and could be as mundane as a field clearing or a pile of rocks thrown over a dead cow to keep the crows off it. Thomas, of course, had his own explanation, and it swam up now from that disowned part of Gerard's memory. In ancient times the people of Clare were besieged by an enemy from across the sea. Gerard couldn't remember what the name of the invaders was, but he knew that they had cat heads. They marched across Clare and overthrew all in their path, and the survivors beat a retreat until they ended up on the island and could retreat no further. When the time came for them to go down to the shore to make a last stand against the invaders, every man, woman and child picked a stone and they piled them together in a heap. Only those who survived returned and removed their stone. The cairn, with its hundreds of stones remaining, told the rest of the story.

Remembering it brought a catch to Gerard's throat, as it had done when he was a child. Sometimes it seemed as though Ireland was nothing but an enormous burial ground. Why wouldn't strange things happen? He blocked off the thought quickly, fearful of where his imagination seemed to be leading him.

'Martina!'

Gerard stood still and listened. A long, moaning call answered from far behind him and he swung round, his nerves a-jangle. The cattle had followed him back across the causeway and were standing at the bottom of the hill, watching. It was one of them that had answered him.

Specks turned neither left nor right but kept steadfastly on along the Ennis road. Tractors passed with rattling trailers and lorries thundered by without consideration but the cob paid not the slightest attention. He was safe as houses, safer than a bicycle and a lot safer than the jittery youngsters that Trish rode every day. She patted his neck and praised him. He listened with one ear and kept the other on the road ahead.

Brigid went out through the gate and closed it behind her. For a moment she leant on her stick and, as if in salute, a lark climbed the steep steps of the sky and hung in the heights, ringing bubbling glass bells for her. Brigid's heart lifted towards it until it took her breath away with a headlong plunge towards the rocky ground. At the last minute it saved itself and landed as lightly as a moth. When she turned to leave it was sitting on the wall with its crest standing up in punky spikes, and it was still singing.

Gerard had climbed up the hill and was not far from the fort when, sure enough, Popeye put up a hare. Gerard groaned and called a couple of times, quite uselessly. The dog's only master now was its instincts.

Hare and hound were well matched; both lean and muscular and powerful. Gerard was stunned by their speed. He became mesmerised and, despite himself, found that he sided with the hare. The dog's head was down, straining towards the hare's heel. No matter how she twisted and turned, Popeye twisted and turned behind her. She led him into the fort but doubled back when she met the inner ditch. His nose followed her but the rest of him was still set on a different course and his legs went out from under him. He yelped and rolled over three times, but with astonishing speed he was on his feet and gaining on the hare again.

She was heading down the hill now and Gerard was sure that she was making for the trees. But suddenly Popeye was upon her and she was jinking and dodging and leading him back up across the field towards the fort. She leaped the outer bank, the dog snapping at her heels. She leaped the inner bank, hardly seeming to touch it. And then she was sprinting across the enclosure, straight towards the sheer drop which hung over the lake.

Gerard couldn't believe it. He wanted to warn the dog

but it was all happening too fast; his diaphragm seemed to have seized and he couldn't find breath. The hare was certain to go straight out over the edge, but she didn't. With breath-taking agility she doubled, right on the brink. Far too late, Popeye saw the danger and put on the brakes. His front feet dug into the ground an inch from the edge but his back end went up over him and he flew in a somersault out into midair and down.

Gerard drew a sharp breath and began to run across the grass. He looked for the hare, expecting to see her loping off towards her home again. But she was gone. Gerard stopped, unable to believe his eyes. There was no sign of her at all. She had vanished.

Specks was still swinging along in the same mood and Trish was beginning to wonder whether he wouldn't keep going on like that till he came to the sea. They had travelled at least a mile and passed several turns but the horse hadn't shown the slightest inclination to go down any of them. Trish lit another cigarette and dropped her feet out of the stirrups to let the blood back into her toes, but put them back in again as a blue Hi-ace van pulled up beside her. There were three Travellers in the front; a middle-aged woman in the passenger seat, a child of about Aine's age in the middle and a man driving. He leaned across as the woman rolled down the window. He was a lot younger than the woman was, more likely to be her son, Trish thought, than her husband.

'Are you selling the horse?' he asked.

Trish shook her head. 'He's not mine.'

'Whose is he?'

'He belongs to my boss's daughter.'

'Will she sell him?'

Specks looked at his reflection in the wing-mirror, then blew on it and misted it up.

'She's missing,' said Trish.

'What d'you mean, missing?'

Trish told the story and the woman listened. She didn't move except to prevent Specks from taking a bite out of the wing-mirror. Beside her the child was silent, picking at a fraying hole in his jeans.

''Tis very strange,' said the woman, when Trish finished.

''Tis strange all right,' said the young man.

'You didn't see anything?' said Trish.

They both shook their heads.

'Will you keep your ears open? Put the word out?'

'We will, of course,' said the woman. 'What was the girl's name at all?'

'Martina,' said Trish. 'Martina Keane.'

The woman repeated it. The man started the engine.

'Good luck, now,' he said.

The van pulled off and Specks set out again, as purposeful as ever.

The cow's skeleton, when he came across it, threatened to breach the stout walls of Gerard's rationality. He forgot all about the dog. He had not admitted to himself that this search might end with the discovery of a death but he knew it none the less. And then, although he satisfied himself immediately that it was not his daughter, it was some time before he succeeded in working out what, in fact, it was.

She must have died on her back with her legs in the air. Gerard didn't know why animals died like that but he had seen it before. He had seen sheep on several occasions and then there had been Thomas's donkey, a long time ago now, but still a vivid memory.

Whatever creatures had been feeding on the cow's carcass must have eaten through the ligaments so that the legs had slipped straight down and created the appearance of something that walked upright. A nine-foot cow. Or a bull spirit.

Gerard turned away, disliking the direction of his thoughts. A year ago she would not have been left there like that. Anthony would have dragged her down behind the tractor and the knacker-lorry would have paid him to take her away. But since BSE the boot had been on the other foot. The rendering plants were not equipped to dispose of carcasses in accordance with the new regulations and the knacker-man didn't come any more. To bury a dead cow required a vet's certificate and a licence, every time. Between paper-work and digger drivers a lot of time and money could be spent. It was generally easier to turn a blind eye. He had already done it himself, more than once.

As the shock receded, Gerard remembered the dog again, and walked on around the outer bank of the fort. At the westernmost side the bank disappeared; the steepness of the cliff below being sufficient defence for anyone. Gerard looked down to the dark waters of the lake, far below. Popeye was clambering out on to the rocks and Gerard laughed and called. The dog shook himself so hard that he nearly fell over, then looked around eagerly, ready to obey Gerard's call but not sure where it had come from. Gerard dropped to his knees on the grass, then down on to his stomach, leaning out over the edge. Below him the dog found its bearings and raced around the rocky shore to climb the hill again. Gerard continued to look down. There were wet splashes where the dog had been and a few small waves ran into the narrow shore, remembering him. Gerard watched them as they lulled and slowed and forgot. He had rarely seen the lake so still. If he stretched out just a bit further he would be able to see his own reflection. He was tempted to chuck a stone but refrained, shamed by a sudden memory of his youth. He and Peadar had once dismantled a whole section of the outer bank of the fort and thrown the smaller stone into the lake. He stood up and walked over to the place. The grass had long since grown over it again but one or two of the bigger stones, the ones they could not lift, still broke the surface. They hadn't, before. Gerard was about to turn away when he remembered that they had found something, the two of them. What had it been? A model, a little statue. A bull. Peadar had wanted to take it home and show it to their parents and teachers, but Gerard had been ashamed of it and had sworn him to secrecy. He couldn't remember why, now. It must have been because of the forbidden destruction of the fort.

But where was it now? The memory came back so suddenly and so sharply that the grass itself seemed to live and to glow more brightly, the way it had when he was a child. He walked over to where the ground fell away and followed the slope until he came to the souterrain. They had hidden the bull there; the memory was so clear that it might have been yesterday. Beside the rocks that had been thrown in to block the entrance to the ancient chambers there was, or there had been, a little cavity. Gerard dropped on to his hands and knees at the edge of the depression. The grass was long around the edge of the stones where the cattle couldn't easily reach it, and a few primroses clung to the thin soil. Gerard pushed his hand between them and felt around. The hole was still there, but as he leaned forward to reach into it, the stone he was kneeling against shifted suddenly, causing the ones beside it to slide and wobble and knock against each other. Gerard stood up quickly. Those stones had been there for generations; no one knew how long. Thomas, of course, had some story about the place, but then he had stories about everything. It had probably been blocked to stop cattle from falling into it, or maybe to stop children going down. If it was on his land, he would block it, too.

He stepped back. Where the stones had moved they had left bare edges of earth showing among the grass, almost as if someone had taken them out and put them back in again. But he was sure that they hadn't been like that when he had first knelt down beside them.

Or was he?

'Martina!'

The fear, the desperation in his voice surprised him. Surely to God she was at home by now? Behind him he could hear the dog galloping over the meadow and then it was upon him, its wet nose and tongue shoving against his hand, its paws on his legs, delighted to have found him.

Gerard pushed him away. The cattle had followed up behind them and now stood in a ragged phalanx, watching. Popeye watched them back and then, as Gerard was about to set off down the hill, he discovered the souterrain. Gerard called him but he went down into the hollow until only his tail was showing. Gerard called him again, but he wouldn't come. He was scrabbling about between the stones with his paws, the terrier in him now winning out over the greyhound. Gerard strode over and grabbed him by the scruff, pulled him out, then stood examining the hole. What the hell was the dog looking for? There was nowhere that he could see for the hare to have gone, but there was bare earth beside the stones where the dog had been scratching. There could no longer be any doubt that those stones had moved or been moved recently. Gerard tried to picture how they had looked when he first saw them a few minutes ago but he couldn't be sure. The dog was in there again and digging. Gerard lifted him and hurled him across the grass. Popeye yelped and tumbled and stood looking hurt, his tail between his legs. Gerard advanced on him and shouted and sent him scuttling off down the hillside. When the dog was safely on its way he followed and, although he turned round often and looked back up the hill, he could not get rid of the hideous feeling that there was something behind him, every step of the way.

When Thomas heard the front door bell ring he was afraid that it was the Guards.

'There's a swan at the back,' said Brigid when he opened the door. 'I didn't like to chase it off.'

'No,' said Thomas. 'I wouldn't, either.'

'They can break your arm,' said Brigid.

'They can,' said Thomas.

Brigid propped the hazel rod against the wall beside the kitchen door. She was surprised that she had brought it from the car. She hadn't meant to.

Thomas sat down again. 'Put the kettle on there, for your mother,' he said.

Aine filled it from the tap and took out one of the comic annuals that Thomas kept there for her.

'There's no one at the house,' said Brigid.

'No. They're all gone. Off around the place. A good crowd.'

Brigid stared out of the window. The swan had come round the side of the house and was watching the front door, its head on one side.

'What does it want?' she said.

'You wouldn't know with swans,' said Thomas. 'They can get spoiled by tourists and such. I'd say it found some food belonging to Popeye. He's very fussy, you know, always leaving bits after him. I'd say that's what it's after.'

'Shall I give him some bread?' said Aine.

'No,' said Thomas. 'Then we'd never be rid of it.'

They watched in silence as the swan waddled away down the path. At the edge of the lake it shook itself and straightened a few feathers under one wing. Then it waded into the shallows and settled itself on to the water, as gently as a hen on to a clutch of eggs.

The kettle started whining and Aine slipped outside before

Thomas could command her to make the tea. The swan had been heavy and waddly on land like a big, white goose, but on the water it was pure grace. Its neck curved elegantly and its wings were folded more crisply than Japanese paper. It swam in pulses as it was propelled by first one foot, then the other. A clean, even wake spread out behind it in a long, narrow triangle. As it swam it turned its head, first to the left and then to the right, looking back at Aine with one black eye and then the other. Then, without any reason that Aine could see, it stood up on the surface and beat its great wings, creating temporary chaos in the surrounding waters. Aine ran down to the shore and clambered out to the prow of Thomas's boat, but it was too late. The swan was already running along the water, reaching and flapping, and a moment later it was in the air. As soon as it was high enough it banked and circled and flew right back over Aine's head. She thought at first that it was honking to her, but it was only the noise of its wings.

Inside the house Brigid was very quiet. She thanked Thomas for the tea that he gave her, but she didn't drink it.

'I expect there'll be news soon,' he said.

Joseph and Father Fogarty by-passed the reeds and returned to the lakeside where it became stony again. Rounding a curve of the shoreline they came to the small bay where John Mannion's cruiser lay moored. Joseph scuffed out along the newly-constructed landing stage and looked down into the neat, clean little skiff that was tethered there. Its appearance was always one of the first signs of spring.

Fifty yards away the priest had climbed the steps of the Mannions' split-level bungalow and was standing between Greco-Roman pillars, waiting for someone to answer the door. The big area below was a games room with snooker and ping-pong tables for the boys when they were home from boarding school. Joseph had never seen it but Stephen said that he had.

Mannion himself was a Dubliner and still spent most of his time on the east coast. It was rumoured that he had made a fortune out of software. Nobody really knew him at all, but his wife was a member of the ICA and was popular enough in the village.

It was she who now opened the door. Joseph couldn't hear what she said but he saw her put a hand to her hair and the other one to her neckline, checking. She had a good body and did little to hide it. Joseph made a mental note to tell Steve that he wouldn't mind playing with her in the games room. He smiled to himself and looked down into the murky water. From the lake-bed something white waved up at him.

He discerned that it was only a plastic bag, but not before the most awful, paralysing fear had leached all the strength from his knees. He turned and walked, slowly at first, faster as his legs recovered, back along the landing-stage. The door of the house was closed and the priest was skipping down the steps towards him. Joseph walked straight past him.

'I'm going home,' he said.

There were no flowers on the fuchsia but there were plenty among the ruined houses: primroses, violets, clouds of white thorn blossom, slipping towards pink. Popeye sniffed under the thick growth of brambles and elder that stood within the fallen walls and Gerard wished that he hadn't been so hard on him. When he called him now he shrank away and refused to be directed. Gerard had to beat his way in himself.

Beneath the bushes a layer of rich leaf-mould covered the floors. A broad flag marked a fireplace; a broken lintel indicated a window. There was little else.

Thomas said that the houses had been empty for the whole of his life but that his mother could remember smoke in the chimneys of both of them. He said that it wasn't emigration or hunger or changes in the land laws that drove the people out, but the houses themselves. They had been built with stones brought down from the fort and nothing but bad luck ever attended anyone who lived in them. One crop after another failed on the land. One child after another died. But it wasn't until a man from one of the houses was killed by a bull that the occupants made the decision to move out. The houses fell in directly, he said, and some of the stones found their way back to the fort. You could never be sure with Thomas, but Gerard suspected that part of the story stretched even his credulity. All the same, there was something dark and mysterious about the atmosphere around the houses, and Gerard called up the dog and struck out for home. By now someone was sure to have some news. He wasn't at all sure, though, that he would want to hear it.

Just as Trish was about to turn back, Specks swung into an open gateway and walked straight over a cattle grid. Trish sat still and waited for disaster; the slip, the clatter, the broken leg. But if Specks was aware that crossing a cattle grid was an equine achievement he gave no indication of it. He went on at the same pace, up a slight incline and around to the back of the small, neat bungalow that stood at the top.

He stopped at the back door and when Trish slid off, he shifted restlessly, his big feet only inches from the tidy beds and borders that surrounded the house. Trish growled at him and looked around, wondering what to do next. Before she could make up her mind the door opened and an old lady in a blue nylon housecoat came out.

It seemed as if the cob had been expecting her because he shifted forward and, quite politely, removed a brown bread-crust from her hand.

'You're not Martina,' said the woman.

Trish nipped a sarcastic comment in the bud. 'No.'

'But that's Specks, isn't it? That's you, isn't it, Specks?'

She bent down, hands on knees trying to get closer to the level of the cob's head, which was now not far from the ground. He was scraping the crust backwards and forwards along the gravel trying to break it. Trish took hold of it and he tore his half away.

'I know who you are, now,' said Trish. Martina had often told her of the aunt that she rode over to visit. 'I'm Trish. I work for Gerard, with the horses.'

'And where's Martina?' said the old woman.

She looked too frail to hear the truth.

'I'm not sure.' said Trish. 'I was just riding the horse and he brought me here.'

'Good old Specks! You came to see Lena!'

Specks began to make for the lawn but Trish restrained him.

'Let him,' said Lena. 'Come in and have a cup of tea.'

When Joseph got home he went straight upstairs to his room. He turned on his portable television but there was nothing he wanted to watch. For a minute or two he sat on the bed, listening to the sounds of the house, then he stood up again and took a dog-eared magazine from its place behind his shirt-drawer. Again he listened. Then he plumped up his pillows and settled himself on the bed. The magazine fell open co-operatively and he leaned back.

Downstairs Father Fogarty waited. Brigid found him there when she came up to the house with Aine. The sun was still bright but there was a nip of frost in the air. It was time to light the range.

Gerard drove back up the track to the fork and stopped. He left the dog in the pick-up and walked the hundred yards down to the quarry, where a startled heron lifted on to broad wings and flapped out over his head.

The water stilled as he approached its edge. A couple of silt-filled barrels rusted in the shallows but there was no sign of any recent activity there. He wondered what the young lads got up to these days. It seemed to be all computers and videos; indoor stuff, all inside their heads. Joseph had been his shadow when he was younger; his right-hand man, up on the tractor, up on the horses, wide-eyed and willing and worshipful. Now he hardly knew him. Didn't know what he thought or what he liked or what he wanted to do with his life. Nothing, it seemed.

Gerard stepped closer to the quarry and looked into it. The water was murky. In the soft mud underneath it, indistinct pond life moved. The end of a flat strap emerged from a tangle of green weeds a couple of feet from the edge. Gerard held his breath as he reached for it and pulled it clear, but it was ancient and slimy; had been there for years. He threw it back and washed his hands in the wriggling water. He was glad that Joseph didn't get involved with the place or places like it. He also wished that he did.

'Martina!'

He had brought her here, once, to look at the tadpoles. It seemed like yesterday, but it was years; a lifetime, perhaps. She was about three, a tiny thing in a short frock and fine pigtails. She had clung to his trousers for the first ten minutes, afraid of the gloomy water, reluctant to explore. But after that it had been he who had to keep a grip on her.

'Martina!'

The quarry walls echoed his voice back to him, round and round and round.

Lena laid the table with side-plates and knives and spoons.

'I won't have anything to eat, Mrs,' said Trish. 'A cup of tea in my hand, that's all.'

Lena ignored her and opened the fridge. She took out ham, lettuce, tomatoes, butter, pickled beetroot. Trish noticed that there was a box of corn flakes in there as well and smiled at the wall.

'I've no sweet cake,' said Lena. 'I gave the last of it to Specks yesterday.'

'Yesterday?' said Trish.

'I think it was yesterday,' said Lena. 'Maybe it was the day before.'

Trish didn't like to push. The old woman was very thin and frail.

'Biscuits,' she said, pouring them out of a tin on to a plate. They were so soft that they drooped over each other, but Lena didn't seem to notice.

'Where is she, then?' she said.

'Martina?' said Trish. 'She's . . . Well, we're not sure. She didn't come home last night.'

Lena sat down. The kettle, which seemed to Trish to have been on the hot plate of the range for half an hour, had eventually come to the boil.

'Didn't come home?' said Lena. 'Why not?'

'We're not sure,' said Trish. 'Was she definitely here yesterday?'

The kettle continued to boil furiously. Lena made drying motions with her hands in the skirt of her housecoat.

'Is today Saturday?' she asked.

'It is,' said Trish. She could imagine the days stretching back, one blurring into the other with sameness. It was a sentence she wouldn't have wished on her worst enemy.

'It was, em, let me see, now.' Lena was like someone taking an exam. Trish felt sorry for her.

'I was in at the doctor's in the morning. Paddy Barry brought me in. He's very good. Then we had some soup there, in the hotel. So if it was after that I should remember it, shouldn't I?'

She noticed the kettle at last and got up to make the tea. Trish let her take her time, and it wasn't until they were both finishing their ham sandwiches that Trish brought Lena back to the matter in hand.

'So what did you do when you got back from town? Yesterday?'

Lena looked at her with a blank expression behind which light slowly dawned.

'I'm awful stupid, you know,' she said. 'I wasn't here at all. Senior citizens' day in the community centre. Every whole Friday.'

Her face was child-like in its delight. She had passed her exam.

Throughout the afternoon the searchers came and went. Maureen's sandwiches got finished. The teapot was filled and emptied, filled and emptied. Sam taped together a load of the photocopies to make a master map which was pinned to the wall and shaded in, bit by bit. When Joseph came downstairs again, looking anaemic, he elected to take charge of it, provided that he didn't have to go out again.

Father Fogarty left to make a few calls before evening mass. In a gesture that clearly moved him profoundly he left Brigid his own personal copy of the Bible, still warm from his pocket and very much creased and battered. After he had gone, Brigid put it on the table and looked through it. There were many notes and underlinings. She read a few favourite passages then put it aside. In the context of her current situation Thomas's fairy stories made far more sense.

The phone rang and Joseph answered it. It was ringing more and more frequently as word of Martina's disappearance spread and people wanted to know the latest news. Brigid listened as she washed up for the fourth time that afternoon.

'No. No news. Nothing.'

His tone was flat and betrayed no feeling. Brigid wondered if he had any. She sighed, remembering Martina again. It happened every few minutes and was accompanied by the same stab of panic, the same hopeless casting around in her mind for unexplored possibilities, the same sense of unreality. Somewhere there was an answer, a solution that would free her from the fear that was mushrooming out of control in her consciousness. Facing it was fruitless. The only relief lay in turning away from it, in avoiding thoughts of Martina. Increasingly she found herself taking refuge in that part of her mind that she had not visited since childhood. There was comfort in its archetypal simplicity, its infinite reach, its lack of resemblance to the washing-up world.

The missing daughter world.

She looked up at the mountains. For years she had stood at that window and not seen them. Now they would not let her go. Next time she would climb higher, and see more. But for the moment, she was grounded. She had left her stick at Thomas's for safe keeping. Gerard would burn it if it was here, or one of the hippies might take it and hang a spotted handkerchief from it. Brigid laughed at the idea and then, like a flagellation, remembered Martina again.

Gerard came in with Popeye.

'Any news?'

'Nothing.'

Gerard shrugged out of his jacket and collapsed into a chair.

'Where the feck can she be?'

Brigid handed him a cup of tea. Popeye found a warm corner beside the range, followed himself in three tight circles and was asleep before he hit the ground.

'Shall I shade in the island, then?' said Joseph.

'What?'

'The map.' Joseph showed him. 'Did you cover the whole of the island?'

'Oh, feck off with your colours!' said Gerard, getting to his feet again. 'What are you doing standing around the kitchen, anyway? Do you not realise what's happening?'

Joseph blushed and backed away from the wall.

'Shade it in, Joseph.' Brigid was as surprised to hear herself speak like that as Joseph was, and Gerard.

'Go on,' she said. 'You're doing a job that needs to be done.'

Gerard stared at her, not sure whether he could trust his senses. He pushed the mug of tea away.

'I'm going out again,' he said. 'I can't sit around the kitchen and the girl still out there somewhere.'

Brigid nodded towards the map where Joseph was at work again.

'That'll show you what's been covered and what hasn't,' she said.

'I don't need any map,' he said, pulling his jacket from the chair back.

'Do it your own way,' said Brigid. 'You always do.'

Gerard walked out of the house and got into the car. His heart was pounding and his face was burning. Between rage and terror he was all but paralysed. Somehow he managed to put the car into gear and drive slowly up the boirin. He had no idea at all where he was going. Nor had he any idea how his life could have been thrown out of kilter so completely. He tried to remember yesterday and Martina's presence in it, but he couldn't bring life to his recollections. There was only a generic memory of her; of jeans and big sweaters. It seemed to him now that he took no more notice of her than of a radio in the background. There had to be more than that. Some unusual interaction, a conversation they had been having, a shared joke perhaps. But all that would come to his mind was the adrenalin-charged memory of his struggle with Trish in the muddy field, the fury that followed, the blaze of murderous intent that was coupled with the desire in his loins.

He stopped the car and looked around him. Yesterday. Where was yesterday?

He had lunged The Nipper. That much he remembered. The horse was sound and he was impatient. He had intended to trot him over a few poles but he had seemed so keen, he had jumped so well. A glow returned to Gerard's heart as he remembered. The Nipper was the star of the yard, a jumping genius. And Gerard hadn't been able to resist putting the bar up, and up, and up. When he came back later and found that the heat had returned to the horse's leg, a rage had come upon him. Again. Another one. As though the horse was to blame he had let fly at him with all that he had. Fists, boots . . .

Gerard pulled down a shutter on the memory, dropped his head on to the steering wheel and prayed. The benign, white-robed figure in his mind's eye never knew rage, never knew lust. Like a child he begged to be relieved of all his sins and to become like Him.

As they headed for home, Specks settled into a steady, energy-saving jog which felt to Trish as if it could have gone on for ever. The cob was wasted. Such strength and stamina, standing all day in the field. He should have been pulling a cart or a plough or a dray. He would have loved it. All the work you could give him wouldn't tire a horse like that nor shorten his life by a day. A few oats and a bit of grass was all he needed; the battle every summer was to keep the weight off him, not put it on. All those tractors and cars and lorries, all roaring and stinking and poisoning the world while horses like Specks stood idle. It wasn't fair on him. Never mind him, it wasn't fair on God. She was smiling as she turned down the boirin but her face straightened when she saw Gerard, slumped over the wheel of his car.

Gerard looked up when he heard the sound of hooves on the

stony surface of the track. For a moment he was certain that it was Martina and that the whole thing was a mistake. Then he realised who it was. He flushed and dropped his eyes to his hands, which were gripping the steering wheel. He nodded briefly to Trish as she drew level with the open window.

'Any news, Mr Keane?'

'No. You?'

'No.'

Trish moved on. Behind her she heard the car engine start up. She was sorry for Gerard. There was a lot she didn't like about him; the way he treated the horses sometimes and his tomcat attitude towards women and sex. But there was a lot of good in him, too. If he sold a horse well he gave her a good bonus. If she needed time off she got it. He doted on little Aine and was always bringing her around the place with him.

And she could imagine what it was like living with that Brigid. She didn't like the woman at all. She tried to imagine the two of them having sex and felt slightly disgusted and then guilty. Whatever the Keanes were like, they didn't deserve what was happening to them now.

At the yard gate she slipped out of the saddle. Behind her a contingent of hippies pulled up in a battered van. She led Specks over.

'Any luck?'

Sam was in the passenger seat. 'No.' he said, getting out. 'That's Specks, isn't it?'

'Yeah,' said Trish. The whole county seemed to know the horse.

'Martina sometimes rode him up past our place,' said Sam. 'He was great friends with my Lucy.'

Trish wondered who Lucy was, but decided it wasn't relevant.

'Did you see Martina up around your place recently, then?' she said.

Sam shook his head. 'Not for ages.'

At the top of the drive Gerard stopped and looked right and left. Somehow, he felt, there ought to be a way of knowing which way she had gone. He waited for intuition but he was still there with his engine idling when Brian Burke and Mick pulled up.

Brian got out and leaned in to Gerard's window.

'Any news, Ger?'

'Nothing at all.'

'Jays.' Brian looked round at the mountains and back to Gerard. 'I'm only after hearing,' he said. 'I was working till now. Is there anything I can do?'

Gerard shrugged. 'Half the county's out there looking, sure.'

'And come here, what about the Guards?'

'I told David.'

'Ah, never mind David,' said Brian. 'That lad was in the jacks when they handed out the brains. Are you going somewhere now?'

'Not really. I was just—'

'Come on, so,' said Brian. 'We'll go and report it.'

He went back to his car, collected his jacket and gave the

keys to Mick. Then he got into the passenger side of the pick-up.

Brian had no land. His father did casual labour for Thomas in the distant past. Gerard would not have considered him close; would hardly have considered him a friend. But at that moment he could have kissed the hem of his garment.

Soon after Gerard left, Sam and his friends came into the house. Joseph went over the maps. Maureen came back from the village with a stone of bacon, a sack of potatoes and a box of cabbages. Brigid wanted to make at least a token protest but she had no energy. She went into the sitting room and sat on the sofa with Aine. Neither of them had the slightest interst in sports but they both watched the afternoon results round-up avidly. When the ads came on Aine said:

'Mam?'

'Mmm?'

'How can you tell if a swan is a boy or a girl?'

'A swan? I really have no idea. Why do you want to know?'

Aine shrugged. Together they watched the news.

Joseph answered the knock on the door and found Mick on the doorstep, tossing his father's car keys up and down. Joseph looked past him into the empty car.

'Did you drive over?'

Mick nodded.

'You didn't.'

'I did.'

'How come? Did your dad let you?'

Mick nodded again.

Joseph shook his head in wonder. 'Can I have a go?'

'Better not,' said Mick. 'Any news of your sister?'

'No.'

'Want some help looking?'

'I don't know, really.'

They went inside and studied the map. Most of the nearby parts were shaded; searched or being searched, but there was a triangle of about twenty-five acres between the quarry and Anthony Ryan's house that hadn't yet been covered.

'We'll do it, so,' said Mick.

They told Maureen where they were going. Every pot in the house was bubbling on the range and the kitchen was spotlessly clean despite the crowds.

'Any scones, Mrs?' said Mick. Maureen slugged him with a damp tea-towel.

They drove down to the quarry and walked from there.

'Did your da kill you last night?' said Joseph. It seemed like weeks ago.

'Na. He sent me to bed. I could hear them getting off on it afterwards.'

'What do you mean?' said Joseph.

'What do you think I mean?' said Mick, pumping his pelvis.

'Yeah? You heard them?'

'Worse luck.'

Joseph had never heard his mother and father. It hadn't

occurred to him that they had ever done it, let alone that they might do it still.

'And didn't they say anything?'

'Course they did. They said "ooh, uuh, yesss".' He mimicked sexual ecstasy until Joseph pounded him in the arm and the two of them ran off some steam across the fields. When they stopped and got their breath back Mick said: 'My ma took it back to Duffy's and complained. She said that kind of film should be banned. Betty said that kind of film is banned and she couldn't understand how it came to be in the shop.'

'Did she say she'd look into it?' asked Joseph, and they both collapsed laughing.

People continued to come and go. Sam's friends went out again but he stayed behind and took over the map in Joseph's absence. The coloured areas expanded.

The kitchen filled up with steam and Maureen opened the window. The Kellys returned their map and went home. Another group of hippies came back and their dog got into a fight with Popeye. By the time order was restored Maureen had set out heaped plates of bacon and cabbage for them all. When they explained that they were vegetarians and that they'd get something at home she was deeply shocked. She had heard of vegetarians but she thought they were fictional, like snake charmers. Aine said she would have a dinner and she persuaded her mother to come and have one as well. The hippies went home and Maureen went off to get Trish and Thomas to eat the other two meals. By the time she got back to the kitchen another group of searchers had arrived and she set about feeding them. Brigid wished she could keep her; have her sit beside the range and knit sweaters and mother them all, for ever and ever.

In Ennis Garda Barracks, Sergeant Peter Mullins listened in silence as Gerard poured out the story. From time to time he glanced up at Brian. When Gerard had finished he opened the door into a private office and led them into it. Then he sat at the desk with a pen and paper and they started all over again.

Joseph hadn't much of his mind on what they were doing, but Mick took it seriously and combed the hedgerows and searched every area of jumbled stones and tangled scrub created by old field clearings. The ruin of the big house was in the area they had mapped out to search and they approached it from the back, climbing over a high stone wall in the shadow of a row of beeches. Mick went into military mode, flattening himself against the wall beside the gaping front door and whirling round, hands outstretched, holding an imaginary pistol. Joseph followed him, trying to get into the mood of the game, but his heart was dropping towards his feet and he couldn't get a grip on his feelings at all. The house gave him the creeps.

Afterwards, Mick found money in the glove compartment of the car and they drove to O'Loughlin's.

Emma Duignan was working at the bar. She looked on with disdain as Mick tossed the keys on to the bar and ordered two pints. She had been to school with Martina.

'Any news?' she asked Joseph.

He was sick of hearing the phrase.

'No.' They had decided on lager because it was quicker to pull than stout. With their glasses in their hands they turned their backs to the bar and leaned against it.

'I was over at Mannion's today,' said Joseph.

'What for?'

'Checking the lake. With Doggy Fogarty.'

'With Doggy? Were you?'

'Yeah. I saw that Mrs Mannion.' He leaned closer to Mick. 'She had hardly anything on. She was dead embarrassed when she saw the priest.'

'Was she?'

'I wouldn't mind playing with her in the games room.'

'You dirty dog.'

Joseph laughed. He hadn't eaten anything since breakfast and the beer was going to his head very fast.

'I'd show her a thing or two,' he said.

'Have you got two, then?' said Emma from behind them. 'D'you hear that, Mrs Mannion?' She looked across into the lounge as she said it.

Joseph stood up straight and the colour flooded his face but there was no one there. The lounge was empty.

Emma turned her back on him.

'It's good to see that you're so concerned about your sister,' she said.

When Maureen had fed everyone who wanted to be fed she cleared up and went home. There was still enough food left in the pots to supply a small army.

Thomas went down to his house, laden with scraps for Popeye. Aine went with him to see if the swan had come back.

'How do you know if a swan is a boy or a girl?' she asked.

'God, I don't know,' said Thomas. 'Why?'

Aine said nothing, and Thomas went on: 'Sure, it's gone now anyway, isn't it? It flew away.'

'She might come back,' said Aine.

Trish went back to the yard just as dusk was falling. The frost that had been threatening earlier had gone and the air was warm and damp beneath a heavy cloud cover. She opened the paddock gate for the new fillies who returned to their box eagerly as if they were afraid of the coming dark. Specks called after them from the jumps field but they had each other for company, and they didn't reply. Trish went round with hay and nuts and topped up all the water buckets, then stood looking out into the gathering night. It wasn't cold. The old mare would be all right without her rug.

Suddenly, unexpectedly, the house was empty. Brigid thought of the mountains again, but they were hidden by the blue dusk outside the kitchen window. She went upstairs with the intention of looking for clues in Martina's room. A circled address. A letter, perhaps. She prayed for a letter. But as she passed Joseph's room she found that she couldn't remember where he was. She knocked on the closed door, and when there was no answer she went in.

The place was dishevelled, even though it was only a day or two since she had cleaned up. Automatically, she went in and started to pick the dirty laundry off the floor, underwear with yellowy stains, stiff socks, a white shirt with a grey collar and biro-marks all over the sleeves. The only thing in the room that was tidy was the bed. The duvet had been pulled up neatly over the pillows.

Brigid couldn't remember when she had last changed the bedclothes. She pulled the duvet back to see and it was then that she discovered the magazine. She picked it up and looked through it, horrified. She had found a few copies of *Playboy* once, among a pile of *Ideal Homes* that someone had given to the parish sale of work. They had been bad enough. This was many times worse.

It was a blow, and the fact that it was a blow reminded her of that other one. Every time she thought of Martina now the hope seemed less and the pain was worse. She couldn't stand to have those obscene pictures in the house. Quickly, before anyone could come in and see what she was doing, she ran downstairs and dropped the magazine into the range.

Gerard and Brian stopped at O'Loughlin's on the way home, just for a quick one. The pub was beginning to fill up, but Joseph was the first person that Gerard saw. Brian saw him stop, saw what he was looking at, put a hand on his arm that was both a support and a restraint.

'Jaysus,' he said. 'See what happens when you give them the keys.'

Joseph heard the hush and turned to see his father in the

123

doorway. He wished he were dead and then he wished that he hadn't had the second pint, and then he saw Brian. Now his father would know everything. He had one wish left. He started to laugh.

Brian threw the two lads out and told them to sit in the car. He got a pint and a couple of shorts into Gerard and put the blame of Mick and the tense situation they were all in. Gerard began to calm down and get things into proportion. He was glad Brian was there. He was glad there was someone else to decide when it was time to leave.

Joseph felt slightly nauseous on the way home. He wasn't sure whether it was because of the two pints or the poisonous silence in the car. He felt considerably worse when they got home and found a police car parked in front of the house. Gerard ran in. Joseph crept in behind him.

A young officer was standing inside the kitchen door and Sergeant Mullins was sitting at the table with Brigid. He had a lot of handwritten notes in front of him.

'What's going on?' said Gerard.

'I'm just trying to put a picture together,' said Peter.

'What sort of picture do you mean?'

'He was just asking a few questions,' said Brigid.

'About what? I already told him. It was a riding accident.'

'What was?' said Peter.

'But what . . . what else could have happened her?'

'We don't know, Mr Keane. We have to be open to all

eventualities.'

Gerard had kept his own worst fears in the dark. They emerged even as the sergeant spoke them.

'It's possible that she might have encountered someone.'

Gerard sat down heavily. Encountered. The word rang around his head.

'I'll go over and have a word with the stable girl, if you have no objections, Mr Keane?'

'Of course not.'

'Thank you for your help, Mrs Keane. I may have a word with Thomas as well.'

'Thomas has a bad heart,' said Gerard.

'I'll bear that in mind,' said Peter.

Aine was allowed to give Popeye his dinner.

'Good dog,' she said. 'Good Popeye.'

The dog tried to be polite but for once in his life he had an appetite and it needed all his attention.

'Maybe Martina is hiding,' said Aine.

'By God,' said Thomas. 'Maybe she is.'

'I might have known where you were,' said Brigid to Gerard. 'But I'm surprised at you, Joseph.'

'Ah, 'twasn't like that, for God's sake,' said Gerard. 'I was with Brian. We just stopped off for a quick one.'

'A lesson in how to deal with difficulties, is it?'

'Oh, for Christ's sake.'

There was a despairing moan behind them and Joseph shuffled off upstairs. In the silence that followed, both Gerard and Brigid were aware of the gulf between them but neither of them was able to bridge it.

Trish wouldn't let Peter in. She hated men in uniform, no matter what colour it was and she had no intention of entertaining two of them on her own at this time of the day. She said that she'd be happy to talk to them in the morning. Peter Mullins didn't push the matter. There was, after all, no evidence of a crime. Yet.

Brigid gave Joseph a few moments and went upstairs. She didn't have to go to the door. She could hear him from the top of the stairs, sobbing in a voice that was no longer that of a child but not yet that of a man. She had no experience of what he was going through, and she found that she was too distressed herself to be able to offer any help. Reluctantly she left him and went back downstairs.

Night

Aine held tight to Thomas's hand as they walked up the track between the bungalow and her house. Sometimes Thomas played teasing games in the dark but he wasn't in the mood for it now and she was glad. The night seemed full of horrors closing in behind them as they walked. She turned. Thomas's outside light was on. It cast a faint glimmer out on to the lake behind it and it seemed to Aine that something white glided slowly across it.

She pressed her cheek against Thomas's sleeve; warm wool smelling of tobacco and turf smoke. She skipped a couple of steps, hanging off his arm.

'Grandda?'

'Yes?'

'Shall we play a joke?'

'What kind of joke?'

'Let's pretend we found her!'

But Thomas had lost track of what she was saying. There was a car moving away up the boirin and it looked to him like a police car. He needed all his concentration to breathe deeply and to keep his knees from buckling.

Her granddad seemed to be tilting. Aine put his arm around her narrow shoulders and helped him along, and after a minute he was straight again. She ran on ahead to open the door.

The television was on. Gerard and Brigid were both looking at it but neither of them was watching. Aine ran in and jumped on to the sofa. Thomas followed, breathing with difficulty. Gerard jumped up and guided him into his own chair.

'Was that a police car?' he gasped.

''Twas, yes. But there was no news, Dad. It wasn't bad news.'

Thomas nodded. Everyone waited. The concerns of Pat Kenny's guests in the background seemed absurd. Brigid brought Thomas a small glass of brandy.

'Your dog put up a hare on the island,' said Gerard.

'Did he?' said Thomas.

'He did. But it ran him off the edge, doubled back. He went right over and down into the lake.'

'My God,' said Thomas. He was recovering fast, and making short work of the brandy.

Gerard looked into the fire for a moment. 'And then she vanished,' he said.

There was a pause. Someone on the television tried to sell them toilet paper. Then Thomas said: 'There's magic in hares.'

Brigid looked up at him. 'Is there?' she asked.

Joseph's room was silent as Brigid passed by with Aine. She hoped he was asleep.

Aine's room was all a-clutter. She looked anxiously at her mother but for once she didn't seem to have noticed.

'I could be picking up my things while you got me a hot water bottle?' she said.

'Oh, no. Not tonight, sweetheart. I'll be your hot water bottle.'

Aine changed into her pyjamas the way her friends had taught her on school trips to the swimming pool; without exposing any of the 'naughty bits'. She always got changed that way, even when there was no one in the room. God might have been looking.

Brigid picked a few clothes off the floor and dropped them on to the spare bed then went over and stood at the open window. There was no moon. The mountains were just visible, black against black. A light breeze huffed at her and swayed the curtains. She closed the window.

Aine jumped into bed. 'What shall we read?'

'Let's not read tonight. Do you mind?'

Aine shrugged and wriggled into the bed. Her mother stood for another moment then pulled the curtains. The springs creaked as she sat down on the edge of the bed and removed her shoes. Aine squeezed over as Brigid got in, lifting the covers high and snuggling them in around her shoulders.

She was slightly embarrassed. For years her mother had laid down with her at bed-time, to read a story or just to chat. But not recently. Not for a long time. Her bed was her castle, now, her nest, her place for private feelings

129

and dreams and explorations. Her mother didn't fit into it any more.

She pursued her own thoughts, but didn't get far. She had heard Gerard and Thomas talking about the police before she had come up.

'What does "encountered" mean?' she asked.

Brigid drew a big breath. 'Well. It means "met", I suppose.'

Aine nodded, but it was an unsatisfactory answer. Martina might have met someone. So what? Who might she have met? Somehow she knew that it was not a question that she should ask. Her mother's distress was heavier than Thomas's. It was definitely much too big for the bed.

She turned on to her side and closed her eyes. Brigid stroked the back of her neck with gentle, possessive fingers. Aine allowed the pleasure to claim her until it became an irritant, then she lay still with great concentration, the way she did on Christmas Eve when her father was sneaking around, pretending to be Santa. It worked, and soon Brigid stopped. Aine felt her raise herself on to her elbow, look down at her, then get up slowly and carefully. She tucked the bedclothes in around Aine's shoulders then went out of the room. Aine waited for a moment, then turned on to her back and stared up at the ceiling.

Brigid listened at Joseph's door. She was just about to creep away when she recognised the faint leakage of electronic sound from a Walkman. She knocked.

'Yeah?'

She went in. Joseph sat up on the bed and the earphones fell off. He fumbled with the controls.

'Are you all right?' said Brigid.

'Yeah. Fine.'

'Have you had any dinner?'

'No.'

'Why don't you come down. I'll heat something up for you.'

'I'm all right. I'm not hungry.'

'Come down anyway. Sit by the fire.'

He shook his head and put the earphones back on, closing her out.

Thomas insisted on going home and Gerard walked down with him. The breeze lifted their hair and the hem of Gerard's jacket and dropped them again.

'The wind's getting up,' said Thomas. 'I'd say there'll be rain.'

Gerard lifted the beam of the sheep lamp towards the clouds. Thomas laughed.

''Tisn't that good a lamp,' he said.

They had come to his door. Popeye bounded around their feet and Gerard put out a fond hand to him as though there had never been anger between them.

'Are you sure you'll be all right?'

'I'm certain,' said Thomas. 'You look after yourself, now. And your wife.' He called the dog and went in. Gerard turned away and gave a wry laugh at the idea that Brigid might need looking after. She was tough as old boots, that one, a strapping woman, made to go the distance. If he had realised how tough, he reflected, he would never have married her. But that was life. They laid their traps and you walked into them.

He walked on down to the lake and shone the torch out over the water. The island was just beyond the reach of the beam. He turned it off and waited for his eyes to adjust. The light from Thomas's house cast a glimmer on the black water. It was moving now, under the influence of the wind. Tiny, regular waves ran and danced. The black hump of the island appeared out beyond them. Gerard didn't know why he was looking at it or what he expected to see. But when he remembered the dog scrabbling at the mouth of the souterrain a black wave of fear closed over him and he switched on the lamp and shone its light around him in a full circle. The wind flicked the collar of his jacket against his cheek and tossed his hair right off his forehead. It was going to be a wild night.

The old house was full of silverfish and small, dark moths. By day they sat on the rough, whitewashed walls. By night the silverfish scuttled and the moths flew lightly against the bare bulbs or the screen of the television.

Mildew stained the walls. A spider city expanded slowly in the larder. In the unused parlour, the wallpaper hung off the walls.

Gerard had never intended that Trish should live like that. He had offered to get a plasterer in and to paint the place himself if she would choose the colours. Somehow she hadn't got round to it, but now she wished that she had.

Normally she didn't see much beyond the sink, the cooker and the television. Tonight she saw everything. She saw the dark, smoke-stained ceiling and the dirty brown paint on the doors and windows, the flimsy wiring, the ancient fuse-box above the fridge. She saw a bent, ineffectual bolt inside the front door and a broken catch on the rotten sash window. It was not a safe place to be.

The gutter-pipe that Gerard had promised to fix started to rattle. Trish turned on the telly. The wind snuffled at the window. She turned the volume up. Pat Kenny smiled benignly upon a pair of singing nuns. Trish tried to work out if it was supposed to be funny. The rain came like a wave to batter against the window and Trish swore. Whatever was or was not out there, the yard would have to be prepared for the storm.

She searched out her torch, put on her coat and fastened all the zips and toggles. She left Pat Kenny and the nuns grinning at each other and went out into the night. The torch had new batteries but it was still practically useless. Trish had to knock it against her hand to get it to work, and then it flared and dimmed and flickered. As she reached inside the tack room for the light switch it went off again, leaving her to grope in a gaping darkness while the wind behind her snatched at her jacket. When she found the switch the whole place lit up in a blaze and The Nipper, whose appetite was vulpine, called softly in the hope of breakfast.

Trish shut the top doors, one by one. The new fillies were huddled together in the corner, peering out apprehensively.

Trish flattered them with baby-talk as she closed them in, envying their comfort and their friendship. A bucket blew across the yard and she ran to catch it. When she put it back into the feed shed she saw the old mare's rug, neatly folded as she had left it.

Trish almost turned away; almost succeeded in convincing herself that she hadn't seen it, that the thought of the old mare standing out in the storm had not crossed her mind. But she failed. If she didn't put the rug on the mare, she wouldn't sleep.

Gerard saw the stable lights go on and turned off his lamp. He watched Trish's silhouette as she closed the top doors and felt a surge of warmth towards her. She was a good girl, without doubt, and one of the best riders in the county. He wished he could tell her that. He wished he could start again. He couldn't get it out of his mind that his lust, his sinful intentions were somehow connected with the disappearance of Martina. If only he could put it right, wipe the slate clean.

Trish folded the heavy green canvas rug over her arm. The wind snatched the tack-room door from her hand as she went out and slammed it against the wall. She closed it and shot the bolt home before the next gust could rise. Crossing the paddock, bent forward against the storm, she scolded herself for trusting the weather. The lake was notorious for its rapid changes of mood. Boats got into trouble quite regularly, capsized or driven aground by the sudden squalls. A few years ago a German tourist and his young son had been drowned there.

How many years ago?

Seven?

Trish shook the thought out of her mind and glanced around. The torch was making things worse with its flickering, creating shadows which bloomed and bulged. She turned it off and trusted to her eyes.

Thomas wished he had accepted when Brigid had offered to have oil-fired heating put in for him. No matter how well he succeeded in shielding his mind, his body seemed to be absorbing the day's shocks and reacting to them. He was exhausted. Lighting the fire seemed to be a mammoth undertaking, but he was cold. He needed it. As though in agreement, Popeye had parked himself so close to the fireplace that he was practically inside it.

'You could light it yourself if you weren't so stupid,' said Thomas.

Popeye pricked up his ears and listened intently.

'Or perhaps if you weren't so smart,' said Thomas.

Trish had forgotten that Specks was in the jumps field and she got the fright of her life when she came across him beside the far gate. With his red coat and white flecks and spots he was more ghostly than a grey. His tail was to the wind and his head to the east. Trish spoke to him but, to her surprise, he paid no attention to her at all.

The gate was all tied up with twine so she climbed over. The ground was rutted on the other side but her night eyes were still improving and she could see where she was going.

The mares had gathered at the other side of the field where two good hedges met and gave some shelter. They didn't move as she approached. They didn't even look at her.

She found it strange. It was as though the entirety of their attention was focused on something that she could neither see nor hear. The old mare didn't even seem to notice as Trish threw the wildly flapping rug across her back and felt around beneath her belly for the straps. When she had finished she stood back. Still the horses hadn't moved. They were relaxed yet concentrated, but on what? On their own metabolisms, perhaps, on the business of keeping warm. Or on the wind; the sounds it brought from wherever it originated or the signs of its intentions? Or something else?

Trish was struck by the realisation that in that hour, in that storm, she did not exist for the horses. She was not part of their umwelt. This world was not her world of ropes and sticks and jumps. These rules were not her rules. Some other truth existed in this darkness, which was here long before her and would be here long after. She did not know its name, or whether it was terrible or beautiful or both. She was blind, but the horses were not. They knew and they communed and she had no significance.

But if Trish didn't know that power in the night, she knew the terror that came in its wake. Suddenly and inexplicably the darkness was full of menace. Whatever had taken Martina was out there still, unknown and unnamed and watching. It was all the childhood terrors that were banished by lightbulbs, by the rational mind, by the false security of a booming economy. She turned on her torch but it was worse than useless. Whichever way she turned, the nameless threat was behind her.

Gerard looked into the pots at the cold potatoes and congealed bacon-grease. He scraped away some of the fat and cut thick slices for sandwiches.

In the sitting room, *Kenny Live* was just ending. Brigid looked up briefly as Gerard came in with the tea-tray, then turned back to the television.

'She's sure to turn up, isn't she, Ger?'

'Of course. Of course she will.'

'Where could she be?'

Neither of them, for all their wishing, could come up with any possibilities.

Gerard poured tea. The ads ended and a traditional music programme started. They both watched for a while, but neither of them saw.

'What did the police ask you?' said Gerard.

Brigid sighed and rubbed her eyes. 'Some strange things,' she said. 'I think they wanted to be sure that she hasn't just run off with some young man.'

'My God. What made them think that?'

'They didn't think that. They just wanted to consider it.'

'And did they?'

Brigid shrugged. 'They asked if she was happy.'

'What sort of a question is that?' said Gerard. 'Of course she was happy.'

Brigid walked across to the television and turned it off. She stood for a while with her back to Gerard, trying to focus, searching for courage. Behind her he munched and slurped. She found the sounds repulsive.

'I don't think she was,' she said at last.

'Was what?'

'I don't think Martina was happy here. I think that we just didn't notice.'

'Oh, God,' said Gerard. 'What kind of talk is that? How could you say that? She had everything she wanted. She would do anything for us.'

'Yes. She was good, all right. I won't deny that. But I don't think it means she was happy.'

'This is ridiculous,' said Gerard. 'Just because she came back from that training college? Just because she couldn't make up her mind what she wanted to do?'

'No. Not because of that.'

'Why, then?'

'I don't know. I think she was afraid. I think she had no confidence.'

Gerard was angry, and Brigid realised for the first time that he always became angry when someone didn't agree with him. If he couldn't win an argument with reason he would win it with force. He had to be right.

'So we're going to analyse her now, are we? Shall I phone a psychiatrist?'

Brigid said nothing.

'That's right, Doctor,' Gerard went on, a parody of himself in his righteous fury. 'Our daughter had everything that she wanted in life but she didn't like teaching so she threw herself into the lake. Is that it?'

He was losing it. Brigid walked away, heading for the kitchen, but he pursued her.

'Did you tell the police that? Did you? That our daughter was wasting away with misery and just waiting for an opportunity to—'

Brigid cut across his tirade. It was the first time in her life that she had done such a thing. 'Do you think she's in the lake, Ger?'

He was stunned. 'What?'

'Do you think she's in the lake.'

He deflated, painfully. 'I don't know what to think.'

A gust of wind hit the front of the house like a shock wave. For a long time neither of them spoke. Eventually Gerard said: 'It would be better if she had, wouldn't it?'

'Had what?'

'Run off with some fella.'

Rain hit the window like a handful of gravel. Without a word Gerard went out to the kitchen and put his wet coat back on.

Thomas's house was nearer than her own; just the other side of the orchard. Trish held her breath as she passed among the trees. They were losing their blossom to the wind. By the fistful, by the bucketful it blew like white moths across the feeble beam of her torch. The black terror still pursued her, with claws always inches from her shoulders, beak poised at her throat. At Thomas's back door she didn't wait for an answer to her knock.

He was sitting up in bewilderment as she came through

to the sitting room, but it was clear that he had been dozing in his chair. Popeye was curled up in a shivering heap. He got up reluctantly to greet her and brought orange ashes on his paws.

'I'm sorry, Thomas,' she said. 'I got a fright. Can I sit down for a minute?'

'You can of course. Longer, if you like.'

Thomas's voice lacked it usual strength and it was only then that Trish realised how pale he was and how cold it was in the room. She felt his hand, then went into the kitchen for the bottle-gas heater.

Gerard swung the beam of the sheep lamp up around the girders of the hay shed. Biddy was up there, the little black bantam, a throwback to the days when Martina had kept a few hens. Biddy's fondness for the high perch had saved her life when the fox came and took the rest. Aine called her Biddy Banty and fed her from her hand. Gerard said she was a nuisance, sitting up there every night and shitting down on top of the bales. Once he caught her picking up spilled horse nuts in the corner of the feed-shed and made to wring her neck and have done with her. But she was so tiny, her body so thin and light, that it was like killing a song bird. He had let her go and she had looked up at him with a bland, indifferent eye that suggested he had done her no favour. And though he complained about her whenever he saw her, he knew that he would miss her when she was gone.

The horse box was shoved in under the hay-shed out of the weather. Gerard shone his lamp into it and under it. He walked round the buck rake and the transport box parked beside it then began to climb the bales. There were a couple of hundred left out of the thousand or so that they had made in the summer. Most of them had gone on the horses. The few cattle that weren't on the mountain were fed on silage.

There were gaps between the hay bales and down beside them at the edges of the barn. Gerard shone his torch into them and kicked at anything suspect. A wiry cat shot out and vanished into the darkness. Gerard came down again and went round the back to where the remaining plastic-wrapped silage bales stood. Behind them a heap of empty bottles and paint tins leaned against a breeze block wall. Nettles grew up through the heap, thick and dark. Gerard trampled them down and shone the light over the wall and into the sludgy ditch on the other side where the run-off from the septic tank was supposed to drain away. Rank grass and rushes grew out of it. It was in bad need of half an hour with a shovel.

He walked on around the back of the stone buildings where an unkempt hedge leaned over and met the gutters and made a dark tunnel. There were more paint tins in there, and the white plastic bottles and tubs and drums that agro-chemicals and pharmaceuticals came in. The tunnel gave him the creeps. He went through quickly and around the other side into the low, damp building that had once been a pigsty. It was full of other kinds of junk: broken fridges and washing machines and a couple of valve radios, their wooden cases rotting. He had a long-standing intention to take a trailer-load to the dump. One day he would. The place smelled of rats, but there was nothing out of place.

The old dairy was full of feedstuffs in bins and bags, and bulk containers of veterinary medicines. Beside it the stone cowshed was another junk room. Gerard switched on the light in it and turned off the torch. He never threw anything away. There was a complete trap harness hanging against the wall and quietly rotting. There were jars and cans of nails and screws and nuts and bolts and staples and rivets. Spanners and chisels rusted in wooden butter-boxes and better kept tools hung in rows on a board. An old dresser was loaded with paint-tins, all upside down so the skin would form on the bottom. There were brushes and scrapers and bottles of turps, rolls of wire and coils of rope and drums of cable. Everything was useful, or might be, one day. Gerard told Aine that he might not be able to build a space rocket with the contents of that shed but he'd certainly be able to fix one.

'You would not.'

'I would, indeed. Just so long as there was a decent bit of two by four handy.'

'Two by four?'

'Two by four. The basic building block of the universe.'

But as Gerard looked around him now, nothing had any relevance to the hole that gaped in his life. The realisation that he couldn't fix it filled him with despair.

Brigid thought of the mountains; of the goats and the hazel and the hare. There was a vibrancy associated with them in her mind. It was a magic place, florid and bright, and something up there operated on a disused but still functional frequency in her being. A whole new world stood on her doorstep, just discovered, not yet explored. Her life of servitude here in the middle of nowhere, her monotonous, cabbage-smelling job would never rule her again. She knew that her daughter had somehow come to be governed by the same set of rules. Now that she was gone, Brigid didn't want to play by them any more.

The embers settled in the fire and she sat up. She supposed that she must be very tired, but she couldn't tell; couldn't remember what tired felt like or, for the moment, the difference between waking and sleeping. Nightmares were no longer confined to one, nor was clarity a certain property of the other. Martina was lost. She was in some kind of never-never land. Brigid hoped that when she came home she would remember to bring all those odd socks with her; the ones that got beamed up by the washing machine.

She laughed and her laughter brought her back again to the fire-side, where the embers were dimming. Gerard was outside somewhere and she was frightened; frightened of being alone, frightened of his return. She hoped the children wouldn't wake up because she couldn't be a mother to them now. Where was Maureen with her bacon-fed bosom and her great, dew-lapped arms, always bare, always warm. Where was her own mother, the one whose image we should carry with us always, to enfold and encourage, to comfort and care. She was up on the wall in a pale blue cowl, smiling down upon a male infant sprung from her virgin loins. She was up to her elbows in Sunlight Soap, looking down her nose in disdain at her eldest daughter, and she spoke of the sins of Eve and said that God was male and divinity was male, and woman was second best in every respect.

With a sinking feeling she knew that she believed it. She knew that she had given Kevin the best of herself, and that Martina had been given little, if anything. Even now, the thought of her eldest son brought a warm glow to her heart and a little, involuntary smile came to her lips. Martina never evoked feelings like that. Martina earned grudging acceptance at best.

Brigid sat up again. The embers were grey. A gale was blowing around the house. She hoped that Joseph wouldn't come down to sit by the fire. She didn't know him any more. He was a stranger. His room was warm and musky like a burrow or a lair. He read bad books in there and looked at bad pictures. Already he was thinking like his father. She was afraid of him. Afraid of everything. Of Gerard coming back with drink on his breath and lust in his loins, bruising and persistent, on and on to some goal that she once knew but had forgotten. She remembered how fresh it had been, once. Fresh and new as the clean air in the mountains, waiting to be breathed.

It was cold. She curled up on the sofa and pulled the patchwork quilt down around her. When she closed her eyes she could see the round, dark, shadowy place inside her head where she didn't want to go. There was something terrible there, something that sent adrenalin-shocks through her bones. If she stayed in the bright places, well away from it, she could survive. Her mind was closing its doors.

*   *   *

Gerard heard Martina's voice on the wind, calling him. He stood stock-still outside the buildings and listened. It didn't come again until he let out his breath, and then it did, distant, faint.

'Dad!'

The rain ran down inside his jacket. He couldn't tell where the sound had come from. He walked a little way along the boirin to be clear of trees and buildings, but he couldn't hear it now. He waited for a while, then turned into a field at random and began searching all over again.

Trish brought Thomas a blanket despite his protests and put the gas on high and lit the fire as well. Under Thomas's instruction she dug out bottles of stout, and cut slices of rubbery brack from a loaf and spread it with vegetable butter, yellow and slick.

As the room heated up, Popeye stretched out and began to relive, or perhaps to revise the hunt of the hare.

'It's a bad night,' said Trish.

''Tis,' said Thomas. 'Very bad.'

'I got a fright.'

'Why wouldn't you?' Colour was beginning to return to Thomas's cheeks. He refilled his glass from a fresh bottle. Trish was relieved to see that he wasn't quite ready to give up on life. But he wasn't really quite with her, either, not quite on the surface of the planet. They listened to the wind coming in off the lake, until Popeye yelped and sat up looking bewildered, then relieved and then embarrassed. Trish rubbed his head reassuringly and they listened to the wind some more until Thomas said: 'Something is mad out there anyway.'

'What is it?' said Trish.

'Oh, you wouldn't know,' said Thomas. 'There are all kinds of stories about the lake. And about the island.'

'Martina told me a lot of them,' said Trish, 'when we'd be out riding together. About Cormac and the bull and the city under the water.'

''Tis how he still hunts the bull,' said Thomas. 'On nights like this. That's what my mother used say. If you listen you can hear him blowing his horn and the bull bellowing and sometimes you can hear hounds.'

Popeye pricked up his ears and looked towards the door and Trish laughed. 'He can hear them, anyway.'

Popeye barked and stood up as the door flew open and Gerard swept in, driven by the wind at his back. Trish jumped to her feet in a reflex action, her heart in her mouth. When Gerard saw her he froze, and the wind blew in and caused the gas heater to gutter and the fire to billow smoke into the room. Then his features hardened and he closed the door. Trish put a hand to her heart and exhaled.

'You gave me a fright.'

'I was just seeing how Dad was getting on. Are you all okay?'

'Grand, sure,' said Thomas. 'Any news?'

'Nothing.' He was soaking wet and haggard. Trish looked into the fire, knowing that the events of that recent night had no relevance now; ashamed all the same of being the object of his desire.

'My lamp is running out, Dad,' he went on. 'Can I borrow yours?'

'Work away.'

He took Thomas's torch from beside the door and left his own dripping on to the floor. Trish would have taken the opportunity to get company on the way home but she was afraid that she would be taken up wrong. When Gerard was gone she felt awkward about being there with the old man. She would give it a few more minutes and then make a run for it.

Joseph dreamed that he met Stephen and Martina in the pub. They were going out together. They all leaned against the bar, having a great time, but Joseph suddenly realised that what he was drinking was piss and he felt sick. The other two were gone. He went to the jacks at the back. It had a big window and he could see Stephen walking down the motorway. He had a bridle slung over his shoulder.

Joseph sat up in bed and fumbled for the light but it was already on. His earphone cable was twisted around his neck and he was sweating and cold at the same time. He felt desperately sick.

Aine was checking the good hiding places in the house. She had already looked under the coats in the porch, inside the broken freezer and in the hot press. She had looked in the bottom of the dresser even though Martina was probably too big to fit into it any more, and under the sofa where her mother was sleeping, and inside the big corner cabinet.

Upstairs she had searched under her own, Martina's, and her parents' beds. Martina wasn't in any of those places. There was only Joseph's room, which she would have to leave until the next day, and the big linen press in the bathroom. She had just opened its door when she heard footsteps coming rapidly down the landing. Reacting without thought, she slipped into the cupboard and pulled the door closed behind her.

Through a crack she saw Joseph burst in and lean over the toilet bowl, heaving. The sound was dreadful; the smell was worse. She held her breath. Joseph blew his nose and coughed, then flushed the cistern. Aine breathed through her mouth and watched as Joseph unzipped his fly and pissed into the bowl. When he was finished he seemed to turn towards the cupboard and make a face at her, but he didn't stop. When he left, he turned out the light.

Aine sat in the darkness, still hardly daring to breathe. She was sure that Joseph had seen her and that now he was angry and waiting for her outside in the dark hall. The wind buffeted the house. The cistern hissed as it filled. Aine was sitting on a folded blanket and her feet were on two more. Holding her breath, she tugged one out and wrapped it around her and tucked her thumb into her mouth. She thought of Martina; could not imagine any place for her in the black, roaring world of the night. The blanket was scratchy. Aine wriggled into comfort and closed her eyes and saw a white swan which ran across the water and flew into the sun.

Joseph left his light on. One of the ear jacks had broken off his walkman. He dropped it down beside the bed and stared

at the white ceiling for a moment, then got up and began
to search again for the lost magazine.

Thomas's lamp lasted for a cursory search of the orchard.
Defeated, Gerard returned to the house. His coat was heavy
with rain. When he hung it on the back of a chair, the chair
fell over. He left it there.

Brigid was asleep in the sitting room. If she had been any
kind of a decent woman she would have stayed awake and
kept the fire going, waiting for him. His own mother would
have. There would have been hot soup on the range. If Brigid
had been any kind of a decent woman she would have had
kindness for him. Any man had a right to that.

He dropped into an armchair beside the dead fire. His wet
clothes soaked the upholstery. He peeled off his socks and
dropped them on to the hearth, where they made a puddle
on the tiles.

What had that policeman meant by 'encountered'? Who
had she encountered? What did he mean? Gerard shivered
but the energy to get himself upstairs and undressed was
not there. He crossed his arms and sank deeper into the
chair. The light seemed to dim and without standing up he
somehow moved the chair to the window, where the waters
of the lake were deep and dark and where a drowning dog
was grasping a bridle, dragging it down, dragging down the
white hand which still clung on to the reins, trying to pull
it back towards the surface. Failing.

Gerard gasped and opened his eyes, still beside the fire
and under the bright triple bulbs of his own cut-glass

149

centrepiece. He wrenched himself out of the chair and went into the kitchen, where he put on the kettle and got out of his wet clothes.

Joseph stripped the bed, dragged the mattress off the base and pulled the base away from the wall. There was thick dust down there, a few missing socks and underpants, his geometry set, *Marvel* comics with their pages set in crumpled fans. He picked up the geometry box and kicked the rest of the stuff around. The magazine was not there. He pulled the base out further, exposing a crate of dusty Lego and more comics. Frustrated, he shoved the base home and put everything back together again. For the sixth time he checked behind the shirt drawer.

'You bastard!' he screamed into the empty room. The injustice hurt. He didn't want the damned magazine. He wanted to destroy it.

In the kitchen, where he sat beside the range wrapped in a spare duvet, Gerard heard Joseph's anguished cry. His first reaction was rage; the boy shouldn't make a noise like that at night. When he calmed down he was sorry. He ought to go and see what the trouble was, but he couldn't. He was afraid that the rage would return and sabotage his attempts at friendship, at fatherhood, as it had done so many times before. It was easier to forget.

Thomas threw another few sods on to the fire and turned off the gas.

'Help yourself to another bottle there, Trish,' he said.

Trish was glad of the excuse to stay. 'Are you sure?'

'Course. Make a sandwich for yourself if you want one.'

'Do you want one?'

'No. No, but help yourself.'

Trish reached for the bottle opener. 'How did the bull come to be on the island in the first place?'

'Ah,' said Thomas. 'That's a long story.'

'Will you tell it?'

'I don't know, mind. I don't know if it's a story for the night that's in it.'

Thomas stayed quiet for a moment, then seemed to have changed his mind.

'Before Cormac came, Airmed, who was a daughter of Diancecht, had a sidhe on the island. It's said that people who were sick could go to a holy well that was there, and she would come out by night and heal them. But all that stopped when Cormac came.'

Trish poured beer into their glasses and Thomas waited until she had finished before he went on.

'He was a proud and bloodthirsty man, you see, and he would hear of no power greater than himself. Bit like one or two of our politicians today.' He paused for a moment, as though for her laughter, as though it was a line from a play, well-rehearsed and reliable. 'Anyway,' he went on, 'Cormac was out hunting one day and his hounds ran down a beautiful doe and held her while Cormac caught up to them. He drew his knife and was about to kill the doe when it began to call out. "Save me, Cormac, don't harm me!" Cormac was amazed, and put away his knife and called his hounds off and where the doe had been a beautiful woman was standing instead. A bit like yourself.'

Trish laughed. 'Get away with your old plamas and tell the story.' She noted that his colour was good now, revived more by the talk than by the fire or the beer.

'Right, so,' he said. 'Well. Cormac had no intention of letting the beautiful woman go. "I'll spare you from my knife," he said, "if you will consent to become my wife." "I'll be your wife for a year," says she, "and I would consider that a fair exchange." So Cormac agreed. After the year was up she said to him that it was time for her to return to the sidhe, but he wouldn't consent to it. He put a chain around her ankle and tied the other end to the doorpost of his house and then he went off about his daily business. But when he came back, there was the chain still tied to the door post and no woman on the end of it.'

Thomas paused for effect and took a swig from his glass.

'Cormac asked the women of the household if they had seen his wife. They said that they had not, but one of them said that she had seen a hare disappearing into a hole in the hillside near the well. So Cormac set men to dig her out of the hill, but no matter how hard and how long they dug they could not find the sidhe and as night fell they went back to the dun to sleep.

'But that night the fairy woman came to Cormac in his chamber. She begged Cormac to leave her alone. She had returned to her own lord in the sidhe and would never leave his side again. Cormac took out his sword and struck at her, but she turned herself into a swan and flew out of his reach. He swore that she would never return to her faery lord and ordered his men to block up the well and to throw stones down into the entrance to the sidhe where they had been digging that day.

'God.' Trish shuddered and realised why Thomas had said it wasn't a great story for the night. Being trapped underground had always been one of her greatest fears. Like being buried alive.

'It was after that the trouble began with the bull. That very night there was a roaring and a bellowing the like of which was never before heard in Munster. The whole island shook with the thundering of hooves and the crashing of rocks as though it were being knocked down from the inside. Cormac's men and their wives pleaded with him to take away the stones again but he would not consent. And all through the night the roaring went on and the white swan flew round and round the island and would not settle.

'The following day all seemed to be quiet and the fairy woman came humbly back to live with Cormac in his dun. And as time went by it was clear that she was with child, and Cormac was well pleased. But when the day came for her to give birth, the midwife and the serving women came out of her chamber in an awful state, for it wasn't a baby that had been born to her but a bull calf.'

'Yeuch!' said Trish. 'Freaky.'

'Freaky all right,' said Thomas. 'No sooner was the calf

born than the mother turned back into a swan and flew away out of the window. The womenfolk said Cormac should kill the calf but he was a stubborn man and he kept it. For a year it lived outside his dun and grazed with the other cattle. In the second year it began to grow into a mighty bull, the best he had, and Cormac put a ring through its nose and tried to tame it. But the bull fought with him and bolted and the rope got twisted, and before he knew what was happening the bull had dragged Cormac across the island and over the edge into the lake. And neither of them was ever seen again.'

'My God,' said Trish. 'And is that them out there again tonight, still battling it out?'

'It is,' said Thomas. 'It is, exactly.'

'And what happened to the swan?'

'Sure, isn't the swan on the lake to this day?' said Thomas. 'Didn't I see her this evening myself?'

'You did not!'

Thomas laughed and emptied the dregs of the last bottle into his glass. Popeye got up, a little stiffly, and went to the door. Thomas followed and let him out into the storm.

'You're on your own tonight, lad,' he said.

Not long afterwards Thomas went off to bed and Trish kipped down on the couch with Popeye. In the big house, Gerard sat at the kitchen table with the duvet round his shoulders and finally lost his battle against sleep.

In the surrounding meadows the horses and the cattle stood firm against the bellowing storm until, at last, it tired itself out and retreated to wherever it had come from.

Day

Joseph was woken by his mother who put her head around the door and said: 'Is Aine here? Have you see Aine?'

It was like a nightmare repetition of the previous day. Brigid went off without waiting for an answer and Joseph heard his father's voice downstairs calling for Aine.

He got up quickly, still in yesterday's clothes, and went out on to the landing. By the time he got there the panic was over. His mother was on her knees with her arms around Aine, who peered with sleepy indifference over her shoulder and straight at him. His father, outside now, was still calling. Joseph ran down to enlighten him.

Trish was woken by the sound of a helicopter flying low over the house. For a moment she didn't know where she was, then everything came back like a tightening noose.

Thomas was standing at the door watching the helicopter as it made a pass over the lake and swept away inland. Trish joined him.

'Never thought I'd be so glad to see one of those,' said Trish. 'They're sure to find her with that.'

'If she's on the ground,' said Thomas. He went back into the kitchen. Trish stepped outside. The air was fresh, scoured by the storm. A few branches had broken and a new complement of tattered silage plastic was wrapped around the bushes and fence posts. It seemed to Trish as though she spent half her life picking it up.

In the morning light the island looked clean and innocent. A figure was walking up the hill beside the church. Anthony, no doubt, checking his cattle. Trish put on her boots and set off up the boirin towards the yard.

On the island, Anthony watched the chopper swing away and steepened his ascent, heading for the fort. The smell of the dead cow wafted towards him on the wind. Before the helicopter could come back he wanted it gone, over the edge and into the lake. There was no sense in confusing the issue.

Peter Mullins and his young sidekick called to tell Gerard and Brigid that everything possible was being done. Afterwards they went over to talk to Trish. She was in the yard, trying to ascertain how lame The Nipper was.

'Nice horse,' said the young officer.

'Except that he's lame,' said Trish. 'Needs a holiday.'

'Don't we all,' said the Guard, then remembered himself and straightened up.

'Do you mind if we ask you a few questions?' said Peter Mullins.

It was the usual stuff: when did she last see Martina, what was she doing, did she have a boyfriend. Trish showed them the saddle and the broken martingale but they didn't want to see the horse and were content with a description of him. Afterwards they went down to see Thomas and asked him the same things.

Trish finally got round to turning the horses out into the paddock and mucking out the boxes, one by one. The helicopter buzzed backwards and forwards like a trapped bee. She hoped it would find Martina, and then she changed her mind and hoped that it would not.

Breakfast was practically silent. Joseph wondered which one of them had found the magazine. It was like waiting for a blow to land.

Brigid's behaviour was driving Gerard up the wall. She was vague and fluttery, going through the motions of things without any energy, getting things back to front. She started to gather the plates and cups before anyone had eaten anything and she dropped a net of fresh oranges into the pedal bin. When they had all finished she put bread into the toaster. He wanted to shout at her but he was afraid.

When they heard the helicopter coming Joseph raced Aine to the door. They watched it fly over and Aine jumped up and down like a crash survivor.

'If they don't find her no one will,' said Joseph, returning to the table. His words were greeted by a despairing silence and he wished he hadn't said it.

Gerard made a dozen phone calls to friends and relatives outside the area, just on the off-chance. None of them knew anything and they all wanted to know too much. He found it a terrible strain. By the time he got round to phoning Kevin in Stuttgart he was shaking.

Brigid watched the helicopter as it floated across the lower slopes of the mountain like a big dragon fly. She wondered what the goats would think of it.

Aine was quiet and wouldn't respond to suggestions; wouldn't read her book or help her mother to make ginger-bread men. She turned on the television but she didn't watch it. Instead she wandered round the house for a while, looking under things and into things until she came across a long-lost sliotar and brought it into the kitch-en.

'What happens to people when they die?' she said.

Brigid flinched and reached for her rubber gloves even though the washing-up was all finished.

'Well,' she said. 'Well ...' She struggled, but could not bring herself to repeat empty dogma, even for the sake of her daughter.

'Do they come alive again?' Aine asked.

'Martina isn't dead, Aine,' said Brigid. She said it with certainty, with authority. It seemed to be the best answer for everyone. It eased the panic around the dark place in her mind.

'I never said she was.' Aine tossed the battered sliotar from hand to hand, then dropped it and ran after it.

'Can I give this to Popeye?' she said.

'Of course you can! Go down and give it to Popeye.'

The helicopter made another pass of the mountainside, so

159

low that it seemed to be skimming the rocks. Gerard came in from the hall. 'Go and talk to Kevin,' he said.

'Kevin?'

'On the phone. Tell him there's no need to come home.'

Brigid was delighted to hear him. She asked how he was getting on in the job and whether he had found a girlfriend and what he did in the evenings and at weekends. He answered her brightly, her Kevin, always kind and forthcoming. But then he asked if he should come home and stay with them until they found out what had happened to Martina. She was off guard and the shock went through her like an electric current.

'No,' she said. 'No, don't come home. Martina will be back soon, I'm sure of that.'

There was a silence on the other end of the line, then Kevin said: 'There's a nice priest here. I'll have a mass said for her.'

'Send us a postcard,' said Brigid.

Gerard sent Joseph to check on the cattle in the roadside meadows, even though he usually complained that the boy couldn't tell a live one from a dead one unless it was on his plate. He located his wellingtons, but his feet had grown since he had last worn them. He borrowed the pair that Father Fogarty had worn the previous day, feeling slightly queasy about it.

Around the gates the earth was slimy and sucky, and soon the wellingtons were heavy with mud. He would never be a farmer. He was certain of that. Nor would Kevin, not in a million years. The only one of them who showed any interest was Martina. If she didn't come back . . .

One of the wellingtons got stuck and he stepped out of it and into the sludgy mud. Joseph swore, then swore again, then roared and shouted until his voice went soft and whiny, like a child.

Aine collected the milk from the box at the top of the drive and ran all the way back to the house. She dropped four cartons on the kitchen table and ran with the fifth down to Thomas's house.

'Good girl yourself,' he said, taking the milk from her. 'Now I can make myself a rice pudding.'

'Will you?' said Aine.

'I might,' said Thomas. 'Later. I might.'

Aine gave the sliotar to Popeye who took it, gently and politely, then dropped it on the floor. Aine called him outside and threw the sliotar down the path which led to the lake. Popeye sat beside her and watched it come to a halt on the shingle.

'Go fetch it, Popeye! Go fetch it.'

The dog licked her face earnestly and went back inside.

'Why won't he play, Granddad?'

'Don't mind him, Aine. He's very stupid.'

'He is not. Are you, Popeye?'

Popeye rolled over on to his back.

'See?' said Thomas. 'What did I tell you?'

Aine shrugged and threw the ball up and caught it.

'What happens to people after they die?' she said.

Thomas thought for a moment. 'Who says they die?' he said.

'Everybody dies, stupid!'

'Who says?' said Thomas. 'Tuan Mac Cairill didn't die, did he? And he was one of the very first men in Ireland.'

'Who?'

'Sure, you have that story in a book. I know that because I gave it to you myself. And I read it to you as well. I remember it.'

Aine bit her lip and frowned.

'He went to sleep and when he woke up he was a stag, isn't that right?'

'Oh, yeah,' said Aine. 'And then he was a hawk, and then he was king of the salmon and then, and then . . .'

'I don't recall,' said Thomas. 'But didn't he come back as a man again and tell the old abbot a thing or two?'

Aine was clearly pleased with the answer. She threw the sliotar to Popeye. It hit him on the nose and he yelped.

'A very stupid dog,' said Thomas.

Joseph left the wellies and the muddy sock outside the back door. He hadn't enjoyed going around the cattle but it had made him feel more solid; more like a part of things.

'Someone should go and count the cattle on the winterage,' he said to Brigid. 'After the storm.'

Brigid nodded. She wanted it to be her. On her own.

'Dad's going off his nut,' said Joseph. 'He's tearing the place apart.'

'You should help him,' said Brigid.

'He's too cross,' said Joseph.

Gerard felt the need to see into the middle of the piles of rusted wire which lay beside the boirin so he was sorting them out at last. But they had been there for a long time. Nettles and brambles had woven themselves into a sort of vegetable knotwork and were reluctant to be disturbed. In places the fallen leaves and stalks of years had made new soil and the wire lay underneath it. Most tenacious of all were the tough, yellow roots of the nettles.

Gerard knew the right way to do the job. The right way was to use wire-cutters or pliers or even to use the tractor to drag the wire clear, undergrowth and all. But he hadn't the patience to get the tools. Instead he made a horse of himself, hauling on the wire till it gave and he staggered, or yanking at it until his muscles ached and his hands bled. When Sergeant Mullins arrived he found Gerard in a frenzy that took some time to subside. He waited until he caught his breath.

'Someone rang in to say they saw Martina riding down beside the lake that day,' said Peter. 'We have dogs down on the lake-shore. And a few divers,' he added, almost apologetically. 'They're gone on down to the lake beside the causeway. I thought I should tell you.'

It seemed that they were nearly the last to know. By the time they got down to the lake half the neighbourhood was already there. When people saw Brigid and Gerard coming they lowered their eyes and stepped back deferentially. It made Joseph feel important. He walked an inch taller.

Anthony was among the crowd. He told the Keanes that the story had gone out on local radio, along with an appeal for information. Mullins confirmed it. There were already a number of calls about sightings of riders, he told them. They were all being followed up, but none of them looked very promising.

Two bright orange rubber dinghies were being unloaded from their trailers and launched into the shallows, one on each side of the causeway. Four frogmen in wet-suits attended each craft, wading out with it until it was clear of the shingle, then loading it with flippers and cylinders and anoraks. It took them a long time to get going. There was a lot of standing around and talking. Brigid noticed that the helicopter was gone and asked Joseph how long it was since he had seen it. He couldn't remember, either. He went to ask Peter Mullins, who was leaning on the bonnet of his own car with his arms folded, but Gerard intercepted him and told him not to be wasting the sergeant's time.

Joseph lost the inch he had gained. He went over and poked the tyres of the boat trailers with his toe and spun their rubber rollers. Then he went for a walk along the causeway towards the island. Anthony's cattle were standing in a line like a second tier of spectators. They moved aside to let him through and watched him for a while before returning their attention to the madness on the water.

Gerard asked Sergeant Mullins what had happened to the helicopter. Mullins said it had done all it could and gone back to base.

'Does that mean she's nowhere out there?' asked Gerard.

'It means the guys in the helicopter didn't see her, anyway.'

Gerard wanted to tell Joseph but when he looked around he couldn't see him. Brigid was sitting on one of the trailers staring into the shallow water which lapped against the wheels. He couldn't handle her fear. It was making her a stranger and it frightened him. It was easier to stay away. He was sure that she must feel the same.

He watched the small stones moving this way and that beneath the waves. It wasn't like the sea, where the tide acted like a great mill and rounded the pebbles on its shores. These stones were the same shape as when they were first brought here by horse and cart from the quarry. Broken by hand. Gerard thought of the famine workers, the ones who made the repairs here. There were famine roads everywhere, some of them in regular use, some leading into the back of beyond, still others unfinished, monuments to tragedy. If each of those starving builders had brought a stone and made a pile of them, and if those who survived the famine took their stone away, what kind of a pile would remain? One like the one on the island? Or one like the unexcavated mound on Slieve Cairn, visible for miles around.

Gerard returned to the present as the first boat's engine started up. When it was well clear of the shore, two men in waders went out into the shallows with hooks and drag lines.

As soon as she realised what they were doing, Brigid decided that she didn't want to watch. She didn't want to see anything that might be dredged up from those bleak, invisible depths.

She took the keys from Gerard and walked back up the track to the car.

Aine ran up to the yard and found Trish sitting on a feed bin, smoking a cigarette.

'Who are you going to be riding today?' she asked.

'It's Sunday,' said Trish. 'Sunday is a rest day.'

'But they had a Sunday yesterday, and the day before.'

'Won't do them any harm,' said Trish.

'Does Specks have to rest on a Sunday?'

'Why? Do you want to ride him?'

Aine nodded eagerly.

'I'll make a deal with you, then. If you ride Specks you have to clean his tack for him afterwards.'

'Even on a Sunday?'

'Especially on a Sunday.'

Trish stuffed folded newspaper into her own helmet to get it to fit Aine, then tacked up the cob and let them off together in the paddock. Specks stood at the gate for a while, ignoring Aine's feeble kicks and watching Trish sweep the yard.

'He won't go,' said Aine, petulantly.

'He will, once you show him that you really mean it.'

Aine got mad and gave three huge kicks, practically jumping out of the saddle. Specks gave a martyred sigh and moved off.

Thomas walked along the shore with Popeye but turned back when he saw the bright boats and their dark crews. A pair of swans stood on the bank beneath a tall sycamore, watching Popeye carefully. He kept on the safe side of Thomas. He had experience with swans.

Thomas hoped that they would stay. For as long as he could remember pairs had nested among the rushes along the shore. He had always taken great delight in the cygnets swimming along in a line like little grey ducks. But last year he hadn't seen any. He was afraid that it was another sign that the lake was becoming incapable of supporting life. For there were many. There had been no wading birds for years, now. He couldn't remember the last time he had seen a grebe, and he missed the annual visits of the lapwings, more spectacular than starlings in their flocking displays.

And it seemed that there were hardly any fish. There were angry meetings in the village where farmers defended their right to use all the nitrates they wanted and local business people, who made their entire year's income during the short tourist season, insisted that something had to be done. Environmentalists, most of them incomers to the area, came on board and confused the issue further. The argument divided the community, each side suspicious of the other. Some of the farmers quietly capitulated and joined the EU Rural Environment Protection Schemes which made it worth their while to farm in a way that didn't damage the environment. But others did not.

The divers put on their flippers and their cylinders and their masks. One by one they dropped backwards off the edge of the dinghies and vanished.

167

Peter Mullins introduced Gerard to a Detective Costelloe, who was in charge of the underwater operation. He wasn't in uniform. He was friendly, explaining how the search was carried out, how long the men could stay under, how they were trained for their job. It was designed to take Gerard's mind off what they were down there looking for, but it didn't.

'You must have had some kind of a tip off,' he said.

Costelloe looked surprised.

'Ah, no,' he said. 'Nothing like that.'

Gerard shook his head. 'It's a lot of divers to be dragging out on a Sunday just on spec.'

Peter Mullins looked at his feet, then glanced over each shoulder in turn, then moved a step closer to Gerard.

''Tis sort of a joint operation, you could say,' he said. ''Tis a bit hush-hush, you know.'

'What kind of a joint operation?' said Gerard, too loudly for Mullins' liking. 'Is there someone else missing?'

'No, no,' said Costelloe, stepping in quickly and trying to defuse Gerard. 'Nothing like that, nothing like that.'

'What, then?' said Gerard.

Costelloe shook his head. 'Nothing like that at all.'

Soon afterwards, Sergeant Mullins left. They were conducting door-to-door interviews, looking for sightings. Costelloe's walkie-talkie bleeped and he moved out of Gerard's earshot to talk into it. Gerard looked around at the familiar faces still hanging on. With a terrible shock he wondered if he ought to be suspicious of any of them. He felt dreadfully alone.

Joseph stood beside the church and looked down on the

frogmen. He had a good view from there. He could see the men in their dark suits beneath the water, at least for the first couple of feet. They were not a bit like frogs, despite their flippers, but one of them moved a bit like a seal or a dolphin, undulating his body. There was something attractive about it and Joseph dreamed about doing it himself, except that he would discover that he could breathe down there without those cumbersome cylinders, like the guy in *Waterworld*. He would be called for whenever there was any trouble underwater. He could go down to great depths, deeper than anyone had ever been. He would discover a beautiful girl held hostage in an underwater kingdom. He would breathe for her. Into her mouth.

But not Martina.

She was not down there, or not alive, anyway. There was no underwater city, despite what Thomas said. If Cormac ever existed he was a hairy man with a sword who kept hairy cattle, and he was long dead.

One of the frogmen had brought something up out of the water and the others were emerging and gathering at the boat-side to examine it. Joseph couldn't see what it was but he had a feeling that it was nothing to do with Martina. He looked across at the other boat but his view was obscured by bushes. He stood up and began to climb higher. He had never had much interest in the island but he was glad to be there now. It was like a place of his own, a quiet spot in a clamouring world.

Costelloe returned to Gerard's side.

'They've found some old bit of a sword or something,' he said.

'How old?' said Gerard.

'Ah, very old, now. Ancient, you know. I said to bring it in when they came, not to be wasting time.'

Gerard nodded. Detective Costelloe looked up at the sky, where light cloud drifted.

'Could be worse, I suppose.' he said.

But Gerard couldn't imagine how.

Thomas wandered up to the stable yard. Aine called out to him.

'Look, Grandda.'

With a considerable amount of kicking and flapping, she succeeded in walking Specks to the far end of the small paddock.

'Watch, watch.'

She turned him round and kicked again. Obligingly, the cob jogged up to the gate.

'Good girl, yourself!'

Aine hauled Specks' head around and set out again.

Brigid left the car at the gate. The water in the tank was overflowing following the heavy rain. It made a muddy patch for a few yards around the tank, then disappeared between the rocks. Brigid circumnavigated it, conscious that yet again she was wearing stupid shoes.

She didn't go up this time, but walked straight around the side of the mountain. To her left, above her, was rock, broken by the extension of her hazel gully until it gradually petered out. Below, to her right, the stony slopes gave on to several acres of small, rough meadows and thick, hazel scrub. One or two of the cattle were visible and Brigid made her way down to look for the rest.

As she did so, she realised that she had forgotten to bring the stick that she had found. She missed it as though it were an animate thing or perhaps, more pertinently, a symbol of her acceptance by whatever, or whoever inhabited the hazel woods. She was about to enter one of them now, but there was no point of entry on the tack that she was pursuing. Squat sentries of blackthorn stood guard, two or three deep in some places, barring her way. She could have pushed past them at the cost of a few pricks and scratches but somehow it would have seemed like an insult.

She followed the edge of the scrub for a while. There was an entrance for smaller creatures; a little path which disappeared into a tiny tunnel beneath the blackthorn. Brigid laughed at its neatness, feeling like Alice with the Drink Me bottle, too big for the world in which she found herself. But she went on and, sure enough, she found a way in. As soon as she was inside, the bushes stopped crowding each other and left plenty of space for her to move around. But now that she had become aware of it, it seemed that there was some sort of system in operation; a set of subtle rules for visitors. A path would end abruptly, blocked by a fallen branch or a boulder or a thorn bush. In most cases Brigid could have pushed or clambered a way through but, as at the edge of the wood, there was never a need. If she took her time, there was always a way that she could take that didn't involve effort or force. For a while she just followed these paths, testing the hypothesis; proving it, delighting in it. A few drops of rain began to fall. They touched her skin like a tingle of excitement, like the promise of a baptism into ecstasy. She raised her face to the falling drops and stuck out her tongue to catch them, then nearly bit it off as her foot slipped from under her and she landed heavily on her rump.

Shamefaced she stood up and made silent apology for her presumption. She had found the cattle or, at least, very recent traces of them. It was cowshit that she had trodden in, and a very muddy pathway that she had landed on. Like a main road it marched through the woods. Heavy hooves had broken young bushes and scraped the moss from a stone here and there. The smell was rich and fetid. Brigid brushed ineffectually at the large, muddy stain on her clean, beige skirt and followed along the trail.

Joseph climbed towards the fort. Some time before he got there the wind began to bring him snatches of a bad smell. Something up there was dead. He hesitated. Surely a body wouldn't begin to decompose so fast? He didn't know. He wondered if he should go back and get his father.

The boat on the farm side of the causeway had moved further out into the lake. One diver was in it and another one hung by his folded arms on to the side. The other boat was visible now as well, rocking severely as a frogman climbed aboard. It was out in the middle of the lake where the water was said to be bottomless. How did they think Martina could have

172

got out there? Joseph could see Gerard on the causeway, his head bowed close to that of another man, deep in conversation. There was no point in asking him. He would just be told to stop wasting his time.

The smell came again and curiosity tempted Joseph to climb on. The grass was short, still wet from the storm, slippery in places. The smell was evasive, sometimes there and sometimes not, until Joseph was no longer certain that he could smell anything at all. Up at the fort it was at its strongest, but apart from a patch of stained and trampled grass there was nothing to be seen. He stood for a while looking out over the lake, the fishman again, lord of it all. Then he set off to go home.

On the town side of the causeway a diver rose to the surface and threw something fairly heavy in over the side of the boat. Costelloe saw him and moved away from Gerard. Gerard watched the expression on his face, but it was inscrutable. Eventually he rejoined him.

'Ox bones,' he said.

'Ox bones?'

'Hundreds of them. Stacks of them.'

'What are they doing there?'

'We often find them. Some lakes are practically lined with them, sure. Ancient. From the last time there was mad cow disease in Ireland.'

Gerard missed the joke. He was watching as a diver in the boat played out a rope.

'A hundred cart-loads of them came out of Lough Gur in

Limerick,' Costelloe went on. 'Back in the nineteenth century. All the skulls were broken just here.' He pointed to his own forehead. 'Where they gave them a belt with something or other. To kill them, like.'

As if in illustration a long, hornless skull came up on the end of the rope. It was dark with sludge and decay.

'But . . . What are they fishing those out for?' said Gerard. 'That's not what they're here for!'

Detective Costelloe looked towards the heavens. 'Sure, they think they're Jacques Cousteau, some of that lot.'

Brigid counted cattle. She didn't know how many there were supposed to be, but she etched the number on to her brain. They all looked sleek and well, none the worse for the storm. Nor was she surprised by that. If she had been outside in last night's weather she could think of no better place to be. Because apart from the thick growth of hazel and blackthorn there were all kinds of nooks and hollows where a warm-blooded creature might find shelter. Even on the bare pavement plain beyond the meadows there were erratics; huge boulders dumped by the last glaciers, eons ago. Brigid thought they looked a bit sad, a bit embarrassed at being left. She noticed a large band of goats out there, some grazing, others lying down and being used by their kids for climbing practice. Brigid had always assumed that they were vermin but the more she saw of them the closer she came to changing her mind. She remembered Martina telling her that all the wild goats in Ireland were feral; either they or their ancestors had been domesticated. She said that no matter how many generations of domesticity lay behind any individual goat, it would revert to the wild without any difficulty if the circumstances allowed. And it would survive.

For some reason the thought gave Brigid hope.

She was still walking through the meadows making sure that she hadn't missed any cattle when she came across the ruins of Colmkille's church. She knew it was there; she had visited it many times, but always from the other side where an OPW sign marked the pathway in from the public road.

It wasn't on their land but it was close to their boundary. Brigid crossed the wall at its lowest point and walked through the coarse grass towards the stout, stone cross that marked the place. The church itself was no more than a few low walls which could easily have been mistaken for a ruined cabin or shed, but the more recent cross defined it and gave it an air of sanctity. Not far from its westernmost end a square flagstone marked the holy well. It no longer held water, but the stream that still ran through the bottom of it was considered by some to have healing properties, and the hawthorn tree which overhung it was adorned with votive offerings of red wool. On the opposite bank a single, plaster virgin was lodged among the rocks, her features blunted by weather and time. Brigid realised that she didn't understand the significance of the red wool, nor did she know who put it there. It was like a dim echo coming through from ancient times, when Ireland was closer to Asia than to Rome.

The thoughts, like the rain, both chilled and excited her. They came from layers of her mind that had been long unused, like files in a dusty attic, forgotten. They pleased her, like the sudden discovery of an inheritance and she wondered about the people who had built this church and lived an austere and solitary life devoted to it.

She wanted to drink the water. She believed that it could heal, maybe even reach that frightening wound that gaped darkly inside her mind. But she remembered reading somewhere that water on the surface of the land was often contaminated by cattle and you could get liver fluke if you drank it.

Brigid didn't want to get liver fluke. She sat on a protruding root of the big old hawthorn, but the peace that she expected did not descend. Instead, she became restless, drawn by a sound far behind the church in the woods that clothed the lower slopes of the mountain. She had gone a long way back into the past, but not yet far enough.

Aine insisted that Thomas get a pole for Specks to jump. He brought a light one from the next field while Trish went to the yard and fetched a couple of buckets to rest it on.

Aine was becoming more confident and getting more action out of the horse. While Trish and Thomas smoked and watched she built him up to a fairly lively trot and faced him at the pole. The first time he sailed straight past. Aine swore at him and drove him round again. This time he slowed to a walk and stopped, looking innocent. Aine screamed and slapped him with the reins. As she set him up for it again, Trish came though the gate, intending to give some assistance. Specks guessed her thoughts and pre-empted her. A good six feet from the jump he sprang, sailing way out over the pole and leaving Aine behind so that she toppled backwards and sideways out of the saddle.

Trish reached her almost before she landed. The ground was soft and she was more embarrassed than hurt. She got up and marched towards the fence, refusing to look at Trish. Trish let her go and went to catch Specks, who stood nearby, looking apologetic.

'Specks is sorry, Aine,' said Trish. 'He says to give him another try.'

Aine said nothing but continued to hide her face.

'Let you get up on him, Trish,' said Thomas. 'He can fairly pop, that lad. You can take him into the jumps field and give him a spin.'

'No!' Aine's voice was shrill and determined. She came out of her sulk, her face still red and tear-stained, and took hold of Specks' bridle.

'He's mine, now,' she said. 'Now that Martina's gone. He's mine.'

Joseph came down from the island and on to the causeway. The cattle had got bored with watching the boats and were making their way back towards the higher pastures. They gave him a wide berth, bunching up together in alarm as though they suspected his intentions.

With his hands in his pockets he slipped in among the crowds still waiting to be there when the headlines happened. He didn't need to ask whether there had been any developments. The listless expressions gave him the answer.

Gerard saw him and nodded. He knew that there was

something he wanted to tell him and tried to remember what it was. But he forgot about it when a diver popped up beside one of the boats and waved across at Detective Costelloe.

Off he went again with his walkie-talkie. It was absurd, his little, private game. He spoke into the phone and listened and nodded gravely and listened again. Gerard waited anxiously, but Costelloe didn't return to him. He went instead to his car where Gerard could see him go through the whole set of motions again on a different phone, a different wave-length.

He felt sick. They had clearly found something. He felt sick and then he felt angry, that not once during those two phone conversations had that man looked in his direction. He might have been a fence post. When Costelloe finally came over, Gerard was dizzy with apprehension.

'Not to worry,' said Costelloe. 'Nothing to do with this case.'

'What do you mean? Have they found something?'

'They have. They have found something. But it isn't . . . I mean . . . you know.'

'What have they found?'

'I can't tell you, I'm afraid. I've told them to leave it where it is for the moment and to get on with this case. It shouldn't be much longer, now.'

Gerard shook his head in bewilderment. It was like some sort of macabre lucky dip down there, every pick a winner. God only knew what else they would find.

As the first crew set up a marker-buoy above whatever it was that had caused the excitement, there was a shout from the other boat. They were hauling up a tangle of something that made Gerard's heart lurch until he saw, even at that distance, that it was too big to be a bridle.

He realised that he didn't want to know what it was. There was a lead weight in his innards and he couldn't take many more frights. He looked around for Joseph but he seemed to have gone. And Brigid was gone, too, with the car. He asked a police driver to give him a lift home.

Aine was back in the saddle and on her way again. This time Trish ran along beside her, holding her knee and clucking at Specks.

Thomas couldn't watch. He wandered aimlessly around the back of the big house, just in time to see the police car coming down the drive. He sat down on a low pile of breeze blocks and stayed there while the car pulled up beside the back door. Gerard got out. A few drops of rain began to fall.

The car pulled away. Gerard shook his head hopelessly at Thomas and went inside. From the paddock came the sounds of delighted laughter. Trish was doing a great job.

The wood behind the church was darker than the glade with closer growth and taller trees; ash and holly and the occasional spindle as well as the ubiquitous hazel. The ground was more uneven, shaped here by huge chunks of limestone which had fallen in the distant past from the towering crag behind. They were all moss-covered, though, all soft and richly green in the filtered light.

The sound that had attracted Brigid's attention was the rushing of water. The stream that fed St Colmkille's well disappeared underground very close to the edge of the wood but there was an earlier emergence further on in. Brigid moved towards it. There seemed to be no pathways in this wood, though there was plenty of evidence of life. Fresh earth at the base of rocks marked the entrance to lairs, and everywhere that a rock created a little sheltered overhang, hazel-cup litter had been gathered in large quantities.

Brigid followed the highway code she had established earlier and found that it still held good. It was right that there should be no struggle in there; no pressure. She would travel along ways that were open and avoid ones that were closed. She would not go anywhere that wasn't allowed.

In that way she came to the place where the stream first came out of the ground. It wasn't a great amount of water, though the roaring which now came from above made it sound as though it was. It was unusual to find any part of a stream above ground in the Burren, since most of the water-courses ran far beneath the surface, hollowing out circular tunnels and occasional colossal caverns, emerging rarely and randomly.

Above the disappearing stream the terrain rose steeply, a jumble of mossy rocks and scrubby hazel which somehow found anchorage between them. Beyond that the crag rose almost sheer to the top of the mountain. From where she stood Brigid could see no sign of water on the face of it, so the sound must be coming, somehow, from underneath the rocks.

She had no inclination to go any further. She did, though, decide to ignore the danger of liver fluke, and she stooped and collected water in her cupped palms and drank it. It was so cold that it made her gasp. It was wilder, fresher, more delicious than anything she had ever tasted. She drank more, and then more again. It wasn't a thirst that needed to be satisfied but another kind of craving that she couldn't name but knew was associated with what she felt when she was in these woods.

The water ran down her chin and spilled on to her chest. She drank until her stomach was stretched and she could drink no more. As she straightened up, a scything sound above her head made her flinch and look up. It was the raven, just barely clearing the tops of the branches. Behind it came another one.

The house was empty. Gerard remembered his mother standing at the range boiling up small potatoes in a bucket for the pig. Then he wondered if he really remembered it or just wished that he did. It would have to have been a very early memory. He was sure that if she hadn't died so young she would have been at the range still and that the range would never have been cold. Brigid was not that kind of woman. It was small wonder that things went wrong.

The back door rattled and Joseph came in, his trainers and the hems of his jeans wet from walking across the fields. He looked shocked when he saw his father.

'How did you get here?' he said.

'What do you mean, how did I get here? I flew, that's how.'

It might have been a joke but it wasn't. Joseph edged across the kitchen into the hall.

'Take off those wet shoes before you go upstairs,' Gerard went on.

Joseph mumbled something in a hollow voice, then the front door opened and closed.

Gerard grimaced and shook his head and slumped on to one of the kitchen chairs. He knew what he had said and how he had sounded but he hadn't been able to stop himself. The boy drove him mad. He was like a lodger, coming and going as he pleased, turning up at meal-times and sloping off again. He was useless to him; worse than useless. He didn't even seem to realise that there was anything going on.

And where the hell was that woman? He was starving; weak with the hunger. The three cold pots were still sitting on top of the cooker but he didn't want cold food. He began to slam around the kitchen, pulling out sausages and beans and a frozen loaf. Thomas came in.

'No news?' he said.

'Don't you think I'd tell you if there was?'

'You'd never know what you would or wouldn't do,' said Thomas. He patted the range, then leaned against it. 'Where's Brigid?' he asked.

Gerard lifted the pots off the stove and banged a frying pan on to the front ring.

'How the feck am I supposed to know where Brigid is?'

'Well if you're not supposed to know, I don't know who is!'

Gerard concentrated on the sausages, breathing deeply. Fury and terror fought a blood-red battle inside his forehead, wave upon wave, clash upon clash.

'Someone would want to watch out for her, anyway,' Thomas went on. 'Or she'll be away with the fairies.'

'There's only one person around here away with the fairies,' said Gerard. 'Don't you know that women don't want anyone to look after them any more?'

'I didn't say look after,' said Thomas. 'I said look out for.'

'Same difference,' said Gerard. 'They don't want it. They want jobs and freedom and money of their own. Sure, half of them don't want men at all!'

'Well,' said Thomas, standing up straight again and heading for the door. 'It's well for you that you know so much about everything. I hope you're right.'

He closed the door behind him. Gerard looked at the fat, pink fingers sitting in the pan. His appetite had vanished, but he reached out for matches and lit the gas.

As Brigid walked back across the mountainside she startled a solitary goat kid that was sleeping beside a rock. It ran a few yards from her then stopped, staring around in bewilderment. Brigid stood very still. The kid bleated, a small sound in the mountain's grey silence.

Brigid looked around. She couldn't see any more goats. The kid seemed to be completely on its own, as if abandoned. It wandered forward a few steps, then bleated again. There was no answering call, but from the nearby slopes a small troop of goats appeared. They saw Brigid and gave her a wide, wide berth, as such goat bands always did. But to Brigid's surprise, one of them didn't. An old, black goat and her small, black kid broke away from the group and made a wary detour past the solitary youngster. It bounded up to them, bleating urgently but the goat walked on past with apparent indifference. The kid was disappointed, but it tagged along behind the pair as they altered their course again and rejoined the herd.

It was a neat little exercise and Brigid was moved. She wanted to stay, to wander in the hazel, to learn more about the goats, to drink the wild water at the foot of the crag. But she couldn't, not yet. There was a reason for her to go back, even though she wasn't willing to think about what it was.

On automatic pilot she walked to the car and drove home. The rain started in earnest as she pulled up beside the house and she ran from the car to the door. The kitchen stank of burnt fat. Gerard sat at the table in front a black and greasy plate.

'Where have you been?'

'I was . . .' for a moment she forgot. 'I was up at the winterage. Counting the cattle.'

'Good of you. Were they all there?'

The number that she had filed so carefully was gone. 'How many were there supposed to be?'

'Twenty-nine.'

'That's right. There were twenty-nine.'

'Good.'

Gerard picked up the empty plate. 'They didn't find her, yet.'

It was like a small explosion in Brigid's solar plexus, hot flack spreading outwards to her arms and her temples and her calves. She sat down at the table and remembered to breathe, and waited for it to go away.

*   *   *

Aine and Trish had beans on toast and jam tarts and hot, milky tea. Then they cleaned the tack. Gerard came to check on Aine but he didn't stay. Aine was happy with that. There was a storm blowing through the heart of the family. Her father was standing straight in rigid defiance of it, but he was exhausted; he might just crack in the middle. Her mother had bent so far in front of it that she had become misshapen. Neither of them offered any shelter. Worse, they made her uncomfortable. Thomas was better and Trish was better than Thomas, but Specks was the best. He was her pal.

She cleaned the tack with a thoroughness that surprised Trish. Afterwards she stayed and helped to tidy up the tack room, rolling up bandages and finding pairs for the brushing boots. When they were finished they had more tea and more jam tarts. Aine would have stayed but Trish said it was time for her to go home. To be on the safe side, she brought her to the door.

The phone was ringing as Aine went in and she grabbed it, but Gerard was beside her and taking the handset away before she could find out who it was. He always seemed to say the same things: No, no news. I will, I will. Thanks for ringing. She wondered why none of her friends rang up any more. Perhaps they did. Perhaps she just wasn't allowed to speak to them.

She went into the sitting room to look for the book. Her mother was sitting beside a cold fire. She reached out for Aine when she saw her but Aine pretended not to see and searched out the book from beneath the pile of RTE Guides.

Fairy Stories by James Stephens. She looked at some of the coloured pictures inside then turned to the first story. It wasn't easy to read, but she was determined.

The fire was lit by the time Peter Mullins came round that evening. Brigid looked frightened when he came in and went off to make a cup of tea, even though he insisted that he didn't want one. Aine stayed very quiet on the sofa.

'There's nothing in the lake, anyway. Nor in the quarry.'

'There's something in the lake,' said Gerard. 'But no one will tell me what it is.'

Peter looked pointedly at Aine and then down at his feet. 'No bearing on this case,' he said.

'Aine, go and help your mother,' said Gerard.

She didn't even try to resist but took the heavy book with her. Brigid wasn't making tea. She wasn't even in the kitchen. Aine found her on the upstairs landing, looking out of the window at the lake. There were frogmen still working there, out in the middle. On the surface of the water a dozen brightly coloured balls were bobbing around like lost footballs.

'What are they?' said Aine.

'Markers,' said her mother. 'Buoys.'

Neither of the words fitted what Aine was seeing, so she ignored them. They went downstairs and while her mother made the tea Aine said: 'Tuan Mac Cairill went to sleep one night and dreamed he was a stag, and when he woke up the dream was true and he was a stag.'

'Really?' Brigid sounded a little like a robot.

'He did. And then he was a boar, and after that he was a

hawk and then a salmon. A woman ate the salmon and that was how he got into her tummy and then he was born as a man again.'

Brigid smiled, dimly.

'Silly, isn't it?' said Aine. 'You don't get pregnant like that, do you?'

'You never know,' said Brigid. 'You never know what might happen.'

Aine had hoped that she wouldn't say that. She had been nearly sure, but now she would have to watch what she ate.

She tried again.

'Do you think that was how Our Lady got pregnant?'

Peter Mullins put his head around the door.

'I'm off now, Mrs,' he said. 'I was saying there to your husband that it mightn't be a bad idea to get a few sleeping pills from your doctor. Your nerves must be in an awful state.'

Brigid made no reply but looked anxiously towards Gerard who was standing behind the sergeant.

'Ah, no,' said Peter. 'It isn't that. We haven't found anything. It's just the waiting, you know. Not knowing.' He smiled at Aine. 'You'll look after them, sure, won't you?'

He was gone without his tea, but Aine made it anyway for her mother and father, quite proud of the new responsibility she had been given.

'He says there's no more looking they can do,' said Gerard. 'They said they'll put out a report and a photograph and she'll be on some missing persons list or some such. But they have no leads. Nothing.'

Aine bustled importantly with cups and spoons, and put

milk in a jug to be specially good. Abruptly, her father began to laugh. He laughed until tears came into his eyes.

'What?' said Brigid. 'What is it?'

But he was unable to answer, helpless with laughter, alleviating the tension of the last days. Aine started laughing herself and even Brigid could not prevent a few smiles. When Gerard finally pulled himself together enough to be able to talk he was still in thrall to the humour of it.

'Do you know what they found in the lake?' he said.

'No,' said Brigid and Aine together.

'Drugs. Black fecking plastic bales of drugs.'

He started laughing again. Aine couldn't see what was funny. She thought drugs were very serious. Brigid was just shaking her head. And suddenly Gerard was serious again.

'So much for their fecking "joint operation". I don't believe the bastards were looking for Martina out there at all.'

Joseph and Thomas were watching the recovery operation from the shore. Earlier they had rowed out in the boat and only narrowly avoided getting arrested. Some of the same frogmen were working there but they were under orders of Customs and Excise now, not the police.

An army Land-Rover pulled up beside Thomas's house and a pair of young lads got out. They stood at a distance from Joseph and Thomas as though they were scornful of civilians.

'How much of it is in there?' said Thomas.

The taller of the soldiers shrugged his shoulders.

'Hard to say,' he said.

'You must be expecting trouble.'

'Not really.'

Thomas laughed. 'If I had a big gun like that, I'd be expecting trouble.'

He returned to the house and Popeye followed with a few anxious, backward glances. For a while Joseph watched on his own, self-consciously, then Trish wandered down.

'How's it going, Queen Wellie,' said Joseph.

'Not so bad, Wanking Walter. And yourself?'

Joseph blushed and looked away.

'What's going on, lads?' said Trish to the soldiers.

'Not a lot,' said the shorter of the two. Trish noticed that he had a pierced ear.

'Lost your earring?' she asked.

He grinned and shook his head.

''Cos I've a few in the house if you want one.'

He shook his head again and neither of them spoke for a few moments and then they both spoke at once, which made them laugh. Trish thought that she could get to like him, despite her hatred of uniforms, but he got official and stiff and said that he was on duty and shouldn't be talking to anyone.

Trish moved away, surprised by how embarrassed it made her feel. Out on the water the activity had ceased and the frogmen were hanging off the sides of the boats as if waiting for something to happen.

Father Fogarty came to the house to give the family communion.

'I hope you won't think me presumptuous,' he said, 'but I can understand that it was difficult for you to get to mass today.'

'We're honoured, father,' said Gerard. 'It's good of you to come.'

The priest spread a small cloth on the table in the sitting room and set out the host. Brigid watched Gerard during the brief service. His face was grave and still, as though he was really in contact with the mass and its meaning. She wished that she was. She couldn't even remember what it had felt like. It was mumbo-jumbo, without meaning. She had trouble taking communion, struck by the priest's arrogance in coming here, his assumption that he was wanted, that he had something to offer. As he handed out the wafers, they all heard the sound of the helicopter overhead.

Thomas heard it, too, but he stayed where he was. The radio was on in the kitchen and was reporting the drugs find. It referred to the fact that the police had discovered the drugs while searching for a missing teenager. It was sensationalist and cruel. Thomas hoped that Brigid wasn't listening.

It wasn't the same helicopter. This one belonged to the Irish Customs. Aine ran down the boirin after it as the priest drove away. It seemed newer and bigger, but it probably wasn't.

A pantechnicon lorry and a forklift truck stood on the causeway. Three men in overalls waited beside it. The helicopter wasted no time but dropped a line to a waiting frogman, who dived and attached it to something beneath the water.

Gerard came down to watch. Aine ran from Trish's side and grabbed hold of his hand. He stood between Joseph and the two soldiers and he didn't acknowledge Trish at all. She felt awkward, unwanted. She had been too nice to the soldier boy and not nice enough to Gerard. She stayed where she was, a little behind the others, but determined not to be frozen out of it.

The divers resurfaced and waved to the chopper crew, who began to winch up the load. The bale emerged black and dripping from the water. When it was well clear it was carried across to the truck and lowered gently on to the causeway behind the lorry.

It was dramatic and engaging. For a few minutes at a time, Gerard found he was able to forget about Martina.

Thomas rejoined the group at the shore just as one of the bales burst and scattered smaller packages into the lake.

'Jaysus,' said Gerard. 'Now we'll have some fish kill.'

'Not a bad way to go,' said Joseph.

'Hi lads,' Thomas called to the soldiers. 'Have you empty bottles?'

They laughed.

'Better than any poteen,' Thomas went on.

'Can't they bring their own bottles,' said Gerard. 'We'll charge them at the top of the road. We could get the lake drained fast, that way.'

It was a bit close to the bone and they all fell silent. Trish was suddenly disgusted by the whole operation and went back up to the yard to check on the horses. Afterwards she sat in the armchair while she waited for the kettle to boil. When she woke up it was dusk. The helicopter was gone and the lake was silent again. It was all over.

Night

Thomas and Popeye went out as night fell. The sky was rapidly darkening but the surface of the lake was bright as though it had collected all the light of the day and was hoarding it.

There was no evidence of the day's activities. The lake was calm and still. Thomas had an image of the waters absorbing the memory of all that had happened. It wasn't the first time that he had felt that the lake was all-knowing, all-remembering. If he only knew how to interpret, he was sure that those bright waters could tell him about everything; about Aengus and Oscar and Cormac and more. About the penal times, the famine, the civil war. About Martina.

He turned and looked up at the lights of the big house. What was happening was unfair. He was old and tired. If he could have given himself in place of Martina he would have. But he had tried that one before, when Gerard's mother was dying of pneumonia. It hadn't worked then, and it wouldn't work now.

Brigid cooked dinner from the mountains of leftovers. She

brightened while she was doing it and was delighted when Aine showed her the new dance she had learnt, even though she kept forgetting it and having to start again.

But after dinner she returned to her inner world and sat by the fire in silence.

Trish made herself a big, greasy fry. There was nothing on the television and she wished that she had stayed over with Thomas again. Out there in the darkness, no one was innocent until someone was found guilty. If something didn't get sorted out soon she wouldn't stay. She couldn't live with this.

Brigid knew that she didn't have to be on the mountains; not all the time. Travel to safety, to the bright places within, was always available to her. Provided that she didn't let the people around recover the emotional grip that had made her their property for all these years, she would be all right. They were all the same, with their endless desires and expectations. The only one who had been different, she now saw, was Martina.

Joseph phoned Mick and learned the latest rumour. The Mannions had done a bunk; picked up their boys from boarding school and fled the country.

'Are you serious?' said Joseph, but he didn't get to hear Mick's answer before Gerard ordered him off the phone.

'Someone could be trying to get through!'

Joseph looked into the sitting room and said goodnight. His mother whimpered like a child and looked up at him with frightened eyes. He turned quickly and ran upstairs. In his bedroom he tried to fix the Walkman again, without success. He listened to it with one ear. He wanted to masturbate but the pictures he was used to imagining scared him now, and disgusted him. He knew that Stephen could have had nothing to do with Martina's disappearance but he couldn't get the dream association out of his head. He was worried as well about his mother, who seemed to be on another planet. He wished he were Kevin. If he was Kevin he would know what to do. But he wasn't, and he didn't.

Gerard had the television turned to sport all evening, but he didn't get to watch much of it because the phone kept ringing. Each time, the others would look up, then hear the usual patter begin and look down again. Aine read her book until she went to sleep.

Thomas settled in front of the fire. He slept little at the best of times, and these days barely at all. His heart seemed mostly to be sleeping, but occasionally gave a little jump or flutter to remind itself to keep going. He wished that Trish would come over again. For the first time in his life he could enjoy female company without feeling bashful or sinful, and he could see women for who they were instead of for what they might do for him. There was no end to learning in life. It was one of the exciting things he had discovered about growing old.

Gerard carried Aine up to her bedroom. Brigid stared at the empty room for a few minutes, then picked up Aine's book and flipped through it. She was surprised that she had never paid any attention to it before. The text was by James Stephens and it had beautiful illustrations by Arthur Rackham; some colour, some line. A lot of the stories in it were familiar, but the style of the telling was new to her. She read a few lines at random.

'In truth we do not go to Faery, we become Faery, and in the beating of a pulse we may live for a year or a thousand years. But when we return the memory is quickly clouded and we seem to have had a dream or seen a vision, although we have verily been in Faery.'

When Gerard came down he found his wife absorbed in a book; a children's book. If you paid him he couldn't have read a book at that moment. For the first time it occurred to him that Thomas was right. Maybe Brigid did need support in this. He was slowly coming around to asking her how she was when the phone rang again. And when he came back, she had gone to bed.

There was no end to learning, but there was still no way of knowing. As Thomas dozed and woke through the long, dark, dog-scented night he dreamed and he thought, not of the knowledge that he did have but of the knowledge that he didn't. He would never be able to hear the stories that the lake told or the island, or the wind. He would never be able to contact the mind of another being, to speak and to listen without words, though he knew that the animals did it, and maybe even the birds and the fish. Specks knew what had happened to Martina but Thomas would never be able to learn from him. Nor would he ever be able to know; just know, the way a mind that was old and expanded ought to, somehow. He had lived a long time and he knew a lot, but it would never be enough.

Part 2

Eternity

Sometimes the days and nights got mixed up. Brigid wasn't sure of the order in which things happened, or whether some of them happened at all, but time slid by and there was no stopping it. Wild horses, galloping unsteadily, carried her along. Waking was a horror, sleep was lost, prayer was a dim memory. She had little or no power over herself or those around her, and they had minimal influence upon her. For the moment at least, she had to be where Martina was, and if that place was between the planets; if it was the place where fairies reside or gods or other ethereal beings, so be it. And if it was not easy to be there, she knew that there was nowhere that would be easier. As for what others thought, she didn't care.

In the darkness of the night Brigid and Gerard lay together but separate. Their bodies touched but their minds did not. Gerard dreamed of fish and things that floated and decayed in an oily gloom. He could not breathe, but he could not die, either.

Brigid dreamed by day, not by night. But once, as she waited for dawn, she felt a hand alight gently on her arm and she knew it was Gerard's. The touch was full of kindness and consolation and Brigid experienced an enormous sense of relief. But it was an illusion. He had turned in his sleep on to his back and his elbow had come to rest on her arm. His mouth was open. As Brigid looked at him he began to snore.

Thomas was woken by the sound of his own breathing; slow, distant, rattling, like waves breaking on a pebbly beach. He sat up and coughed. The fire was dim and he was growing cold. His thoughts surprised him. He couldn't go yet. Not with all this going on. He couldn't go yet because of Aine.

On the island the primroses died away and orchids flowered, and spring gentians. Wind and rain closed in again. Between them, the family kept the farm ticking over. Just about.

The days that passed were watched and numbered; Day Four, Day Twelve, Day Seventeen. Soon after that, time started to be measured in weeks, but it made no difference to the family. Their meagre hopes could no longer anchor them. In their different ways, they were all swimming hard against the currents of the Styx.

Whether his parents wanted him to or not, Kevin came home. Around the same time, Brigid's sister Mary was deputised by her other siblings to come and stay. Between them, Kevin and Mary took over and did their best to manage the tragedy. The house became a centre of operations again.

Kevin brought new energy and new ideas. He got posters printed with Martina's photograph and had them pasted up in all the neighbouring towns and villages. He contacted the Missing Persons helpline and sent them details for their files, and he drummed up interest in the media.

Gerard agreed to go on the radio to talk about what had happened and put out an appeal for information. He remembered similar items he had heard and was quite certain that he would remain composed and not break down like others did. Those people were looking for attention and sympathy. He wasn't like that.

He didn't break down, but he didn't speak, either. A trembling came over him as soon as he was in front of the microphone, and Brigid had to manage the interview on her own. They were all sure that something would come of it, but nothing did. The waiting grew worse, not better.

People returned, and the searches resumed and widened. Ground was covered and recovered. The map was hatched and cross-hatched, highlighted, blocked, and finally blackened.

The New Agers were among the most consistent of the searchers. They had no jobs or farm-work to claim their attention and their various building projects and their craft-work would wait. It was often quite late in the day when they arrived, but they put in long hours around the fields and tracks and mountainsides and were often the last to return at night. But Mary didn't like them with their doggy clothes and roll-ups and bits of string. She didn't say anything to the others in the house except how marvellous it was that they turned up every day, but she made the New Agers so uncomfortable about their smokes and their muddy boots and their food preferences that they became wary of her and began taking their tea and their smokes outside. And one damp day, Trish discovered them there and invited them into her house.

Gerard's life began to be ruled by the souterrain. The energy that he expended in not thinking about it exhausted him and he often became stuck during a chain of thought that was leading him, as they usually did, towards it. When Kevin suggested a new search of the island he agreed that it was a good idea but declined to join it. While Kevin and the others were gone he could hardly tear his mind away from them until they returned. They had been there for most of the day, walking all the shoreline and rowing Thomas's boat around the shallows, but they had found nothing. There was no mention of the souterrain or its stones. Gerard could not bring himself to ask.

Aine stopped going to school, but Joseph hated being at home all day and found life easier with a routine to follow. His Irish teacher took him aside one afternoon. His name was Mr Pettigrew but most of the students called him GAA Joe on account of his fanatical support of Gaelic games and all things Irish in origin.

'I'm sorry about your sister, Joseph,' he said. 'No news, I suppose.'

'No, sir.'

'How long is it now? A few weeks?'

'I don't know, sir.'

'Very sad, very sad. Please God she'll turn up.'

'Please God,' said Joseph.

There was a moment when Joseph might have made a successful escape, but he missed it.

'The world is going mad, Joseph,' said Pettigrew. 'Yeats foresaw it, you know.'

'He did, I suppose.'

'He did, you can be sure. "The falcon cannot hear the falconer. The centre cannot hold."' He paused, and Joseph nodded gravely.

'It is almost upon us you know,' he went on. 'We must rediscover the old gods, the vigorous spirits of the Celtic world? We must resist greed and individualism, Joseph. We must make a stand against the rough beast before it's too late.'

Joseph nodded, glad that there was no one else there to conspire with. The slightest sideways glance would have been enough to induce a fit of laughter.

'I hope that I am wrong, Joseph,' GAA Joe continued. 'I hope your sister will turn up alive and well. But I am afraid . . . Well, let's keep hope alive, shall we?'

When Joseph was back in the classroom with the others, Mick asked what had happened. Joseph shrugged.

'He's pure nuts,' he said. 'Thinks some animal out of one of Yeats's poems has eaten Martina. Or something.'

Aine was careful to be good. The adults who came into the house made a bigger than usual fuss of her, then forgot her entirely. She stayed out of the way and watched a lot of television, and didn't ask the questions that she knew no one wanted her to ask. She listened to the confident chat and felt the underlying urgency. Every tone was earnest, every suggestion careful, every parting apologetic.

But she was all right. As long as she knew where everyone was, and as long as she didn't forget, she was all right.

Gerard went out to do a few jobs around the farm. When he came back in at eleven o'clock, he huddled up against the range, knowing what it was now to feel cold, whatever the weather. The search parties for the day had already departed. It was beginning to be a pattern, but Gerard was not willing to admit that he didn't want to be a part of any more searching, for fear of what he might find. Instead he just disappeared from time to time.

Brigid was where he had left her, still in her dressing-gown. Mary had made her a cup of coffee.

'Would it help to talk to Father Fogarty?' he asked. 'Or maybe a doctor, or a counsellor of some kind?'

Brigid shook her head. 'Not unless they know where Martina is,' she said.

Joseph dreamed about the souterrain. In his dream he was down in the depths of the earth and there was a bull, huge and black and raging with elemental power. He was terrified of it and tried to run out, but it was right behind him and he could feel its furious breath heating his spinal chord. And then it was upon him.

He thought he was dead, but nothing happened. He was

leading the bull by the ring in its nose, out of the souterrain and across the island. Some long-standing problem was solved by it. It made him feel great.

When he woke he was surprised at the dream, because he had forgotten that the souterrain existed. There was another one a couple of miles away on the other side of the town. He had gone down it once with Kevin and Mick. It was years ago, now; he could only have been about seven or eight. Both of the others were afraid to go first, so he did. He remembered it as clearly as if it was yesterday. The first part was like a steep cave going down. After about ten feet it levelled out at the entrance to the first chamber. That was where the fun began. There was only one way in and that was through a crawl-hole. Beyond was an ancient and absolute darkness.

He had lit a candle. The others were above, peering down. They didn't think he'd go in. He didn't think he would, either. But at that moment, almost without his volition, he became someone else. A boy with a mission. The one with the courage to go into the underworld and find the lost treasure. He got down on to his stomach and wriggled forwards. It was much, much further than he had expected and stray fears hovered at the edges of his mind; of a hand grabbing his ankle, of a rock-fall trapping him in the darkness. The candlelight struck a wall in front of him. For a moment he thought it was a dead end. Then he looked up. He stood.

'I'm in!' he called.

The wall was waist-high, a part of the brilliant defence system which meant that no enemy could enter the place with their head intact. Joseph climbed over and dropped down into a stone-lined hall that stretched beyond the reach of his feeble light. Above his head, scorch-marks on the ceiling told of generations of children with candles. Beside the wall a coke bottle had been left by one of the more recent visitors, but there was no other sign of human occupancy.

The others scrambled in behind him, Kevin first and then Mick. They were bolder now but it was still his place, his triumph. It was he who led the way to the end of the chamber and through more crawl-holes into the next one, and the next, on into the bowels of the earth. He was king of the underground halls, and for months afterwards he would not let his brother or his sisters forget it.

A flush of embarrassment raced through him as he remembered that. He must have been an awful pain.

Brigid could not get to the hills those days. No one had said it, but there were no longer any hopes of finding Martina alive and it was unthinkable that her mother might stumble across her remains. She was encouraged to stay at home, and for the moment she put up no resistance. The hills would wait.

Mary made sure she was occupied. When there were no more scones or apple tarts that they could bake they went shopping. When there were no more clothes they could iron they cleaned out the kitchen presses and threw away rusted tins of baking powder and sweetened condensed milk, and then scoured the shelves with Ajax and put everything back in good order. Sometimes Maureen came over to lend a hand. They had great fun with it all, or so Mary kept saying.

Brigid put everything on hold and played along with them.

As though her mind could be so easily distracted. As though anything could possibly fill the waiting that her life had become. But most days she kept an eye on the mountains and she got the message that the lark brought one day, of brightness and hope, of peace beyond the reach of coming and going and endless natter.

The men, when they came in, were worse than the women, because there was nothing they didn't know. If they hadn't got an answer to something then they invented one in order that everyone could go away comfortable and satisfied. Like children, making rules for their games. Strong walls for their houses. Certainties.

But where Brigid was, no certainties were. She listened for the lark and she waited.

Every time someone went shopping they bought something special for Aine. It was better than Christmas. There were all her favourite sweets, bars, little plastic pots of this and that. There was every keep-the-kids-quiet kind of thing: reading books, colouring books, pencils and pastels and paints, stickers and sticker books. Aine knew what they meant. She saw the uncomfortable look in Mary's eyes as she handed over the latest paper bag. And in her mother's as she saw the damage accruing but didn't know how to stop it. Aine ate the sweets and littered her room with the presents.

She avoided her mother when that look came over her face that said she wanted to hold her and talk to her and make it all right. She went looking instead for Thomas and Trish and Specks. Thomas and Trish didn't pretend;

at least, not more than they always did. And Specks never pretended at all.

To keep his mind off the horror that still taunted him from beneath the ground, Gerard took refuge at mass and, on several occasions, brought the family with him. None of them wanted to go. None of them had the courage to say so.

Aine found it boring. Once a week was bad enough, but it was tolerable. More than that was torture. It was torture for Joseph as well. Father Fogarty seemed to single him out as though he needed some sort of special attention. A lot of his comments seemed too close for comfort. He couldn't get rid of the impression that someone was watching him. He could never wait to get out of the place.

Kevin had long since lapsed. He went nowhere near a church in Stuttgart and never gave the matter any thought. He didn't mind attending mass from time to time for his parents' sake, but usually preferred to be out in the fields and the lane-ways, continuing his search.

As for Brigid, she went along because it was easier than not going. But it was as though her subconscious mind was in rebellion. Twice she fell asleep in the pews and once she started snoring. On another occasion her foot slipped as she was kneeling down so that she landed with a thud and was unable to repress a brief gale of laughter. It infuriated Gerard, but Brigid wasn't worried. The church was behind her, now. She had found truth somewhere else.

Of all of them, only Gerard took sustenance from the mass.

'We cannot hope to understand the will of God,' he said one day as they drove homewards. Each of the others searched their mind for an answer of some kind. Not one of them could find one.

The New Agers set up their own centre of operations in Trish's kitchen. They smelled of wood-smoke and chronic dampness but once she got used to that, Trish quite liked their coming and going.

She did the stable jobs in the mornings and managed most days to lunge or school one or two of the young horses. In the afternoons she tacked up Specks and joined in the searches. Every day she took a different route, following any negotiable track or boirin that she found. She even took the cob on to Brigid's mountainside one afternoon, but his reluctance to cross the difficult ground suggested to her that Martina never brought him further than the gate.

Specks enjoyed it all, as happy going out as he was coming home. But they uncovered nothing.

If Aine was around when Trish came back from her afternoon ride she would get up on Specks and go around the paddock or even the jumps field. Sometimes Trish supervised and sometimes she left the two of them to get on with it. More than once she went to look for them and found Specks standing idle, snoozing, while Aine leaned forward with her arms round his neck, talking to him. She loved the heat and the smell of him. He was so big and solid and gentle. She liked it that she could get him to do some of the things she wanted but she liked it as well that there were things he wouldn't do, like going too fast, or over jumps that she wasn't quite certain about. If she put her ear in exactly the right place she could hear the hard 'lub-dub' of his heart, slow and consistent and safe.

One day Thomas found her like that.

'Don't be telling him any secrets now,' he said.

She sat up, dreamy and smiling.

'Why not?'

'Because he won't keep them, that's why.'

'He will, so.'

'No, he won't. He'll tell them to the apple trees in the orchard.'

'He will not.'

'He will. I've heard him whispering to them.'

'Well then,' said Aine. 'So what if he does?'

'So, they'll be written in the apples, then, in the summer time.'

'Huh?'

'When you cut the apple across,' said Thomas. 'It'll be written all through it like a stick of rock. Aine loves whoever it is. Aine thinks her grandda is a right eejit.'

'I don't!'

'I'm delighted to hear it,' said Thomas.

Aine got Specks going again, around the field. Thomas sat on an oil drum and watched.

Only Gerard didn't like Aine riding Specks. He didn't admit it, but somehow, irrationally, he blamed the horse for Martina's loss. He told Brigid that he didn't want Aine riding him. Brigid said nothing, but Joseph was listening.

'You can't wrap her in cotton wool, Dad,' he said. 'She has to get on with her life.'

'You'd know, I suppose,' said Gerard.

'He's right, Dad,' said Kevin.

'I suppose,' said Gerard.

Joseph went up to his room. He loved Kevin but he hated the way his parents idolised him. He had always been the saintly one, and in his presence Joseph felt smaller than ever, no matter what he did.

The wind blew around the lake. It buffeted the tall, square surface of the big house, and whipped round the corners and over the roofs of the smaller ones. At night the rain padded across the fields and along the hedgerows and the standing horses listened to it and smelled the earth's saturation and shifted their feet in the holding mud.

The lake collected the endless rain and held it, invisible as its other secrets. A moorhen educated her chicks in the shallows. Fish were jumping again. Only they knew how deep the middle was.

The fish and the frogmen.

Thomas looked out in the early hours of a sleepless morning and hoped that the new life hadn't come there at a price.

Time ran out for Brigid. She could no longer resist the pull of the mountains. One morning she set out before her sister got up and went into town on her own.

When she came back she walked down to Thomas's house. It was raining slightly. Two swans sailed by close to the shore,

213

then stopped and, one after the other, stood on their heads in the water.

Thomas was listening to the radio, but he turned it off when Brigid put her head around the door.

'Come in, come in,' he said. Popeye joined the welcome, fawning and yawning. Brigid stood awkwardly inside the door.

'I won't stay,' she said.

'Ah, do. You'll have a cup of tea.'

'I just called in for my stick.'

'Oh, yes. But, sure, the tea is in the pot.' He pulled out a vinyl-backed chair for her and she sat down.

'Nearly in the pot, anyway,' he said, putting on the kettle.

He collected the stick from the front room where he had put it for safe keeping. Brigid took it gratefully and looked it up and down, as though to make sure that it hadn't come to any harm. After that she seemed to relax a little.

Thomas put out a cup and a plate for her.

'Will you have a piece of toast?'

'No thanks.'

He put two slices of bread in the toaster. 'You might,' he said.

Brigid returned her attention to the stick.

'Do you believe the stories, Thomas?'

'God,' said Thomas. 'There's a question, now.' He emptied the teapot into the sink and washed away the tea-leaves. 'I don't know did anyone ever ask me that before.'

'I'm sure they did,' said Brigid.

'I wouldn't be sure. They were always just there, part of life. You accepted them the same way you accepted God our Father and Holy Mary.' He laughed. 'I'm not even certain that we were supposed to believe in them. They were for a certain part of your mind, if you take my meaning. You'd be hungry for them and they'd be given to you and then you'd be hungry for more of them.'

Brigid nodded. She was hungry for them, or for what lay behind them, creating them.

'But do you believe them?' she asked.

The toast popped up. Thomas put it on Brigid's plate and pushed the butter towards her.

'Eat that, now,' he said, 'and don't be asking so many questions.' Brigid grinned and obeyed. Thomas made the tea and poured it.

'I don't know whether I believe them or not,' he went on. 'But I'll tell you one thing. My mother believed them and my father did, too, and they weren't any the worse for it. They weren't stupid, either, even though people today might try and make out that they were. They knew a lot of things that I have forgotten and that you'll never learn.'

He turned his face away from her, afraid of betraying a passion and a grief that he rarely admitted. If Brigid noticed she didn't react, but finished her toast and sipped her tea. When Thomas recovered his composure he said, 'If people don't ask for the stories they'll be gone, and they'll never come again.'

Brigid nodded. She stood up and reached for her stick.

'I do believe them,' said Thomas.

215

'So do I,' said Brigid.

On the same day, later on, the sergeant phoned and said that Gerard was wanted at the local station for a few minutes. Gerard said he'd be right there and made for the door, but his innards liquefied and he had to visit the toilet first. He was sure they had found something.

Brigid was remembering what it felt like to be wet. She was remembering the mild, damp days when she would linger on the way home from school to get the most out of the day. Everything was different on those soft evenings. The grass smelled different and the plants in the hedgerows; even the road had a wet smell and a dry smell. The earth was replete, plump with rain but not heavy as it could be on the real rainy days that made your bones cold and sent you indoors. The good days always looked worse when you were looking out on them from indoors. Then, when you went out, because you had to, you didn't want to go back in again. Brigid seemed to remember having more energy on those days; walking faster and running further, but she couldn't be sure that it was true. She would run now, if the going wasn't so dangerous. She felt she could almost remember how.

The sergeant led Gerard into a small, concrete-walled room at the back of the little station. It had a single, high window and felt like a cell, even though it had a table in it. Two men in jeans and casual jackets were in there, one at the table and the other standing. They looked like thugs. Gerard felt fear clutch at him. He was offered a seat and he took it. The sergeant went out again and Gerard felt dreadfully alone.

'Have you found something?' he asked.

The man at the table shook his head. 'Afraid not,' he said. 'This is Detective Neylon and I'm Detective Inspector Clifford. We're down from Dublin, just having a little look into the case.'

He smiled and Gerard smiled back, uneasily.

'Nothing to worry about,' Clifford went on. 'We'd just like to ask you a few questions, that's all.'

Brigid walked over the rocks in her new boots and tried to remember when it happened, the voluntary hobbling. It was associated in her mind with drainpipe skirts and nylon stockings; with her maturity, her womanhood. But she was no longer sure what that meant. When she had first married and come to live at the farm she had been willing, even eager, to lend a hand with the outdoor work. But she hadn't been good at it, and then she had become pregnant with Kevin, and then, somehow, it hadn't seemed appropriate. She drove a car. She stayed indoors. She had spent her life waiting on others.

But now she had boots. Nothing would ever be the same again.

The two detectives ran through the events of the day with Gerard, what he could remember of them. He had fed the horses and the springers beside the road, then gone up to the winterage to check on the cattle there. He had visited Thomas. He had lunged The Nipper. He didn't remember

Martina setting out on the cob. He didn't know what time it had been. Later he had gone out to town for various supplies. Had his dinner. Gone out to the pub.

The detectives listened and nodded and asked the occasional question. Gerard relaxed a bit. They weren't as bad as they looked.

'What kind of relationship did you have with your daughter?' Clifford asked.

'Good. A good relationship,' said Gerard.

'Good in what way?'

'Good, you know. We got on well.'

'She's nineteen, is that right?'

'Nineteen,' said Gerard. 'That's right.'

'Most girls of nineteen are gone off into the world, wouldn't you think?'

'They would be, I suppose.'

'Why was she still at home, then?'

Gerard shrugged. 'She didn't like the course she was doing. She came home again.'

Behind DI Clifford, the other man started to move. He came round to Gerard's side of the table, very slowly, and ended up behind him, out of his sight. He was silent. Gerard could barely even hear him breathing. It made him nervous.

'You were close, so, were you?' said Clifford.

'Well . . . I suppose . . . We were friendly enough, like.'

'The first daughter, wasn't she? Daddy's favourite, perhaps?'

Gerard's skin crawled. A different reality had come into

existence. 'She was my daughter,' he said. 'Of course I was fond of her.'

'Why do you say "was", Mr Keane?'

Gerard stood up and swung round to get Neylon in his sight.

'What's going on here?' he shouted. 'What are you two suggesting? You have no right to treat me like this, do you hear?'

The two men made no response at all, but waited for Gerard's outburst to subside. By the time it had, he was shaking.

'I'd guess that you're used to getting your own way, Mr Keane,' said Clifford. 'Would I be right?'

Brigid walked through the hazel and on over the mountain. She found a way to the top for the first time, and looked out over Clare and Galway in three directions. The boots rubbed a bit, but small pains distracted her from the big pain, and were welcome.

She walked a mile across the uneven plateau of the mountain-top to where the great cairn stood. She had never climbed up to it before. It was much bigger than she had expected and she could only marvel at the race of people who had constructed it. From where she stood beside it she could look out over the sea, and from the sea and the shore anyone could look up and see it; the cairn on the mountain-top. She wondered if it was a message, a beacon of some kind. She wondered if it had served its purpose or was still waiting, for people, or for gods, who might come in from over the sea.

*   *   *

Gerard's interrogation went on for another, gruelling half an hour. It was like a nightmare. He had never been so humiliated in his life. He did not speak to the sergeant as he left the station. If he could help it, he would never speak to him again. He got into the pick-up and drove some distance down the road before pulling into the side and turning off the engine.

For a long, long time he sat there, trying to reconstruct himself. How could they have asked those things? How could they have thought that? Couldn't they see who he was, what he stood for, the values he upheld? He was shaking from head to foot. The fraternity upon which he had based his sense of identity did not exist. He wanted to go home, to be comforted by Brigid, but Brigid wasn't Brigid any more. She had been into town that day and bought a big pair of boots. The world had been turned on its head.

One evening Sam stayed on in Trish's house after the others had gone. They shared a joint and each of them shrank into themselves for a while, then Trish got up and made egg and chips and they ate together. Sam asked her why she worked with horses and why there, for Gerard. Trish found talking about it interesting, because she didn't know some of the answers until she said them. She learned that she loved horses because of their power and their kindness, because they could overcome people with their strength but they chose not to. She was surprised to find herself speaking like that and was slightly embarrassed. But Sam seemed to understand.

'I often think about the horses that used to carry men into battle,' he said. 'Did you see the film of *The Charge of the Light Brigade*?'

Trish shook her head.

'It ends on a freeze-frame image of a horse that has been killed. I cried my eyes out when I saw it.'

Trish had never met a man who cried, or admitted that he did. She didn't know what to think. She made more coffee and Sam rolled another joint.

But neither of them was a great idea. The joint made Trish paranoid and she remembered that no man was in the clear as far as she was concerned until the mystery of Martina's disappearance was solved. She became withdrawn and monosyllabic, and Sam soon left to walk the mile and a half across country to his caravan. Then after he had gone, the coffee kept her awake for hours.

Gerard dreamed that he went down into the souterrain. He was pushing and wriggling down into the hole, like a worm or a mole, and he was nearly there, nearly at the inner chamber. But a dark flood of warm, salty fluid came against him. He was blocking the hole and it couldn't get out. His head was in the fluid and he couldn't breathe. Nor could he turn in the narrow tunnel. All he could do was try and reverse, but as he did so he realised that there were miles and miles of tunnels behind him and he would never make it.

He woke in a sweating, palpitating panic. If Brigid had been there he might have reached for her. But she wasn't.

She was downstairs in the dark kitchen, standing at the

empty sink, watching the slow beginnings of dawn outlining the hills. There were lights up there, gentle, blueish ones, but she could only see them with the corners of her eyes. If she looked straight at them, they disappeared. But it didn't mean that they weren't there.

The next morning Gerard drove Brigid into town to see a counsellor that the family doctor had recommended. She was like a zombie in the car, and in the waiting room where they had to sit for forty-five minutes.

'You all right, Brigid?' said Gerard.

'Grand, sure,' she said.

'It's just, you might like to talk to someone, that's all.'

'Of course.'

'I thought you might like to talk to someone.'

It was him who needed to talk to someone, Brigid thought. But she didn't really care.

Trish had finished the mucking out and had long-reined the colt she was breaking. She was taking a coffee break when Sam arrived with six of the other New Agers. There was a woman with them that Trish hadn't met before. She was small and thin and had hennaed hair.

'She's Janice,' said Sam. 'She has come up from West Cork. She's a psychic.'

Trish shook the cold little hand.

'What does that mean?' she asked. 'What do you do?'

'All kinds of things,' said Janice.

'We're going to have a bit of a session if that's all right with you?' said Sam.

'What's a session?' said Trish.

'Well. We all join hands and Janice guides us and we all concentrate on Martina. With a bit of luck—'

'With a bit of help,' Janice corrected.

'With a bit of help, yeah. With a bit of help from Janice's guides we'll get a picture of where she is.'

Trish turned and busied herself at the sink to hide the amusement on her face. 'Are you going to do that here?' she said.

'With your permission,' said Sam.

'With your blessing,' said Janice. 'Maybe you would join us?'

'I don't think so, somehow,' said Trish, the smile still threatening the edges of her mouth.

'Perhaps you could help us in another way, then,' said one of the other women. She was one of the regular searchers. Her name was Cloud Dancer. She was very English and very earnest, as though she had a driving need to convince everyone of her integrity. She dressed in wraparounds and shawls and carried a huge bag made from heavy brown velvet.

'We need an article of Martina's clothing,' she went on. 'So that Janice can tune into her energies.'

The others all nodded. Sam had gone into the front room with a bundle of hazel and oak twigs and Trish could see him lighting a small fire in the grate.

'I couldn't do anything about that,' she said. 'You'd have to ask her mother.'

Janice shook her head and said, 'No. It would not be right to involve her mother.'

She spoke with great authority for someone so small. Again the others nodded and approved.

'Well I haven't got anything,' said Trish. 'And I'm not going over to the house, poking around.' She was beginning to get a bit irritated with it all and it showed in her tone.

'No, no. It's cool,' said Sam, from the front room. 'We wouldn't ask you to do anything like that.'

Trish was remembering that she did, in fact, have not one but several pieces of Martina's clothing in the house. She was remembering that they often went out together, for a drink or to a disco, and they often exchanged clothes. She was wondering how she could have come to forget that.

'The saddle,' said Cloud Dancer. 'What about a stirrup or a girth? That the horse was wearing when she disappeared?'

'You're all cracked,' she said.

They carried on anyway, lighting incense and covering the floor with rugs and bedspreads that they had brought with them. Trish finished her coffee and went out to start work again. The broken martingale was hanging on the back of the tack-room door. She took it in. Sam was in the kitchen, searching through his knapsack for a map. She gave him the martingale.

'Thanks. Perfect,' he said. 'Are you sure you don't want to join in?'

'No,' said Trish. 'No way. Do you really believe in all this stuff?'

Sam thought for a minute, then said, 'I will if it works.'

As Trish went out again she realised that she liked him.

*　　*　　*

'So, Brigid,' said the counsellor. 'You must be having a terrible time.'

Brigid shrugged. 'I suppose I must,' she said.

He had told her that his name was Tom, and she couldn't remember what the second bit was. He was short and sandy and flat-featured. Brigid didn't take to him at all. She didn't remember giving him permission to use her Christian name, but she tried not to let it matter. She could endure him if she had to.

'I suppose the worst of it must be the not knowing.' When Brigid didn't reply, he went on: 'I mean, about what has happened to Martina?'

'I suppose,' said Brigid.

'What sort of things go through your mind? What do you think might have happened to her?'

'I don't know,' said Brigid. 'Why should you think that you can help me?'

'Well,' said Tom. 'It is my area of expertise.'

'Missing people?'

'Not exactly.'

'Have you lost someone yourself?'

'Well, no. But I understand the kind of problems that people face at such times.'

'How?'

'I beg your pardon?' said the counsellor.

'How do you understand,' said Brigid, 'if you have never experienced it yourself?'

'It's my business to understand,' he said, and Brigid could hear the annoyance in his tone, even though she was sure that he was successfully hiding it from himself. 'It's my training. People often find that by talking about their difficulties they can come to terms with them and feel better.'

'I don't want to feel better,' said Brigid. 'I want to know where my daughter is.'

The Nipper was wearing a track in his bedding, going round and round and round. Trish took him out in the cavesson. He danced all the way down to the lake-shore, then refused to go into the water, then leaped in, soaking himself and Trish in the process. Then he sniffed and pawed, and waded in circles around Trish, then flubbered at the water with loose lips. Trish laughed and he did it again. He had more brains than most people, that horse, but Trish was afraid that he didn't have the constitution to match. She didn't know what would happen to him. She didn't like to think about it.

Eventually they both kept still enough for a fish to rise a few yards away. The ripples spread and washed around their legs and they both watched them until they stopped.

'People are quite often left with feelings of guilt,' said the counsellor. 'In cases like this. Problems that were never resolved. Conflicts, perhaps.'

There was a window in the office but a venetian blind was drawn down over it and Brigid couldn't see anything between the slats. She was trying to listen to what Tom was saying, but she didn't seem to feel anything.

'Did you get on well together?' he went on. 'Did you have arguments?'

Unbidden, a string of images flashed through Brigid's mind. Martina lifting a pot from the range and turning towards her. The quick energy she had, the natural strength. She lit a cigarette, the same brand that Trish smoked, and Brigid told her to take it outside. She did. Into the rain.

'She never argued with me,' said Brigid, but she saw no reason to tell Tom that she wished she had.

Thomas watched Trish and The Nipper from his kitchen window. The girl was very strong. She had never expressed any emotion at all about Martina's disappearance, despite the fact that they had been so close. Women were different, these days, he knew that. He hoped that they weren't getting too strong for their own good.

'My relationship with Gerard?' said Brigid. 'Relationship?'

Tom nodded. He waited with professional patience, but Brigid was stuck. Relationship. She looked at the word from all angles, but she couldn't make it mean anything. Eventually she left it parked where it was and allowed her mind to wander off and commune with the green air beyond it.

And Tom, for all his training, could think of no reason for fetching her back again.

When Trish got back from the lakeside the New Agers were piling into the back of their ancient Transit. Cloud Dancer was in her usual place at the wheel. Trish wondered why she wasn't called Van Driver. She decided not to ask.

Sam came over.

'Have you found her?' said Trish.

'We got a picture of a rocky slope near a strange-shaped hill and we found it on the map.'

'Don't forget to bring a picnic.'

'We won't,' said Sam. 'Is it all right if we hold on to the strap for the moment?'

'I don't see why not.'

'Want to come with us? Plenty of room.'

Trish shook her head and Sam rejoined the van.

Inside the house, on the kitchen table, Trish found a little hand-made card with dried flowers on the front and 'Thanks' written on the back.

Gerard had dropped Brigid at the house and was moving some bales across from the hay shed to the stable yard when he saw the hippies drive off in their van. He finished loading the transport box. The next step was simple. All he had to do was to climb up on to the tractor and start it. But somehow he couldn't. He got stuck. He could see no reason for doing it.

The actions of his life circulated in his mind. Feeding cattle. Selling them to someone who would kill them. Breeding more cattle to feed and to sell. Growing grass to feed them. He was struck by a memory of a programme he had seen on the television. Ireland's oldest archaeological site was older than the Pyramids. But it wasn't a tomb or a temple; it wasn't a monument of any kind. It was a place in Mayo called the Ceide Fields. Three thousand acres of stone-walled fields, so old that they were covered by more than two metres of peat bog. Evidence that for as long as there were people in Ireland there were cattle.

And cattle were still central to Irish life, the basis of rural existence. Everywhere Gerard looked he saw scatterings of them on the hills and meadows, but he couldn't think why. Dimly, he remembered the need to eat and to feed the family.

The family. It was no longer quite clear to him what the family was. They were all adrift, like satellites, but there was no centre. What was to prevent them all abandoning their orbits, vanishing into the vacuum of endless night, as Martina had?

The hay, the tractor, the yard. The hay, the tractor, the yard. Gerard had heard of people whose lives had lost their meaning. He had never believed it. He had seen it as an excuse for giving up, copping out, embracing the role of the victim. But he was still stuck half an hour later when Trish rode past on Specks.

'Are you all right, Mr Keane?'

He looked up and a shock ran through him.

'What time is it?' he asked.

Trish looked at her watch and he looked at his.

'Can you manage everything here?' he asked.

'I can, surely,' said Trish.

'Thanks.' He said it as though he meant it. 'I'm going to go to mass.'

Trish rode along the main Ennis road as if she was going to visit Lena, but half a mile before her house she turned right

229

into a narrow lane which led up towards the mountains. It was one of the few times she had ever met with resistance from Specks, who clearly had his heart set on Lena's sweet cake. He stopped and tried to turn back, but under pressure from Trish he soon gave up. By way of consolation he snatched a mouthful of grass out of the hedge and covered his bit with bright-green froth.

The New Agers could hardly have found a more beautiful place for their settlement. The lane was bounded on both sides by high hedges of hazel and hawthorn, behind which the mobile homes and caravans and makeshift wooden houses were practically invisible. The land was poor, all rock, which was why it had been cheap enough for them to be able to buy it from one of those rare farmers who didn't care who he sold to. Trish was surprised. The word locally was that the place was a mess, an eyesore, but she couldn't see it. Some of the buildings were a bit of a shambles, made from scrap timber and re-used corrugated iron but there was no litter, no plastic, none of the rusting cars that often took up space in country farmyards. Here and there a patch had been painstakingly cleared and cultivated. One holding had a polytunnel which was considerably bigger than its owners' caravan. Another had a couple of milking goats tethered in the hazel scrub. And at one place a horse called out to Specks, who stopped dead and called back.

Trish craned her head until she could just see, through the bushes, the horse tethered in a clearing. She was heavy, a real work-horse, but young. As Trish watched she walked around her anchor and called again. Specks answered, his whinny shaking his whole body and Trish's too. She kicked him on and hoped that the mare wouldn't break her tether.

Most of the dwellings appeared to be deserted, but there was smoke rising from one stove pipe. Outside that caravan two small children in thick, hand-knitted jumpers were playing with matchbox cars in a pile of grey sand. Their clothes and faces were grubby but they looked robust and clear-skinned. To her surprise, Trish found herself wondering if one of them was Lucy.

Gerard had missed mass, but he sat in the church for a few minutes on his own. Afterwards he found himself, almost by accident, in O'Loughlin's, and he stayed there for most of the afternoon, watching a basketball match on Sky Sports. It made about as much sense to him as humping bales and silage around the place, feeding more cattle than his family would eat in ten years.

As the first colour of dusk entered the sky that evening, Mary was scrubbing potoatoes in the kitchen when Sam knocked on the door and came in. He had been trawling some valley halfway across the county, for some reason, and had found an Aran sweater, thick and pale blue.

Brigid was sitting at the table. She looked up and shook her head. 'No. That isn't hers.'

Joseph appeared in the doorway. 'She wouldn't be seen dead wearing that,' he said. In the deathly hush that followed his words, Sam slipped out again.

231

He went over to Trish's. He found her in the yard, grooming The Nipper in his box.

'I found a jumper,' he said, 'but it isn't hers.'

'That's good,' said Trish. 'I suppose it's good, anyway. I suppose no news is good news.'

'I'm not sure,' said Sam. He stood for a while, watching her over the stable door. 'I walked over with it.'

'With what?'

'With the jumper. I walked over from Killinagh. That's where we were searching. The others are still there. I probably won't bother going back.'

'But Killinagh is miles away!'

'I came across country. About five miles, I reckon.'

'I said you were cracked,' said Trish. She patted The Nipper and took off his head collar. 'I'd say you could probably do with a cup of tea.'

The Kellys dropped Kevin back from a comprehensive search of all the empty buildings in the area. The dinner was ready and the family sat down together.

Gerard had done a check on the winterage cattle and sobered up in the process. He was suffering the effects of coming down.

'It's over,' he said. 'All this searching. There's no point at all in going on with it.'

No one answered. Everyone knew that he was right.

'It's time you were getting back to Stuttgart,' he went on.

'Oh, Dad!' said Kevin. 'I can't possibly go back.'

'You can, of course,' said Brigid, in total opposition to her feelings. 'And you must. There's no sense in staying here.'

'I can keep on looking,' he said, but his tone lacked conviction. Everyone knew that he would go.

'And we have to bring the cattle down from the mountain,' he went on. 'I'd better stay till you've done that.'

'We have plenty of help,' said Brigid.

'I suppose I'll be getting on home as well, so,' said Mary.

Brigid nodded, careful not to show the relief that she was feeling.

Trish made omelette and chips. Sam sat at the kitchen table and smoked roll-ups. He had run out of draw.

'You should go for a swim and see if the frogmen left any behind,' said Trish.

'I will some day,' said Sam. He concentrated on his smoke for a moment, then said, 'Are you happy, Trish?'

Trish laughed. 'What kind of a question is that?'

Sam shrugged. 'You don't seem happy,' he said. 'Is this job what you want?'

'Not really, I suppose.' She dropped the chips into the hot fat and they fizzed furiously.

'Can I come and help bring the cattle down?' said Aine.

'You can, of course,' said Gerard. 'You can come with me in the pick-up, and Joseph and Trish can walk them down.'

'I don't want to go in the pick-up,' said Aine. 'I want to ride on Specks.'

233

'Ah, now,' said Gerard, 'I don't think so. Not this time.'

'I'd mind her, Dad,' said Joseph. 'I could hold him and she could ride.'

Gerard's jaw went tight and the colour rose in his cheeks.

'Why do you do it?' he said.

'Do what?' said Joseph.

'Why do you keep contradicting me, whatever I say?'

'I don't!'

'There you go again.'

Around the table, the members of the family found themselves taking emotional shelter, ready for the coming storm. But Brigid refused to.

'I'll come myself,' she said. 'I haven't ever done it before. Me and Aine and Specks will follow them down and Trish and Joseph can run and stand in the gaps.'

Gerard stared at Brigid as if she had two heads.

'You're mad, woman, do you know that? Stone mad.'

He left his dinner uneaten and went out. The storm had been averted, but the family was as disturbed as if it had run its usual course.

As Gerard drove up the boirin on his way back to O'Loughlins, Cloud Dancer was driving the van down it. At Trish's house the searchers got out and, along with several dogs, gathered in the kitchen.

Janice was disappointed that the sweater hadn't belonged to Martina.

'We're glad, though, of course,' she said. 'But all the signs are now that there is no point in searching any more, not physically, anyway.'

234

The others nodded, relieved.

'There's nothing to stop more psychic searching, though,' she went on. 'And we must send good energy to Martina. Whether she is still in this life or beyond, she needs it.'

In the silence that followed Gerard's departure, Brigid fussed with plates and dishes until Mary reminded her that the meal was not over. For a while they all ate in silence. Then Joseph dropped his knife and fork.

'I'm sorry,' he said. 'I'm sorry.'

Sam was the last to leave. As the others loaded up into the van he lingered for a moment inside Trish's doorway.

'I'm afraid they're right, you know?' he said. 'About no more searching. We've done all we can.'

Trish nodded. There was a moment's awkward pause.

'I have a young horse,' said Sam. 'Lucy. I want to break her in and get her to pull a cart. I don't suppose you'd help me, would you?'

Trish brightened. 'Yeah. I'd love to. Any time.'

Sam bent and gave her a kiss on the cheek, then left. Trish watched the van as it pulled away into the darkness. Its rear windows were covered with stickers.

The horse was Sam's. It was Lucy. That meant that the kids weren't.

Brigid lay in the darkness beside Gerard. She thought about how she had once slept, like a well-regulated machine, as soon as she put her head down at night. Now she had forgotten how. Her mind manufactured all kinds of comforts and all kinds of horrors. She was becoming afraid of it. But she had nowhere else to go.

Part 3

The Beginning

Before he left, Kevin wrote the number of the Missing Persons Helpline on the wall above the phone and his own beneath it. Beside them both he wrote 'CALL ANYTIME!'

Then he left, which was a far more difficult thing to do than to stay.

Trish dreamed about a minotaur that thundered, bellowing, through labyrinthine halls underneath the house. She had always known that the labyrinth was there. What she had forgotten was how thin the floors were that she walked on. At any minute they could give way and she could drop . . .

She was woken from the dream by the sound of someone moving around in the yard and the horses shifting in their boxes and whickering. Just for an instant she thought that it was Martina and that the whole thing has been part of the nightmare.

She checked the clock. It was early. She got out of bed quickly and pulled on her clothes, then went cautiously out into the yard. It was raining.

Gerard was striding across the concrete with an almost regimental briskness, a bucket of nuts in his hand. As Trish watched he went into the boxes, one after another until his bucket was empty. She tried to judge his mood but found it difficult. He saw her eventually and nodded, brusquely. She nodded back and went into the house. The meaning behind his actions was clear to her now. Life goes on.

Everything was back to normal as far as Gerard was concerned. The winterage cattle were back home, out on the good grass beside the lake. Kevin and Mary were gone. The house was their own again. Their lives would return to the way they had been and everything would be all right. All they had to do was to keep going.

To her amazement, Gerard woke Aine at the old time, the time that was once usual. Life was still broken down as far as she was concerned; she was still stranded on the hard shoulder. But Gerard would hear no objections. She was to get up, have breakfast with Joseph and go to school. And she did.

Brigid didn't go back to work, though. She couldn't understand why she ever did it. She couldn't understand why money mattered and why she would have done a thing that she found so dispiriting just for the sake of it. She stood in the kitchen in her dressing-gown and didn't help at all while the others got organised around her. Gerard came in and out from the farm and raged at them to hurry. He located Aine's uniform and bullied her into her shoes and jacket and packed lunches for her and for Joseph. Then he drove with them up the road in the rain to where they would each catch a different bus, going in opposite directions.

*   *   *

Around mid-morning, Trish watched Brigid drive off up the boirin and wished it could have been her. She was mucking out. The boxes seemed dirtier on damp days, the muck heavier. Now that Gerard had come out and taken charge again, Trish was remembering that she didn't want to be here. A racing yard would be better, or show jumping. Somewhere there was people, and not just Gerard. She emptied yet another barrow-load on to the enormous quagmire of a muck heap and stood back. There was a tiredness deep in her bones that was unfamiliar. It was time for a change.

Brigid's waterproof was efficient but she couldn't bear to have the hood up over her ears. The sound of the mountainside, even the absence of sound, was sacred. Soon water was running down her neck and her legs and feet were soaked, but her walking warmed her and she didn't mind.

It was dryer beneath the hazel. Some of the little dens and nut stores were bone dry but the moss was damp like green sponge. Brigid didn't sit down but kept on slowly wandering, following the open paths and shunning the closed ones, keeping to the hazel wherever she could.

She disturbed some goats who were trying to keep out of the rain, but there were no hares and very few birds. There was other life, though. She spent half an hour watching a strong little mouse move a store of nuts from one hiding place to another, feeling insecure about them, perhaps, or robbing someone else's hoard. It worked with great diligence and though it often stopped and looked around and twitched its whiskers it seemed to have no awareness of Brigid's presence. She wondered if she was invisible, if the sharpness of this newly-discovered world made her as insubstantial as she felt. 'In truth we do not enter Faery, we become Faery . . .'

She wanted to believe that it was true. She wanted to believe that at any moment the hosts might come out of the hillside and invite her into their golden halls and that she might find Martina among them as the dead were said to be. But instead, the thought of her daughter caused reality to return with a whiplash of adrenalin. She must have jumped or gasped, because the mouse thief froze, and dropped its booty, and vanished with astonishing speed among the stones.

Brigid broke out in a sweat, but despite it she was cold. She walked on.

Aine was badgered mercilessly. At first it was a novelty, being the centre of attention, the only person in the school with a missing sister. But after a while it became tiring and then distressing so that she had to take refuge in tears and be rescued by one of the teachers. They considered sending her home, but when they phoned her house there was no answer. The crisis passed and she survived it. Life went on.

Brigid had learned from the goats and found a warm, sheltered corner among the rocks. The earth floor was dry, there, and covered with dusty goat droppings. Brigid barely noticed them. She folded her knees and propped her stick between them and wrapped her arms around the lot. She pulled up the collar of her coat and, though she wasn't warm, she was tolerably cold.

She didn't like what was happening at home with Gerard. It scared her. She said to him, 'Let you be the earth for a change and I'll be the lark.' She climbed above the rounded, planetary bulk of him and was surprised by how light she was, and how strong, and how safe in the air. But she could not sing, not a note, and she knew it was because her daughter was dead and her heart was broken. She turned back towards the earth and began her headlong dive, knowing that she could pull up as she reached the ground.

Knowing that she wouldn't.

She gasped and woke up, clutching at her precious hazel rod.

When Aine came home from school Gerard regretted sending her. She was pale and strained and he couldn't imagine the effect all this was having on her. But she ate the toasted cheese sandwiches that he made for her and half a packet of marshmallow biscuits and when she was finished she put on her jacket again and announced that she was going over to see Trish.

Gerard let her go and, as he cleared up, his mind began to run around the familiar rings. Martina had run off with some young man and was living in sin in Dublin. She had fallen off the horse and was in some old person's house with a broken leg or in a coma, but safe. Or she had encountered someone.

At that stage he baulked, as he always did. Like a recurring nightmare the mouth of the souterrain presented itself to taunt him. It would not go away. With a monstrous effort he wrenched his thoughts from it once again.

He stacked the dishes beside the ones still left from breakfast and wondered where Brigid was. In danger of getting stuck again he ran water into the washing-up bowl. It was cold. He turned it off and set about lighting the range.

Trish was riding a young mare in the jumps field, circling this way and that, trying to get her balanced. Now that life was returning to normal she had moved Specks back into the orchard where he had huffed at the fallen blossom and pretended to eat it. Aine guessed where he was and ran back to the yard to get a head collar.

Specks stopped rubbing his neck on a tree and watched her as she climbed in over the gate. He stood and waited as she ran up, and if he wasn't exactly helpful as she stretched up to him with the head collar he wasn't obstructive, either.

It took a bit of time and a few failed attempts but at last, proud as punch, Aine led her mount through the orchard gate on to the boirin. She didn't close it behind her but took the cob back to it and parked him beside it while she clambered up on the rungs and swung a leg over his wet back. Amazed at her own success, Aine settled herself behind Specks's withers and kicked hard.

Specks set off up the track. At the gate to the yard, Aine hauled on the lead rope attached to the head collar and ordered a halt. Specks took no notice. Tossing his head up and down, delighted to be out of his boring quarters, he set out to see what was on the menu at Lena's.

Aine pulled on the rope and called him names. She considered jumping off but it was a long way down and,

244

since she was in no apparent danger, she stayed where she was. At the top of the boirin Specks turned left. Aine made one more attempt to stop him then gave up and settled down to enjoy the ride.

Nobody saw them go.

Brigid might have seen them if she had still been up among the rocks. But she had gone into the woods again and was slowly making her way back. The ravens flew over, like sentries, and when they were gone, the rain gave rhythm to the quiet.

Thomas noticed the open gate of the orchard when he drove up to Gerard's house. He was going in to town and he wanted to bring Aine with him. He thought they might look at some bicycles together. He thought they might do more than look at them.

It was sill raining. Trish was in the yard, washing off the mare. The session had deteriorated into a bit of a battle and had gone on much longer than Trish had expected. The mare was sweating heavily.

Thomas leaned on the gate. 'Did you bring Specks out of the orchard?'

'No. Is he gone?'

'He is, I'd say. The gate's open anyway.'

'Maybe Gerard moved him?'

'Hardly,' said Thomas.

He went into the house to find out. Gerard was there, sweeping the kitchen floor. Aine was nowhere to be found.

Gerard hit the roof. 'I don't believe it,' he said. 'That fucking horse! If I ever see it again I swear to God I'll murder it!'

'Get a grip on yourself,' said Thomas.

'You bought him,' said Gerard, pointing a finger which shook with rage. 'You bought the bastard, that tinker's horse!'

Thomas wanted to answer but Gerard was striding towards the door, slapping at his pockets, taking out his keys.

Trish saw him come out and ran to stop the car. Gerard rolled down the window.

'I've an idea where they could be,' she said.

Gerard reached across and opened the passenger door. Trish got in. Gerard's face was grim and he pulled off at full acceleration so that the wheels of the pick-up skidded and threw gravel out behind them.

Trish hoped that she was right. The road seemed endless, far longer than a child on a sloppy old cob could cover in half an hour. Gerard drove in a terrible silence, like a boiler about to blow. When a turn in the road brought the horse and its small rider into sight he almost drove into the ditch and Trish made an instinctive grab for the wheel.

'It's all right,' he snapped, swerving clear. 'I'm perfectly capable.'

He pulled over in front of the sauntering cob and got out. Trish got out too, dreading what was about to happen. Gerard took the lead rope from Aine's hand.

'He just went, Daddy!' she said, sensing the coming violence. 'I tried to stop him but he wouldn't!'

Gerard reached up and pulled her off and put her behind him.

'I'll take him,' said Trish, but if Gerard heard he gave no indication of it. She took Aine's hand and led her back to the car as Gerard went for the horse, kicking him in the belly and slapping him around the head.

Aine screamed. 'No, Daddy, no Daddy!'

But Gerard was deaf. He carried on laying into Specks until the cob was running backwards along the road, sending up sparks from his shoes. Trish turned Aine to face her and hugged her tight, blinding her.

'He'll be all right. You'll see.'

Aine sobbed and clung to Trish's arms with hands like claws.

'He didn't do anything bad! It wasn't his fault!'

Gerard's steam ran out. He came back towards the car, dragging the terrified horse behind him. Trish took the lead rope. Gerard picked up Aine and held her, but she pushed away from him and wriggled to get down.

'I thought you were gone, Aine,' he said. 'Like Martina. I thought you were gone.'

She wouldn't answer. Gerard put her into the pick-up and turned it, and drove home.

Specks was steaming in the rain. Trish put a hand on his neck and spoke to him and patted him. After a moment or two he let out a great sigh and dropped his head, and the fear faded away from his kind, brown eyes. He had been hammered before and he would be hammered again. There wasn't much left in life that would surprise him.

Trish found him a few nuts, then jumped up on to his wet back and turned his head towards home.

Aine dreamed that she was riding on a bull that walked on two legs. She was on its back, piggyback, trying to control it with a bridle. It lunged and plunged, and its horns swung wildly within inches of her ears. She knew that if she fell off she was done for. But if she stayed on the bull-man would take her away, to the place where Martina was.

She woke. The door was open a crack and the landing light was on. She listened for sounds from downstairs. There was nothing, just the rumble of the Neolithic fridge in the kitchen. She turned and snuggled down again but it was no use. The thing on the island came back into her mind and she could smell its dead smell and see its long legs and hear its empty hooves rattling on the end of its bare bones. She was making herself more scared, not less. She needed some help.

Outside her parents' room she stopped and listened. Her father had frightened her and she didn't want to be near him. But her mother frightened her more, in some ways, with her tight hugs that went on for too long and her eyes full of dreams.

She looked along the landing. Martina's bedroom was empty. Kevin had gone away again. There was only Joseph. She stood at his door and listened. He was snoring lightly. She pushed the door open. The smell was strong, almost animal, but it was known to her. She crept in and shook him by the shoulder.

'What?' he said. 'What?'

They all slept lightly those days.

'Can I come in with you?'

'Why?' His eyes closed and Aine could tell that he was dropping off again.

'Joseph?'

'What? What is it?'

'I had a bad dream. Can I come into your bed?'

He was awake now. He propped himself on his elbow.

'Why can't you go in with Mam and Dad?'

Aine shrugged. 'I don't know.'

'You can. Why can't you?'

Aine said nothing. Joseph looked at her. She was frightened and terribly alone. The realisation sent a small jolt through him and he understood, without trying too hard, why she couldn't go into their parents' bed. He moved over and held up the covers for her.

She got in carefully, on her back. She smelled of nothing. Biscuits, perhaps. She was warmer than he was and it reminded him that when they were younger they had often shared a bed together. They had been good friends, despite the huge gap in their ages. He was the big brother and she worshipped him; laughed at his worst jokes as hard as at his best. How long ago was that?

'What was your dream about?' he asked.

Aine thought for a minute. In the light from the landing Joseph watched her face. It was grave, guileless.

'I can't tell you,' she said.

'Bad one, eh?'

She nodded. He felt strong and protective, but guilty

as well. There was some reason that they had stopped sharing a bed.

'Do you like going to school, Joseph?' she asked.

He shrugged. 'Do you?'

'Yes.'

'Why?'

'I don't know.'

'I suppose it's a bit more like normal, isn't it?'

'Yes.'

They were silent again and then he remembered. They had been having a fight together, just the two of them, underneath the bedclothes. He had been tickling her and she had been doing a lot of squealing and giggling. How long ago was it? It was great fun. He had always known how to wind her up. But something had made him look up, and he had seen his father standing at the door with a face as hard and as dark as bog oak.

'Come out of there, Aine,' he had said.

'Oh! Why?'

He strode into the room and grabbed her wrist and yanked her bodily from the bed.

'When I say "out" I mean "out".'

She ran off, hurt, crying. Joseph sat on the bed, dreadfully vulnerable, expecting the worst.

'You're too old for that kind of carry-on now, Joseph,' his father had said. 'I don't want to ever catch the two of you in the same bed again. You hear?'

Joseph didn't know why. It had made him and Aine strangers and from that day on he had begun to feel dirty, sinful, and to believe that Aine must be as well. And then the things that began to happen to his body were wrong things, bad things, things to be ashamed of. Dangerous things.

Beside him Aine turned towards him and rested a knee on his thigh and put her thumb in her mouth.

'Any more bad dreams and you wake me up, you hear?' he said.

She nodded, her forehead against his ribs. As her breathing began to slow into a sleeping rhythm, tears of indignation rose to Joseph's eyes. She was his little sister. If anyone suggested there was anything wrong with his feelings for her, he would take their eyes out.

On the day before Aine's birthday Thomas collected her from school and took her into town to the bicycle shop. Aine vanished into the heart of it while Thomas talked to a young salesman. He told him that he wanted the best bicycle money could buy. They discussed bull horns and braking systems and different kinds of gears. By the time they got round to looking at the different models, Aine had already chosen a bright yellow mountain bike with fifteen gears.

'I want this one,' she said.

The assistant explained that there was a newer version of that model with a better gearing system and front fork suspension.

'I want this one,' Aine said again.

'It's also a boy's bike,' said the salesman.

'I don't care if it's a donkey's bike,' said Thomas. 'If she wants it she can have it.'

They left the bike at the shop while they went and had tea and buns in the new smart café under franchise from a popular Dublin chain. Thomas had never been in it before and didn't take long to decide that he would never be in it again. It was full of people of a type he had never seen in town before; executive types in smart suits and skirts. He couldn't imagine what they did with themselves; how they earned money to buy clothes like that; why they would want to. He stood out like a sore thumb in his plain trousers and worn jacket. And the prices shocked him. He would have paid a small fortune for Aine's bike, but eighty pence for a cup of tea was robbery.

Aine finished her own cake and then finished Thomas's. Afterwards they went to buy a pair of shoes for him in the last of the town's old-fashioned drapers. He made a great show of choosing, of humming and hawing and getting Aine's opinion. In the end he bought a pair identical to the ones he had on, which were the same as the last pair he had owned and the one before that.

The bike fitted in the Golf with the front wheel hanging over the passenger seat across Aine's chest. She sniffed the clean rubber smell of the tyre.

'Is Specks mine now as well?' she asked.

'Well, you told me he was!' said Thomas.

'But is he? Really, I mean?'

Thomas thought for a moment. 'He isn't, no,' he said. 'He's Martina's.'

'But we don't know where Martina is.'

'That's for sure,' said Thomas. 'But she's somewhere, anyway.'

'Joseph said she could be dead.'

Aine knew he was trying to conceal his sorrow. 'We don't know where she is,' he said.

There was a long silence. The car chugged along the road, past the new bungalows that lined it for the first mile or so outside the town.

'I think she's a swan,' said Aine.

'Do you, begod?'

'I do.' Aine felt more courageous. 'I think she's a swan like the children of Lir. For nine hundred years.'

'Is that right? And why do you think that?'

'Because I saw her. On the lake. And I heard her singing.'

'I didn't know Martina was one for singing.'

'She is,' said Aine. 'She was singing Tub Thumping.'

'Was she, now? My God.'

'So is Specks mine?'

Thomas laughed. 'Let's just say you're minding him for Martina, shall we?'

'Yeah,' said Aine. 'For nine hundred years.'

When they got back, Brigid said that the dinner was nearly ready and that Thomas's name was in the pot. Aine brought the bike into the kitchen to show her.

'Oh, what a beautiful bike,' said Brigid. 'Can I have a go on it?'

'You can't ride a bike!' said Aine.

'What do you mean I can't ride a bike? Of course I can. I was riding bikes before you were born, young lady!'

Aine was puzzled. It didn't fit her picture of her mother. She looked at the skirt which came below her knees.

'Well, anyway,' she said. 'It's a boys' bike.'

She manoeuvred it, with some difficulty, into the front room, where Gerard and Thomas were watching the six o'clock *News*.

'Look at that!' said Gerard. 'What a bike!'

'It's all right,' said Aine, grinning from ear to ear.

Gerard reached out and scruffled her hair, then turned back to the news.

'Grandda says I can mind Specks for Martina,' she said.

Gerard made no response. The newscaster was talking about the murder of a crime boss in Dublin. He had been shot in the head at point-blank range. There were pictures of the taped-off scene.

'For nine hundred years,' said Aine.

'What?'

'For nine hundred years,' Aine repeated. 'While she's a swan.'

Gerard stared at her.

'Jesus, Dad,' he said. 'Why do you do it? Why do you fill her head with that stuff?'

Thomas nodded towards the television. 'What are you filling her head with, then?'

The newscaster had moved on. In the Four Courts a former Christian Brother had been found guilty on sixty-four counts of abusing children in his care over a period of fifteen years. The cameras showed the court building. Gerard shook his head and looked up to where the statue hung of a dead man on a cross. He looked at Aine, who was staring straight at him, her face betraying an anxiety he had never seen before. She looked away and down at the bike.

'It has fifteen gears,' she said.

Brigid put her head around the door. 'Dinner's ready.'

They all began to get up. 'But no one's having any,' Brigid went on, 'until I get a go on that new bike!'

She stepped into the room. She was wearing a pair of Joseph's tracksuit pants.

'Mam!' said Aine, her face brightening with embarrassment.

'Come on,' said Brigid.

Joseph met them in the hall and followed them out. Everyone watched as Brigid stopped and started and wobbled her way to confidence. She wouldn't get off until Joseph mock-wrestled the bike from her and rode it around himself. Aine stood in the middle of it all and yelled.

'It's my bike! I want a go!'

But she wasn't too serious. She liked what was happening.

Gerard and Thomas stood back, watching. Thomas lit his pipe.

'You'll have to watch your step now, Gerard,' he said. 'Now that your woman is wearing the trousers.'

But when Gerard looked across at Brigid he saw that she had retreated again, back into that awful strained silence that was becoming all too familiar. She was watching the kids larking with the bike, but that wasn't what she was seeing.

*   *   *

When Thomas went down to his house after dinner there were two swans standing at his back door. The sight of them sent a shiver down his spine.

'Not yet,' he said. 'Not yet.'

They moved aside to let him through, then walked off slowly towards the water.

Trish was just finishing up in the yard that evening when Gerard came out. He looked over the half door at the two fillies.

'Time those two were out,' he said.

They put head collars on them and led them dancing along the little green alley which ran beside the field where the mares were and into a further paddock, well hedged and green. There they turned them loose and watched as they raced and bucked around the open space.

'I don't want Aine near that cob unless you're minding her,' said Gerard.

'Fair enough,' said Trish. 'But I can't be expected to know where she is at every moment of the day.'

The fillies were standing still in the centre of the field, their heads high, their blood up, snorting at nothing.

'I hope you've been able to forget what happened,' said Gerard.

'What? With Specks?'

'No, not with Specks.' He sounded exasperated. 'Between you and me. That night.'

'Oh.' Trish nodded. She found that she had, pretty much. 'Misunderstanding,' she said.

The fillies, as one, dropped their heads, wheeled round and hared off again as if their lives depended on it.

'You shouldn't have hit old Specks, though.'

'What?'

'Today. There was no need for that.'

Gerard turned and began to walk away. 'When I want your advice, Trish, I'll ask for it.'

If it hadn't been for the tragedy at work in all their lives, Trish would have given him her resignation on the spot. As it was she followed at a distance in impotent rage. Behind her she could hear the fillies, still playing with the wind.

Sam called round to see Trish the next day. He came on a High Nelly bicycle with Sturmey Archer gears and curved handlebars. Trish was moving the manure heap with the tractor and buck rake from the paddock wall to the corner of the jumps field. When she saw Sam she stopped and turned off the tractor. They were delighted to see each other.

'Great job you have,' said Sam.

'Wonderful.'

Sam gestured towards the manure. 'I'd give my right arm for that lot,' he said.

'What would anybody want with your right arm?' said Trish.

He made a mock swing at her with it.

'I don't know what he does with it,' she went on. 'He hasn't touched it since I've been here.'

'How long is that?'

Trish shrugged. 'Too long. I'm thinking of leaving.'

'Not yet, I hope,' said Sam.

'I suppose,' said Trish.

Sam took out the makings and began to roll a cigarette.

'Do you want a cup of coffee to go with that?' said Trish.

'No, ta. I'm on my way in to get my dole. I was going to ask you if you wanted to come and have dinner with me. I was going to see if I could get a bit of fish.'

'What, tonight?'

'Is tonight no good?'

'Tonight is fine.'

'Great.' Sam lit his cigarette and pedalled off. Trish laughed. The bike suited him.

'What time shall I come?' she called after him.

'It doesn't matter,' he called back. 'I don't have a watch.'

Brigid saw him cycle away towards town from the mountainside. She had seen the hare again and had watched where it seemed to disappear among the rocks. She was examining the place now, but could find no hole large enough to take a hare. What she did find, however, was an ornamental gold pin of the kind once used to secure a cloak at the neck. She turned it over in her fingers. The stem was plain but the head was finely engraved with spirals. She didn't know enough about such things. It could have been dropped last summer by a tourist or a thousand years ago by some member of the Celtic nobility. She couldn't remember why it should matter which. It seemed a lot less important than the hole that she was looking for and couldn't find.

She dropped the pin into her jacket pocket and forgot about it.

Sam's caravan seemed bigger inside than outside. It was neater, too, than Trish had expected. About a third of it was the bedroom, curtained off with a threadbare Persian rug. The rest was for cooking and sitting.

There was no electricity. A wood-burning stove stood on a large flagstone. Its pipe went out through a tidily sealed hole in the wall. Candles of various shapes and sizes and ages stood in heaps of melted and remelted wax.

'Make yourself at home,' said Sam.

Trish couldn't, though. She could never live in such a cramped space.

Sam stoked up the stove with small logs, then went out to get more for the evening. Trish looked more closely around her. There was one built-in seat with a foam cushion and two chairs. One was hand-made from hazel rods bound with plaited grass. The other was a stacking plastic one covered in paint stains.

There were Celtic designs all over the walls; spirals and sunbursts and more complex interwoven animals and snakes. Some of them must have required considerable skill to draw. In the corner, a set of narrow shelves went from floor to ceiling, full of books. When Trish looked more closely she found that every second title seemed to have Celtic in it somewhere. *Celtic Art*, *Celtic Design*, *Celtic Mythology*. In between were the writings of Yeats and Lady Gregory and countless volumes of fairy tales and folklore.

Sam saw her looking at them when he came in.

'That's what brought me here, really,' he said. 'All that stuff.'

'Why?' said Trish.

'Do you want the short answer to that or the thesis?'

'The short answer.'

'Okay,' said Sam. 'I don't know.'

Aine pedalled up to the top of the drive on her bike, then turned and pelted back at top speed. She stood up on the pedals at the bumpiest bits where the bike juddered and bucked, then sat down and pedalled again. Beside her house she jammed on the back brake and skidded to a spectacular halt.

Thomas saw her coming towards his house, legs like little pistons, face set in fierce concentration. She went whizzing past the house and crunched to a stop on the shingle, her front tyre touching the water. Popeye raced up to congratulate her and she bowed to him, gracefully. Thomas hunted for biscuits for her. She delighted him more every day. He wasn't sure how she felt about her sister's disappearance but he wasn't too worried about her. It was clear that she intended to squeeze every last ounce of zest out of her life.

Gerard stood outside the house and watched her go up and down. Since the incident with the horse he was reluctant to let her out of his sight. He had said several decades of the rosary in penance for not missing her sooner that day and in thanks for the safe outcome. Her birthday party on the following day had been a riotous affair, like a celebration of her survival, or a rebellion against the grief that still fogged up the atmosphere of the house.

He saw Thomas come outside and talk to her. They went in together, leaving the bike on its stand on the shore. Beyond it Gerard could see the island. It meant only one thing to him now, and that was the souterrain. The thought of it made him feel sick. He would have to do something about it. He could not go on living in fear of it.

The thought, as it came, was almost a decision to act. But he could not do it alone. He was going to need help.

Aine watched *Father Ted* with Joseph in his room and they both fell about the place laughing. Afterwards they gathered their dirty laundry and took it down to the back kitchen.

Their mother had always done their washing for them, but it seemed that she had resigned. Neither of them knew how to work the machine.

'I bet Martina did,' said Aine, then corrected herself: 'Does.'

'Yeah,' said Joseph.

'Grandda says Martina has turned into a swan.'

'He does not.'

'He does. He says she might have.'

'He does not.'

Aine shrugged. 'Do you miss her?'

Joseph sighed. 'I don't think about it really. Do you?'

Aine shook her head. And then, because she knew she was going to cry, she ran off through the house at top speed; up the stairs and along the landing and then back again. Finally, she burst into the living room where her parents were sitting in front of the television.

'How do you turn on the washing machine?' she asked.

Sam's body was long and thin and pale. His skin was silky. He didn't smell of wood smoke any more, or perhaps it was that Trish did, now, as well.

She hadn't intended to stay; hadn't smoked or drunk anything for the sake of keeping a clear head. But he had listened and heard when she talked about things she hadn't told herself, yet: how scared she was, how lonely, and how she missed Martina. She didn't know how she had succeeded in denying it for so long. She had never much liked working for Gerard, but she had stayed because of Martina.

'She was my best friend,' she found herself saying. 'We did everything together.'

She had cried and cried, knowing that Sam didn't judge her and wasn't embarrassed by her tears. And when she had cried enough they had eaten the fish and laughed at the bones and looked at the darkness that had gathered outside the window.

Then a strange stillness had come down upon them.

It was more about friendship at first, but later their bodies took over and found that they suited each other well. They talked and made love until dawn. For the first time since she had started the job, Trish was late for work.

Now that the cattle were down for the summer, there was no more excuse for Brigid to go up to the winterage, but she went without one. It was changing up there. The gentians were at full strength, bursting with impossible blue, and the first bloody cranesbills were beginning to emerge between the rocks. The hazel was nearly in full leaf but somehow the woods were no darker, just greener. The first, delicate flowers appeared on the wild strawberries, struggling for light between the robust leaves of the garlic.

On one or two of the drier days, Brigid brought a sketchbook and colours with her to the woods, but she never used them. What she went up there for could not be taken home in a book.

It was another week before Gerard got around to acting on his decision to open the souterrain. What held him up was his inability to ask for anyone's help. He knew that no one would refuse him, but he was certain that everyone would think he was mad. Around the middle of the week he struck upon the idea of taking Joseph, but dismissed it as ridiculous. By the weekend he had come to realise that he had no other choice.

On Saturday morning he went to early mass on his own and afterwards waited until the hardware shop opened to get new batteries for the sheep lamps. When he got home, Joseph was still fast asleep, his body appreciating the extra space that Aine had recently vacated.

'Get up! Come on!'

Joseph sat bolt upright, clutching at the covers, peering around in bleary-eyed panic.

'It's after ten o'clock, for God's sake,' said Gerard. 'Get up out of bed.'

Joseph swung his legs out and sat up, relieved that Aine was gone. He was still confused that the protective feelings he held towards her, the best he could find in his nature, had to be kept hidden. He rubbed at his sleep-slack face.

'Now, Joseph! Not next week!'

'All right, all right.' Joseph groped around beside the bed for his jeans. To his relief, his father left. In a small act of rebellion he stretched out on the bed again for a minute that felt like an hour.

Thomas was horrified.

'No good will come of it,' he said.

But he let them take the boat, since they could get closer that way than they could by car, and he helped them load the pick and the shovels and the rusted bit of an old Kango hammer that Gerard used as a crowbar. He helped them push off, too, but he wouldn't go with them nor let them take Popeye, even though he kept jumping into the boat.

'He'll only be in your way,' he said. But the truth, if he admitted it, was a little more complicated than that. If anything came up out of that hole, it should be free to go wherever it wished.

It took two trips to get all the gear up to the top of the hill. Joseph took the heaviest tools and pushed himself to heart-hammering exhaustion, but if Gerard noticed he said nothing. At the side of the souterrain they stopped to get their breath and Joseph took a manly swig from the bottle of Coke they had brought. Gerard looked across the causeway to where Anthony's house stood, pale against the drumlin behind it. He should have asked Anthony's permission at least. It was his land.

But Anthony didn't come near them and nor did his cattle. He had moved them down to fresh pasture and was letting the island rest for a week or two before he put the sheep in. The work, once it began, was uninterrupted.

'You see?' said Gerard. 'See where the stones have been moved?'

Gerard lifted the fringe of grass. Joseph could see nothing.

'I'd say they just settled, maybe,' said Joseph.

'Settled!' Gerard was incredulous. 'After hundreds of years? Settled?'

Even as he said it, Gerard knew his son was right. He also knew that doubt, like a demon, was at work in his mind and he would never rest in peace until he had searched the interior. He picked up the crowbar and thrust it down between two stones, in a manner that put Joseph in mind of a man driving a sword into a dragon.

One by one, the stones came out. Joseph put his back into the work. He helped at haymaking and at moving cattle, but not with anything else. He had memories of Kevin working with his father; building walls and fences, riding the horses. Maybe that was it, the reason his father had no time for him.

But he knew it wasn't just that. It was something more fundamental; something that had always been there. He wasn't like Kevin; never would be. Kevin was like his father, always on the front foot, facing the world square on. Joseph was a skulker at the back, full of dreams, preferring darkness. There was no understanding between them.

None of the stones was too heavy for a man to lift, but it would certainly have been a lot easier to put them into the hole than it was to get them out. They were wedged tight, assisted by gravity, and their smooth, muddy surfaces were almost impossible to grip. It was hot work, and tiring. About halfway through the job Gerard called a halt, and led the way down among the trees, where they ate their lunch. In no time the Coke and the tea were gone.

Joseph took the empty flask and bottle to the well. As he leaned over it he caught a glimpse of movement, a speckled fish that darted into the cover of the weeds in the depths. He watched quietly for a long time but it did not move again.

'I saw the fish in the well,' he said to Gerard when he returned with the water.

'You're as mad as your grandfather, so you are,' said Gerard.

They returned to the hole and worked on, stripping down to their T-shirts in the spring sun. They took more time with the deeper stones, working them up the sides gradually, using their bodies as props. Joseph laboured through his exhaustion, relying on marrow and sinew more than on muscle. And as the day wore on his father's words became less critical and his tone less scornful and, although there was no praise, the work became smoother and more satisfying as they learned to pull together.

When the last stone was gone and the few shovelsful of loose earth thrown out of the bottom, there was still a couple of hours of daylight in the sky. They took another break, sitting at the edge of the hole eating bruised bananas and squished chocolate bars. Afterwards they were still hungry. Their dinner would be ready. Gerard could see the house and Aine bombing up and down the drive on her bike. Behind her a man was cycling down, his knees angled outwards like an insect. That hippy again. He seemed to have practically moved in.

Joseph was looking down into the hole, at the heavy stone lintel at one side and the shallow crawl space beneath.

'I'm sure no one has been in there, Dad,' he said. 'There's no way.'

Gerard knew he was right. But he had to see. 'Sure, we have it open now,' he said.

Joseph shrugged. Gerard's legs felt as if they were filled with hot wax. There was no more time for procrastination. He reached across for the lamps and handed one to Joseph.

'Right,' he said.

He slid down to the bottom of the hole. Joseph stayed where he was on the rim.

'Right, so.' Gerard dropped on to his knees and peered into the darkness. He shone the torch in. All he could see was the flat tunnel and his mind was besieged by the image of dark water, waiting to drown him. He straightened up again, his chest constricted with fear.

'I can't,' he said. 'Oh, Jesus, no way.'

Joseph couldn't believe it. It had never, never occurred to him that his father might ever fail. He stared at him until he realised that he was ashamed and looked away. But he was already moving, stripping off his T-shirt and sliding down the wall of the hollow. Lithe as a snake he twisted on to his belly and began wriggling through the crawl-hole. The lamp in his hand blinded him. He turned it and its light met the wall ahead. When he reached it he turned the beam up and stood. It was just like the other souterrain with its low barrier and long, stone-lined chamber.

'Joseph?' His father's voice sounded small. He waited for a moment, savouring the feeling, king once again of the underground halls.

'I'm in,' he called. 'It's quite safe.'

He climbed the wall and dropped down. A couple of inches of mud had gathered on the floor, smooth as a tide-washed beach. There were no marks in it at all. Joseph walked through, shining the beam up at the coarse stonework, marvelling at its simple efficiency. For the first time he found himself wondering about the people who had built this place and he was seized with an urgent desire to learn. Completely fearless now he dropped on to his belly again to slither through into the next chamber.

Gerard took a deep breath and held it until he got to the end of the crawl-hole. He stood up by careful degrees, expecting the roof to be lower than it was.

'Joseph?'

He shone the torch to the end of the chamber. There was no one there.

Gerard feared that he was losing his grasp on reality, and for an instant he looked into the florid potentials that lay beneath his rigidly held rationality.

'Joseph!' There was panic in his voice, and this time Joseph heard him.

'It's all right, Dad. I'm here.'

His voice was muffled and could have come from anywhere. Gerard scrambled over the wall and discovered the footprints in the mud. He began to follow them realising where Joseph had gone. Realising as well that no one had been down there for a very long time. Then something caught his eye.

It was lying at the edge of one of Joseph's footprints, partly exposed, partly covered by the settled mud. He reached down and picked it up. It was cold and slimy in his hand, the little bull that he had hidden so many years ago up above the stones at the top of the hole.

Joseph discovered that the second chamber was the last. There was a fall of loose earth and small stones that might have concealed the entrance to another one but he had no inclination to disturb it. He followed his own footprints and slithered back into the first chamber again.

Gerard looked up and saw him emerge, his bare belly red-brown with clay, like tribal paint. He looked back at the little brass bull in his hand, trying to work out how it had got there. It was possible that it could have slipped gradually down among the stones or been washed between them by torrential rains. But no amount of help from rain or from gravity could have lifted it over that wall. Gerard wished with all his heart that Peadar was still alive to see this and to confirm his memory of it. Because although it was smaller than he remembered it was otherwise exactly the same. One of its legs was missing and one of the outsweeping horns was snapped halfway down. Otherwise it was perfect, and beautifully executed.

Joseph was beside him. 'What's that?'

'A bull.' At the same moment Gerard remembered why he and Peadar had hidden it and not shown it to anyone.

'Look at the size of his mickey,' said Joseph. He didn't want to laugh but he couldn't stop. Gerard tried to hang on to his paternal gravity but it was swept away by a wave of laughter. And long after the reason for it was forgotten, the man and the boy were still laughing. Their ringing voices, one high and one low, released the hollow hill from a thousand years of silence.

As May advanced Joseph settled in to work on his revision for the exams which were to begin in June. Gerard got the contractors in for the first cut of silage. With Trish's help, Aine and Specks progressed to cantering and jumping the height of half a barrel. Sam spent more and more time at the cottage with Trish. He tidied it up and swept out the cobwebs and began the job of sanding and painting. Then he discovered Thomas and began raiding him for stories. Thomas grumbled and demurred and had to be persuaded, but he was never more alive than when he got into the flow.

Every time the wind blew and sometimes when it didn't, Gerard heard Martina calling him. He no longer tried to follow the sound but it was like a ringing in his ears, like tinnitus. It maddened him. The one place where he was guaranteed not to hear it was in the pub.

There he changed, became one of the lads, a smutty teenager again, laughing at scatological jokes, talking suggestively about women and expertly about sport. He knew that everyone treated him just a little delicately. He also knew that his feelings were safe there, protected from exposure by the rules of male camaraderie. He might get sentimental about his mates from time to time, but Martina would rarely, if ever, be mentioned.

No more was known about her. Because of her absence, she was constantly present and not one of the family moved through an hour without her. She would always be there, not alive and not dead. But they all, none the less, carried on with their lives.

All except Brigid.

One day when she went up to the mountain she noticed that the goats had gone. Sometimes on wet days they sheltered out of sight, but she couldn't remember a dry day when one group or another of them was not spread out across the mountainside. Brigid hoped that no one had hunted them out of it.

She walked through the hazel and into the string of tiny meadows where the coarse grass was beginning to recover from the wintered cattle. The little fields had once been tended and kept clear, but now that farmers had more land they had less time for such work, and blackthorn was invading from every side, gradually diminishing the space. In a few years' time the blackthorn would own this place and the hazel would close in behind it and wild things would live there. Brigid was delighted. There were few enough places in the world where wildness was winning.

A rock among the spreading thorns turned and looked at her. Such things were not so unusual lately, but this time it was not a hallucination. It was a goat kid, grey as limestone and nearly as still. Brigid waited, expecting it to spot her; expecting it to snort and bound away to its mother. But it didn't. It watched her for a while down the neat black triangle of markings on its face, then it turned so it could keep her in sight as it continued to browse.

Brigid laid her stick down on the ground and sat on it. After a while the kid lifted its head, bleated pathetically, listened for a moment, then began to move towards her. It nibbled the dead grass-heads as it came. There was no sign at all of any other goats.

Brigid whistled a few bars of a sad little tune that came into her head. The kid listened and came closer. Brigid whistled again. She could see now that the kid was puny and sick. Its coat was dull, its belly bloated, its hind legs stained with scour. Brigid remembered the straggler she had seen on that other occasion, collected by the old nanny but probably motherless even then. It seemed likely that this was the same kid.

It came still closer, its nose reaching to define the air around her. If she had sprung from her crouching position she could certainly have grabbed it. She wanted to. She could dose it for worms and for gastric infection, she could feed it with the best of everything. She could heal it. But the kid had other ideas. Any life, any death even, was better than captivity. Despite its orphan status and its lack of education the kid was wise. Its searching nose caught Brigid's scent and an ancient memory recognised it. Unnerved, it backed away and moved off, still calling plaintively from time to time; like Hamlyn's crippled child, the one left behind. As for the other goats, it was clear that they were long gone, over the mountain.

Or into it.

Gerard was bringing black bales along the road from the silage meadows to the yard, one at a time. Later on in the evening, he decided, he would give Joseph a lesson on the tractor. It was high time the boy learned to drive.

A convoy of Travellers passed; three vans and a car. Gerard turned to see which way they went. They took the road which wound between the mountains, past the old church and the holy well and on beyond it to Carron.

Gerard reflected that he never seemed to have dealings with the Travellers these days. When he was young they had often called. Thomas had been on good terms with them and had kept old batteries and bits of scrap metal for them to collect. Gerard could just remember the time when they would mend an old bucket or pot, when they were called Tinkers, because that was what they did. What they did now he wasn't at all sure.

As he was about to turn into the boirin he looked back again. A mile or so up the road he could see the vans pulling into the lay-by which served the path to the church. He had heard that they often went up there but he wasn't sure why. He realised that although they were a familiar part of his environment, he knew nothing about the Travellers at all. It struck him now that they were like a separate strain of the same species, awaiting their age to flourish in the Darwinian scheme. Because he was suddenly sure that they would; that if conditions became impossible for the settled majority the Travellers could and would adapt and survive.

The thoughts were strange to him. He wasn't accustomed to thinking like that and he wasn't sure why it was happening. A brief image invaded his mind, of the poisoned lake rising to contaminate the land around it. He remembered his dream of drowning. Perhaps there was, after all, something in what the blow-ins and the other scaremongers were saying. Perhaps he would look again at the REPS schemes on offer.

Something in Brigid's mind was stretched so tight that it hurt. She walked quickly through the woods, followed paths that she knew well now; paths that she had made. Her stick was like a third leg, balancing her, feeling the ground, taking a share of the weight. At the church she heard voices, someone on the track, but it was of no consequence. The church meant nothing to her now. She sought older, rarer nourishment than that.

She followed the stream as it got younger and higher and wilder. At the place where she had drunk on her last visit, she looked up towards the crag above and saw what appeared to be a break in the rock, a shadowy entrance, a door. The longer she looked at it, the more certain she became. Up there were her answers. Up there was peace of mind.

The mossy scree was almost sheer. Brigid clung to fragile branches and braced herself with her stick as the climb became steeper and more treacherous. She stopped often to catch her breath and to gulp the sweet, mossy water; pure fuel for the fire within her.

The climb became precipitous, arduous. It took all Brigid's attention, and she forgot about the portal she had seen. A rock moved beneath her foot and a bough snapped in her hand but her stick, her magical piece of hazel, saved her each time. Mud and moss stained her new jeans; sweat soaked into her blouse. Still she climbed and finally came to where the water broke out at the foot of the crag. She drank there, the wildest and best of all water, tasting of stone and of darkness. And then she looked up.

There was no door, no entrance into the rock. What she had seen was a shadow, an overlap, a joke. She tapped with her hazel rod as if it might change the rock's ancient mind. She knocked harder, then struck, then beat until the rod broke in her hand and became two splintered hazel sticks, no more. Then she sat at the base of the cliff face and wept.

The Travellers had said their prayers. They had added to the offerings around the well and were about to leave when a woman came stumbling out of the woods and in among them. Her clothes were dirty, her hair tangled, her face wild and tear-stained.

The Travellers stood their ground. A calmness in them comforted Brigid. She sat on the broken wall of the church. The little group consulted among themselves, then a woman moved away from the child and the young man she was with and came to sit on the wall beside her.

'Something has you troubled,' she said.

Brigid's tears began again. 'My daughter,' she said.

'Did she die?'

Brigid shook her head. 'Missing.'

The woman looked up and, with a gesture, dismissed the others who were waiting.

'A few weeks, is it?' she said to Brigid.

Brigid turned to her, a spark of hope in her eyes.

'I can see a lot, Mrs, but you must cross my palm, and you must swear not to repeat a word, as God is your witness.'

'As God is my witness,' said Brigid.

The woman's hand was open. Brigid's heart lurched. She did not carry money with her in the mountains, nor food, either. They seemed to weigh too much up there. She felt in her pockets and found, to her surprise, the gold pin that she had picked up near the hare's bolt hole. She put it on the open palm.

The woman nodded. 'Was your daughter riding a horse?' she said.

'Yes,' said Brigid.

'I see him now,' said the woman. 'A grand cob, a speckled cob.'

'Yes!' Brigid's eyes were bright with hope but the woman shook her head.

''Tisn't good, Mrs,' she said. ''Tisn't good at all. You won't see her no more.'

'Is she dead?'

'She is, Mrs. Looking down on the two of us now.'

The woman watched as the passionate light died in Brigid's eyes and was replaced by sadness and certainty.

'She didn't suffer, Mrs, and she isn't suffering no more.

It's us who suffer, who get left behind. I lost two of them myself.'

'Oh, no.'

'I did, sure. In a fire, it was. A long time ago. But you have to let her go, Mrs. Take some thing that was belonging to her and bury it and say a prayer. Have you other children?'

'I have. Two. Three. One's abroad.'

'They need you, Mrs. Your dead daughter doesn't. Go home now, straight away.'

Brigid stood. 'How?' she said.

''Tisn't told to me,' said the woman. 'But it's finished, now. Go home.' The woman gestured, almost angrily. Brigid turned and set off, over the wall and through the bushes. The place was strange to her now, wild and alien. She had no idea what she was doing there.

When she was gone, the Traveller woman inspected the pin in her hand for a long, long time. Eventually she kissed it, then touched it to her forehead, then tossed it into the ruined well. The stream felt it, found a bed for it, and began the long, slow process of covering it over with silt.

Aine met her mother at the top of the boirin and raced down on the bicycle ahead of her. Gerard was in the kitchen, lighting up the range.

'Dad!' Aine shouted, and her voice seemed to have more than the usual excitement in it. 'Mam's back.'

In the early morning, Brigid got up and slipped down to the meadow beside the lake. She brought a small shovel and the little pink wrist band that the hospital had put on Martina when she was born. There had been four of them in the drawer in her bedroom. Now there were three.

No one was about as she dug a hole that was comfortably deep, and dropped the little strap into it, and replaced the rich, brown earth. But the cattle that had come down from the winterage stood in an inquisitive line like mourners, and from the orchard the Tinkers' cob looked on and kept his secret to himself.

And on the water, a single swan watched everything, then drifted slowly away.